Under the Udala Trees

Under the Udala Trees

Chinelo Okparanta

Houghton Mifflin Harcourt

BOSTON · NEW YORK

2015

For information about permission to reproduce selections from this book, write to Permissions, Houghton Mifflin Harcourt Publishing Company, 215 Park Avenue South, New York, New York 10003.

www.hmhco.com

Library of Congress Cataloging-in-Publication Data
Okparanta, Chinelo.
Under the udala trees / Chinelo Okparanta.
pages ; cm
ISBN 978-0-544-00344-6 (hardcover) — ISBN 978-0-544-00336-1 (ebook)
1. Nigeria—Fiction. I. Title.
PS3615.K73U53 2015
813'.6 — dc23
2014044506

Book design by Chrissy Kurpeski
Typeset in Minion Pro
Map by Rachel Newborn

Printed in the United States of America
DOC 10 9 8 7 6 5 4 3 2 1

For Constance, Chibueze, Chinenye, Chidinma

And for Obiora

Faith is the assured expectation of things hoped for,
the evident demonstration of realities, though not beheld.

— HEBREWS 11:1

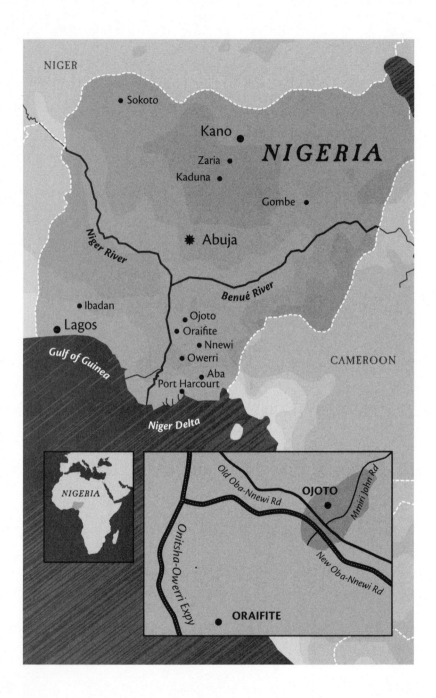

PART I

1

MIDWAY BETWEEN Old Oba-Nnewi Road and New Oba-Nnewi Road, in that general area bound by the village church and the primary school, and where Mmiri John Road drops off only to begin again, stood our house in Ojoto. It was a yellow-painted two-story cement construction built along the dusty brown trails just south of River John, where Papa's mother almost drowned when she was a girl, back when people still washed their clothes on the rocky edges of the river.

Ours was a gated compound, guarded at the front by thickets of rose and hibiscus bushes. Leading up to the bushes, a pair of parallel green hedges grew, dotted heavily in pink by tiny, star-like ixora flowers. Vendors lined the road adjacent to the hedges, as did trees thick with fruit: orange, guava, cashew, and mango trees. In the recesses of the roadsides, where the bushes rose high like a forest, even more trees stood: tall irokos, whistling pines, and a scattering of oil and coconut palms. We had to turn our eyes up toward the sky to see the tops of these trees. So high were the bushes and so tall were the trees.

In the harmattan, the Sahara winds arrived and stirred up the dust, and clouded the air, and rendered the trees and bushes wobbly like a mirage, and made the sun a blurry ball in the sky.

In the rainy season, the rains wheedled the wildness out of the dust, and everything took back its clarity and its shape.

This was the normal cycle of things: the rainy season followed by the dry season, and the harmattan folding itself within the dry. All the while, goats bleated. Dogs barked. Hens and roosters scuttled up and down the roads, staying close to the compounds to which they belonged. Striped swordtails and monarchs, grass yellows and redtops—all the butterflies—flitted leisurely from one flower to the next.

As for us, we moved about in that unhurried way of the butterflies, as if the breeze was sweet, as if the sun on our skin was a caress. As if slow paces allowed for the savoring of both. This was the way things were before the war: our lives, tamely moving forward.

It was 1967 when the war barged in and installed itself all over the place. By 1968, the whole of Ojoto had begun pulsing with the ruckus of armored cars and shelling machines, bomber planes and their loud engines sending shock waves through our ears.

By 1968, our men had begun slinging guns across their shoulders and carrying axes and machetes, blades glistening in the sun; and out on the streets, every hour or two in the afternoons and evenings, their chanting could be heard, loud voices pouring out like libations from their mouths: "Biafra, win the war!"

That second year of the war—1968—Mama sent me off.

By this time, talk of all the festivities that would take place when Biafra defeated Nigeria had already begun to dwindle, supplanted, rather, by a collective fretting over what would become of us when Nigeria prevailed: Would we be stripped of our homes, and of our lands? Would we be forced into menial servitude? Would we be reduced to living on rationed food? How long into the future would we have to bear the burden of our loss? Would we recover?

All these questions, because by 1968, Nigeria was already winning, and everything had already changed.

But there were to be more changes.

There is no way to tell the story of what happened with Amina without first telling the story of Mama's sending me off. Likewise, there is no way to tell the story of Mama's sending me off without also telling of Papa's refusal to go to the bunker. Without his refusal, the sending away might never have occurred, and if the sending away had not occurred, then I might never have met Amina.

If I had not met Amina, who knows, there might be no story at all to tell.

So, the story begins even before the story, on June 23, 1968. *Ubosi chi ji ehihe jie:* the day night fell in the afternoon, as the saying goes. Or as Mama sometimes puts it, the day that night overtook day: the day that Papa took his leave from us.

It was a Sunday, but we had not gone to church that morning on account of the coming raid. The night before, the radios had announced that enemy planes would once more be on the offensive, for the next couple of days at least. It was best for anyone with any sort of common sense to stay home, Papa said. Mama agreed.

Not far from me in the parlor, Papa sat at his desk, hunched over, his elbows on his thighs, his head resting on his fisted hands. The scent of Mama's fried akara, all the way from the kitchen, was bursting into the parlor air.

Papa sat with his forehead furrowed and his nose pinched, as if the sweet and spicy scent of the akara had somehow become a foul odor in the air. Next to him, his radio-gramophone. In front of him, a pile of newspapers.

Early that morning, he had listened to the radio with its volume turned up high, as if he were hard of hearing. He had listened intently as all the voices spilled out from Radio Biafra. Even when Mama had come and asked him to turn it down, that the thing was disturbing her peace, that not everybody wanted to be reminded at every moment of the day that the country was falling apart, still he had listened to it as loudly as it would sound.

But now the radio sat with its volume so low that all that could be heard from it was a thin static sound, a little like the scratching of skin.

Until the war came, Papa looked only lovingly at the radio-gramophone. He cherished it the way things that matter to us are cherished: Bibles and old photos, water and air. It was, after all, the same radio-gramophone passed down to him from his father, who had died the year I was born. All the grandparents had then followed Papa's father's lead—the next year, Papa's mother passed; and the year after, and the one after that, Mama lost both her parents. Papa and Mama were only children, no siblings, which they liked to say was one of the reasons they cherished each other: that they were, aside from me, the only family they had left.

But gone were the days of his looking lovingly at the radio-gramophone. That particular afternoon, he sat glaring at the bulky box of a thing.

He turned to the stack of newspapers that sat above his drawing paper: about a month's worth of the *Daily Times,* their pages wrinkled at the corners and the sides. He picked one up and began flipping through the pages, still with that worried look on his face.

I went up to him at his desk, stood so close that I could not help but take in the smell of his Morgan's hair pomade, the one in the yellow and red tin-capped container, which always reminded me of medicine. If only the war were some sort of illness, if only all that was needed was a little medicine.

He replaced the newspaper he was reading on the pile. On that topmost front page were the words SAVE US. Underneath the words, a photograph of a child with an inflated belly held up by limbs as thin as rails: a kwashiorkor child, a girl who looked as if she could have been my age. She was just another Igbo girl, but she could easily have been me.

Papa was wearing one of his old, loose-fitting sets of buba and sokoto, the color a dull green, faded from a lifetime of washes. He looked up and smiled slightly at me, a smile that was a little like a lie, lacking any emotion, but he smiled it still.

"*Kedu?*" he asked.

He drew me close, and I leaned into him, but I remained silent, unsure of how to respond. *How was I?*

I could have given him the usual response to that question, just answered that I was fine, but how could anyone have been fine during those days? Only a person who was simultaneously blind and deaf and dumb, and generally senseless and unfeeling, could possibly have been fine given the situation with the war and the always-looming raids.

Or if the person were already dead.

We stayed in silence, and I observed the rigidness of his posture, the way his back refused to lean against the chair. His legs appeared to be stuck firmly to the ground. His lips spread, not in a smile, but like a child about to cry. He opened his mouth to speak, but words did not come out.

The night before, late, when I should already have been asleep, but when sleep was refusing to come, I had snuck down to the parlor out of not knowing what else to do with myself. Just outside my bedroom door, I saw that a soft light was coming from the direction of the parlor. I tiptoed toward the light, and toward the soft sounds that were also coming from that direction. Behind the slight wall where the parlor met the dining room, in that little space, barely a nook, I stopped, peeked, and I saw Papa in that now-familiar position, sitting on his chair, leaning on his desk, listening intently to his radio. So late at night, and yet there he was.

I stood quietly and eavesdropped, and I heard the story. Of one Mr. Njoku, an Igbo man who was tied up with a rope, doused with petrol, and then set on fire. Right here in the South, the announcer said. It'd been happening all over the place in the North, but suddenly it had begun happening in the South as well. Hausas setting us on fire, trying hard to destroy us, and our land, and everything we owned.

"Papa? Has something happened?" I asked. By "something" I meant something bad, something like the petrol-dousing that I had heard of the night before.

Papa shook his head as if to try again. In a faint voice, he said, "What can we do? There's not much any one person can do. And to worry over it would be like pouring water over stone. The stone just gets wet. Eventually it dries. But nothing changes."

For a moment, the only sound was the clanging of Mama's pots and pans in the kitchen. Soon the akara would be done, and she would call us to eat the way she always did, even before the war.

Papa took me by both arms, looked me in the eyes. Very softly, he said: "I want to tell you something. It's nothing you don't already know, but I want to tell it to you again, like a reminder. So you don't forget."

"What?" I asked, wondering what it was that I already knew but might soon forget.

He said: "I want you to know that your papa loves you very much. I want you to always know it and to never forget it."

I sighed, out of a sort of disappointment that it should be something so obvious. I said, "Papa, I already know."

In the moment that followed, it seemed as if he were suddenly feeling all the weight and pain and hollowness of the world inside of him. There was a distant look on his face, as if he were estranged from everything he knew and also more profoundly than ever connected to it.

The muttering began. Something about the way Nigeria was already making a skeleton out of Biafra. Nsukka and then Enugu had been seized, followed by Onitsha. And, just last month, Port Harcourt.

He rambled on like that. His voice was a monotone. He seemed to have fallen into a trance.

It wouldn't be much longer before there was no more Biafra left to seize, he said. "Will Ojukwu surrender to Nigeria? Or will he fight until all of us Biafrans are dead and gone?" He looked toward the parlor window, his eyes even more glazed over.

Maybe it had nothing to do with the weight or pain or hollowness of the world. Maybe it was simply about his role in the world. Maybe it was that he could not have imagined himself in a Nigeria in which Biafra had been defeated. Maybe the thought of having to live out his life under a new regime where he would be forced to do without everything he had worked for — all those many years of hard work — a new regime where Biafrans would be considered lesser citizens — slaves — like the rumors claimed, was too much for him to bear.

Whatever the case, he had lost hope. Mama says that war has a way of changing people, that even a brave man occasionally loses hope, and sometimes all the pleading in the world cannot persuade him to begin hoping again.

June 23, 1968. About a year into the war, and the bomber planes were at it again, like lorries that had somehow forgotten the road and were instead tearing through the sky. Papa must have heard it just as it began — the same time that I heard it too — because he stood up from his desk, grabbed my hand. The sun, which had been shining strongly through the open windows, suddenly seemed to disappear. Now the sky seemed overcast.

First he pulled me along with him, the way he usually did when it was time to head to the bunker. But then he did something that he had never done before: at the junction between the dining room and the kitchen, he stopped in his tracks. There was something corpse-like about him, the look of a man who was on the verge of giving up on life. Very pale. More than a little zombie-like.

He let go of my hand and nudged me to go on without him. But I would not go. I remained, and I watched as he went back into the parlor, took a seat on the edge of the sofa, and fixed his gaze in the direction of the windows.

Mama ran into the parlor, hollering, calling out to us, "*Unu abuo, bia ka'yi je!*" You two, come, let's go! "You don't hear the sounds? *Binie!* Get up! Let's go!"

She ran to Papa, pulled him by the arms, and I pulled him too, but Papa continued to sit. In that moment his body could have been a tower of hardened cement, a molding of ice, or maybe even, like Lot's wife, a pillar of salt. "*Unu abuo, gawa.* You two go on," he said. "I'll be all right. Just let me be."

His voice was raspy, something in it like the feel of sandpaper, or like the sound of a crate being dragged down a concrete corridor.

That was the way we left him, sitting on the edge of the sofa, his eyes fixed in the direction of the windows.

The bunker was in the back of our house, a few yards beyond where our fence separated the compound from the bush lot. We ran out the back door without him, stepping over the palm fronds that, months before, he had spread around the compound for camouflage.

At the back gate, Mama stopped once more to call out to Papa. "Uzo! Uzo! Uzo!"

The saying goes that things congealed by cold shall be melted by heat. But even in the heat of the moment, he did not melt.

"Uzo! Uzo! Uzo!" she called again.

If he had heard, still, he refused to come.

2

OUR CHURCH WAS not too far down the road from our
two-story house. It sat at the corner near where the row of
houses ended and the open-air market began.

It was over a year prior to that June 23 that I prayed my first
prayer to God regarding the war. Early March, to be exact. I know,
because it was ripening season for guavas and pepperfruit and vel-
vet tamarinds, that period of the year when the dry season was just
getting over and the wet about to begin. The harmattan winds were
still blowing, but our hair and skin were no longer as dry and brittle
as in mid-harmattan. Our catarrhs had come and gone. It was no
longer too dusty or too cool.

For all the years that we lived in Ojoto, it was to that church, Holy
Sabbath Church of God, that we went every Sunday. It was in that
church that we sat, on the parallel wooden benches that ran in even
rows, listening to Bible sermons. Together with the sermons, we
prayed; and together with the praying, we clapped and we sang. By
the time morning turned into afternoon, we exhausted our prayers,
grew out of breath with singing. Our arms dangled, limp from so
much clapping, all that fervent worship.

It was outside on the concrete steps of the church that I liked to
sit after service and watch as Chibundu Ejiofor and the other boys
played their silly games, like Police: an officer making an arrest.
And Chibundu, with his mischievous childhood eyes, his quick
wit, would always declare himself the policeman. Then, "You're under arrest," he would say eagerly, holding his hand to another boy's
chest, his fingers shaped to resemble a gun.

Sometimes a handful of the girls came out and watched the boys with me. But mostly they preferred to remain inside with their parents so as not to risk having the boys dirty their fine Sunday clothes.

It was in that church, at the tail end of the harmattan, that I prayed my war prayer, because it was there and then, just before the morning service, that Chibundu had joked that soon bomber planes would be everywhere. This was shortly before the war started, and before the bombers began coming into Ojoto. Chibundu made a buzzing sound from his mouth, like an aeroplane engine, and I laughed because of the silly way that his face puffed out, like a blowfish. But it was no laughing matter really, and so I gathered myself and told him, "Not so," that he was wrong, that the planes would never be everywhere. And I was confident in saying this, because those were the days when Papa was going around saying that the war was just a figment of some adults' imaginations, and that chances were that bomber planes would never see the light of day anywhere in Nigeria, let alone in Ojoto. Those were the days when Papa was certain of this, and so I was certain with him.

Chibundu's mother had overheard us, and just as I had finished responding to him, she came up to Chibundu — walked up to him and very offhandedly and unceremoniously slapped him on the side of his head. "*Ishi-gi o mebiri e mebi?*" she asked. Is your head broken? How dare you open your mouth and breathe life into something so terrible!

For the remainder of that day, Chibundu walked around moping like a wounded dog. Later, during the morning service, when the pastor asked us to carry on with our silent prayers, I prayed about the war, pleaded with God to make like a magician and cause all the talk of war, even the idea of it, to disappear. So that Chibundu would not be right. So that the bomber planes would never surround us. So that a day would not come when we had to carry a war everywhere we went, like a second skin, not a single moment of relief.

Dear God, I prayed, *please help us.*

All that time had passed, and Chibundu had been right in the end. It didn't appear that God had been bothered to answer my prayer.

June 23, 1968. We scrambled our way through the shrubbery and down the carved mud steps that led into the bunker. We breathed raspy, thick breaths. We sat in silence in that all-earth room, a space that was hardly big enough to contain a double bed. It was high enough for me to stand upright, but not high enough for Mama, or any other average-sized adult, let alone a tall adult, to do so, not without her head touching the top.

We crouched. Sometimes we turned our eyes to the entranceway above, where a plank of wood concealed by palm fronds served as both cover and camouflage.

In addition to the palm fronds that he had spread all over our compound, Papa had also spread palm fronds on the roof of our house. Maybe the camouflage would work for the house the way it worked for the bunker, I reasoned that day. Maybe the enemy planes would see the palm fronds and would not know to bomb the house.

In the bunker, I prayed to God again: *Dear God, please help Papa. Please make it so that the bomber planes don't go crashing into him.*

Mama remained crouched by my side, not saying a word, as if at any moment she would rush out and go looking for Papa. I scooted nearer to her, bit my lips and my nails. I held my breath and repeated my prayer over and over again: *Dear God, please help Papa. Please make it so that the bomber planes don't go crashing into him.*

I reasoned the way any other child my age might have: maybe this time God would lift His eyes from whatever else was taking up His attention in heaven — maybe disciplining some misbehaving angels or managing some natural disaster, maybe creating more humans, or taking care of dead human souls, or even doing housework (cloud work? heaven work?). What kinds of things occupied Him up there in heaven and kept Him from answering our prayers? He probably didn't sleep or eat, so what, then? What kinds of things were more important to Him than us, His very own children?

Maybe this time, I mused, I would manage to get His attention and He would lift His eyes and look upon me and soak up my prayer the way that a sponge soaks up water, the way that a drunkard soaks up his booze, the way that clothes soak up rainwater, the way that blotting paper soaks up ink. He would soak up my prayer and be full with it so that He would be compelled to do something.

Maybe this time He would be bothered to answer my prayer.

The sounds of the planes grew louder above us, followed by screams, followed by thuds of feet, or of objects, or even of bodies crashing into the land. We shivered through all of it, and the murky, sepulchral soil of the bunker appeared to shiver with us. The raid seemed longer that day than ever before.

3

THE BACK OF our concrete fence had come down in parts, and the shattered cement blocks all around the area made it so that we could not reenter the compound through the back, so we went around the fence and out onto the road, from which we would then make our way to the front of the house and try to reenter that way.

Up and down the road voices were calling out sharply — questioning voices — the way they always called out after a raid. Howling voices, as if all that shouting could somehow restore order.

"Have you seen my veranda chair?" a woman was shouting, a shrill voice, as if she were on the verge of tears. If luck was on her side, she would find the chair — most likely in broken pieces scattered across the road, one shattered limb after another. If luck was on her side, she would find it and be able to piece it back together again.

"Have you seen my son?" a second woman was asking. In between the questioning, she cried out her son's name. "Amanze, where are you? The aeroplanes have come and gone. It's time for you to come out of hiding! Amanze, do you hear me?"

More voices, and soon they all seemed to merge. A chorus of voices, a mixed collection, like an assortment of varying hopes tossed together into one great big wishing well.

"I'm looking for my mother," a small voice now came crying, distinct from all the rest, a girl's, four or five years old. Something Mama used to say: if you are looking for something, chances are you will find it in the last place you think to look. I wondered if the girl would find her mother in the graveyard.

A dog was barking as we hastened across heaps of crumbled con-crete, across fallen tree branches, across pieces of zinc siding and toppled roofs.

The front gate was clear enough. We entered. Behind us the gate door swayed. The sound was something like a wail.

We did not stop on the veranda to dust off our blouses and wrap-pers, the way we always did. We ran, instead, clear past the veranda and into the house, me following close behind Mama.

Later, Mama would say that she had been aware of the scent even from the veranda. Later, she would say that she had been aware of it the way a person is aware of the perch of a mosquito: it would be a moment before she felt its sting.

She says if someone were to have asked her in that very instant, she would have explained it as a musty scent, a little metallic, some-thing like the scent of rusting iron.

Inside the parlor, she caught a glint of the sun reflecting through the windows. Tiptoeing around the shattered glass on the floor, she followed the light with her eyes. I followed close behind.

At the window, only one glass pane remained in its frame, and on it, cracks in an almost circular pattern, as if a spider web had been stretched across its surface. She went up to that pane, touched it, stroked its fissures with her fingers, stared accusingly at it.

At the onset of the war, our social studies teacher, Mrs. Enwere, had, one afternoon, given us a history lesson that, so long as I live, I will not forget.

All the students in class were sitting as they usually did, two to a desk. It was nearing the end of the school day. The day had been stuffy and humid, the kind of weather that seemed to make every-one more miserable than they already were. Mrs. Enwere had cer-tainly been in a miserable mood all of that day, her face so downcast you'd have thought she'd lost a parent or a child. Now she was speak-ing to us, no longer consulting the book in front of her, but speaking freestyle, as if the words of the textbook had somehow registered themselves in her mind.

"First a coup, and then a countercoup. Coup," she said. She repeated the word, "A coup." Then, "Who knows what that means?"

Mrs. Enwere must have pronounced the word correctly, but somehow, in my tired, end-of-school-day child's mind, I heard instead: coop. I could even see it in my mind's eye: a hutch, a cage, red-tailed chickens and golden chickens and white chickens, chickens with wattles of different colors — yellow, brown, pink. A coop.

But what exactly about coops? How was it that chickens were all of a sudden the topic of our social studies class? The context for it, there in the classroom and in the middle of what appeared to be a history lesson, kept me from being sure that I really knew the word.

Mrs. Enwere waited only a moment for a response, and getting none, she continued. "I shall define 'mutiny' for you," she said, looking around the class. She spoke loudly: "Mutiny is a revolt or rebellion against authority."

The classroom was a large cement room, all gray, no paint on the walls. There were three other classroom buildings in the compound, in the midst of which was a courtyard, made up of lush green grass and strategically planted flowers, and a sandy brown area where we had our morning assemblies. The assemblies were the period during which we underwent inspections — the time when the headmistress and teachers checked to see if our fingernails were cut and if our uniforms were ironed and if our hair was combed. During the morning assemblies, we sang the school anthem, and then the national anthem, and from there our teachers led us to class.

The windows were located on the side of the classroom facing the courtyard. This was the way all the windows in all the classrooms in the school were, as if to prevent the students from looking the other way, out into the world.

I was staring out one of those courtyard-facing windows, thinking of the moment when school would be dismissed. What path would I take? The one that cut through the large overgrown field?

Or the path alongside the road, alongside the bicyclists and the occasional motorists?

"Repeat after me," Mrs. Enwere was saying. "Mutiny is a revolt or rebellion against authority." And now I turned back from the window to Mrs. Enwere to find that she was looking directly at me. "Repeat," Mrs. Enwere said, like a reprimand.

I repeated: "Mutiny is a revolt or rebellion against authority."

"Very good. Let me not have to remind you again to pay attention," she said, tapping the cane in her hand on my portion of the desk.

"Now, all of you know of Government House in Ibadan," she continued. This was the way Mrs. Enwere asked her questions, questions that came out more like statements. Questions that were too far above our minds, questions whose answers we could not possibly have known.

The class remained silent.

"Who can tell me about the Prime Minister and about Sardauna of Sokoto?"

More silence.

At this point, Mrs. Enwere began speaking quickly, her words coming out like a storm: *Ahmadu Bello, dead. Tafawa Balewa, dead. Akintola, dead. Dead, dead, dead.*

We listened with alarm, or at least I did, trying to make sense of the words. *Soldiers. Bullets. Head of State. Military.*

Mrs. Enwere went on like that for some time before turning her attention to Ironsi.

"Ironsi," she said. She repeated the name. "Johnson Aguiyi-Ironsi."

Head of State. Ironsi, his body in a forest, still dressed in his military apparel. Holes and holes scattered across his corpse, holes out of which blood flowed like the waters of a fountain, only red.

Ironsi, bullet-riddled and left to decay in the bush.

"A real shame what is happening in this country," Mrs. Enwere said. But in any case, she said, this was how we had arrived at Gowon for Head of State. Before Ironsi, Azikiwe. After Ironsi, Gowon.

We all sat there dumbfounded. You could have heard a pin drop in all that silence.

The silence in the house was as heavy as the one that day in school. Mama calling out Papa's name, and I taking in the dead air that greeted her after each call, complete emptiness in response.

We found him face-down on the black-and-white-tiled floor of the dining room. Mama leapt to him, bent over his body, resumed calling out his name.

His hands and legs were tangled strangely around his body, dying branches twisted around a dying trunk. Pieces of wood from the dining table lay scattered around him. A purple-brown hue had formed where the pool of his blood was collecting.

She stayed bent over his body, the cloth of her wrapper soaking up his blood. *"Uzo, biko, mepe anya gi! Ana m ayo gi!"* I'm begging you, Uzo. Please open your eyes for me!

She continued to call his name, and each new call was louder than the one before. "Open your eyes, my husband. *Mepe, i nu go?"* she said. "Open, do you hear me?!"

Her calling became shouting, and soon the shouting turned into wailing.

I remained where I stood, steps behind her, stunned. My father was dying or already dead, and even if I would have liked to do something to make it otherwise, I must have known already that there was nothing I could do.

In a whisper this time, Mama called Papa again by his name. For minutes she continued that way, just whispering his name, and as she did, she pleaded with him. "My husband, please. Please, get up and walk."

But of course he lay there still.

That evening, a handful of parishioners from church came and lifted Papa's body, cleaned it off, and took it with them. Where they took it I did not exactly know, but I watched as Mama handed to one of the men Papa's gold-patterned isiagu, hanging neatly on a hanger. They must have been the ones who put the isiagu on for him. When they returned with him and laid him back down in our parlor, he was clean and perfect-looking, as if he had gotten all dressed up for a big occasion only to suddenly fall asleep.

4

Papa's name, uzo, meant "door," or "the way." It was a
solid kind of name, strong-like and self-reliant, unlike mine,
Ijeoma (which was just a wish: "safe journey"), or Mama's, Adaora
(which was just saying that she was the daughter of all, daughter of
the community, which was really what all daughters were, when you
thought about it).

Uzo. It was the kind of name I'd have liked to fold up and hold in
the palm of my hand, if names could be folded and held that way.
So that if I were ever lost, all I'd have to do would be to open up my
palm and allow the name, like a torchlight, to show me the way.

In the weeks following Papa's death, it seemed that we had lost our
way, Mama and I. It seemed as if we could no longer tell up from
down, left from right. But no matter how turned around we were,
we at least knew enough to continue running into the bunker as
soon as we heard the sound of the bomber engines. And no matter
how turned around our lives had become, Mama knew enough to
make sure to give Papa a proper send-off, so that he would be able
to take his place among his ancestors.

There was an extensive wake-keeping — people coming in steady
streams to give their condolences. This continued for over a week,
with Papa laid out in the parlor on a four-poster bed, borrowed for
the occasion from one of our church members. Mama, dressed in
white, sat on a chair by his side surrounded by a troop of female
parishioners. She wept and wailed for her dead husband while the
women around her sang their funereal songs in chorus, like an ac-
companiment to her wails.

After Papa had been taken away and buried in the far corner of our backyard, there was the daylong *ikwa ozu* ceremony: trays of kola nuts and jerry cans of palm wine, prayers and libations, village elders invoking the spirits of Papa's ancestors, asking them to guide him into the world of the deceased.

One morning after the *ikwa ozu* had been performed, Mama called me for breakfast.

I went to her, sat with her in our dining room, where she had two bowls of soaked garri ready for us. If it had been before the war, we would have been eating bread with tea and one boiled egg each, or maybe we would have been having some cornflakes with the eggs, the kind of cornflakes that came in the Kellogg's box with the red-combed and yellow-beaked rooster. It was cornflakes imported from out of the country, and we would have been having it with Peak or Carnation evaporated milk, also from out of the country. But it had been some time since we'd had any bread or tea or Kellogg's cornflakes, or Peak milk or Carnation evaporated milk. And as for eggs, they were a thing like peace of mind, like calm, even like a smile. They were a thing we had begun to have only once in a while.

Mama sprinkled some groundnuts in our bowls of garri, and as she did, she said, "The protein in the groundnuts is just as rich as the protein in eggs. It will do the work of any other protein. It will help your brain to work well, think hard, and develop properly."

When Mama had just delivered me — when she was a brand-new mother — she had taken up studying food, for the simple fact that I had been born a little under a month early, and one of the midwives had explained to her that, among other things, it would be important for her to feed me protein. She had not understood what exactly protein was, that abstraction of a thing, like a ghost of a word, a mystery. Not like orange or banana or table or desk, things you could see solidly with your eyes. It was a thing that could not quite be seen.

She had gone and asked people and picked up information on

it here and there—whatever health books or magazines she could find. She wanted me to live. If I were to live, then she must figure out what protein was so that she could feed it to me.

After that, she had decided that if she could do something for a job, she would much rather own a food store than be a nutritionist. All that reading she had done in the name of protein had been quite a lot of work. And she was slow at it—every word a crawl. (All those big words that she did not understand didn't make it any easier on her.) After spending all afternoon reading, she spent her evenings and nights with a headache.

Maybe she herself had needed to be eating some protein back then, I've sometimes told her. Maybe that would have been just the thing to help with the reading and understanding of those big words.

In any case, as I sat there in the kitchen with her, I wondered what exactly it was I needed my brain for anymore, now that the war was making it so that soon enough there would probably no longer be any school for me to use my brain in. School was the reason why I read, and why I memorized the multiplication tables and learned history and geography and followed up with my Bible knowledge. *School* was what was supposed to develop my brain. How was protein supposed to do the work of school?

But Mama said that it would.

"As soon as the war is over," she said, "school will resume full time, and you will see that your brain will be just as intact as ever, even better."

I looked suspiciously at her, and she must have seen the suspicion on my face.

She smiled slightly and said that maybe one day I would use my brain to become a teacher or a doctor or a businesswoman. Because, she hated to break it to me, but I had better begin thinking about these things now. Because, God willing, I would one day marry, but what if one day I found myself like her, suddenly without a husband? "What if?" she asked, staring blankly at a spot behind my head.

After some time, she appeared to collect herself. Her eyes focused on me, and she said, "Well, all I'm saying is that you will have to use your brain for work, that is a fact. And no better way to start than with protein."

We continued to sit there at the table, eating our soaked garri and groundnuts, Mama going on with her lecture on the benefits of protein for my brain, neither of us talking about what was really on our minds, which was that Papa was dead and gone, and no amount of protein could bring him back to life.

5

B Y THE END of July, over a month had passed and Mama had not so much as mentioned Papa.

I took the hint. I resigned myself to just thinking of him. But the way I thought of him, it was the way a starving child thinks about food: he was always on my mind. Each time I heard a man's voice, or each time I saw anyone reading a newspaper, I thought of him. Mama never turned on the radio-gramophone. It was as if she had made it a point not to turn it on. But she didn't need to. Just seeing it was enough of a trigger for me to think of Papa.

One day, when it seemed that I had reached my max of missing him—one day when it seemed that I could not possibly miss him more without dying of the feeling—I found myself, out of the blue, blurting out to Mama, "Mama, do you miss Papa like I do?"

We were at the dining table, eating our dinner of yam porridge.

She snapped, her head whipping up with a sudden, unexpected anger. In a low, grumbling voice she replied: "Why should I miss him? Was he not the same man who made a widow of me and almost an orphan out of you? Tell me, just why should I miss him?"

I went back to my yam porridge.

Some minutes passed, and she said, very quietly: "Anger, that is what I feel toward him. Anger. Sometimes I feel like I will just explode with it."

I listened, not saying a word.

She let it all out then, the words tumbling from her mouth in a sputtering rage: "What kind of man pollutes his own land and his own house by allowing himself to be killed in it? Lucky for him that there's a war going on, so he cannot entirely be blamed for taking his own life. Lucky for him that his death can simply be explained as just another war death. But still, the atrocity!"

Our bedrooms, both on the second story of the house, had been destroyed by the same bombs that had killed Papa, and since there was a chance they might soon be destroyed again, Mama had decided that there was no sense fixing them back up.

We'd pulled down the mattress that Mama and Papa shared from their bedroom to the parlor floor. Each night we slept together on it.

At something like one or two a.m. on the night of Mama's anger confession, her scream came piercing a hole into the darkness, a hole so big that I felt as if I were spiraling at full speed down the length of it.

"Uzo!" she cried. Never before had I heard her scream this way in her sleep.

I grabbed her by the shoulders. "Mama, can you hear me? Mama, it's me, Ijeoma. Quiet down. It's only a dream."

She opened her eyes.

Mama used to say that our dreams were the way in which we resolved our problems, that every problem could be solved if we paid close attention to the tiniest details in our dreams. I used to have those dreams where I would get stuck in my sleep and couldn't move. It was the kind of dream where you were fully aware that you were in a dream, only you were stuck and couldn't get yourself to snap out of it. Sometimes the walls around me were a light shade of green, other times they were a light shade of gray. Either way, they were nothing like the rose-colored walls in our Ojoto house. I would try to scream, to cry out loud so that Mama or Papa would hear and come and wake me up. But neither could I scream in the dream. Eventually I would resign myself to being stuck. Only then would I somehow come out of it.

That night, even after she had opened her eyes, Mama continued to scream. "Uzo!" She turned to me. "Where is your papa?"

She looked frantically around in the darkness. "Uzo!" she called out. "Uzo, do you hear me?"

Had she begun to lose her senses? Had she forgotten that Papa was gone?

I leaned in to her and very gently said, "Papa is dead. Do you forget?" I whispered it to her over and over again.

Papa is dead. Do you forget?

Papa is dead. Do you forget?

Papa is dead. Do you forget?

She began to cry, as if hearing the news for the first time. Her shoulders heaved. Her breaths caught.

I held her, rocked her in my arms.

It was some time before her crying subsided. Finally she looked up at me, looked into my face. "Your papa is gone," she whispered.

"Yes, Mama," I replied, nodding. "Yes, my papa is gone," I said.

6

I PULLED OPEN THE window shutters. It was a cloudless morning, and bright. The swing of the wooden beams sent warm light surging into the room.

In the kitchen the pantry was near empty.

I pulled out a can of sardines and the last remaining tuber of yam.

I had begun to do much of the housework. Mama no longer seemed interested in the day-to-day things of life. It didn't appear that she cared any longer to live. Perhaps she was at a stage in her mourning in which she saw life as a thing she could not possibly go through without Papa. I had no choice but to take over.

It wasn't too difficult to boil things. The hardest part was fetching the wood and lighting the fire. The rest was just keeping an eye out to make sure nothing burned. There had been a small bag of rice, not enough to feed one person, let alone two. I had left it in the cupboard, but now I looked for it and, not seeing it, I remembered that we had already eaten it — mostly me, because Mama was barely eating anything by then.

My eyes fell back on the sardines and yam.

I cut the yam into cubes, removed the burner, filled the stove with wood, replaced the burner. The yam cubes sat boiling while I divided the sardines into two bowls, one for myself and the other for Mama. In the distance a gate was squealing.

I heard a thump, like something heavy falling to the ground, but it was only the door swinging open, hitting the wall.

Mama entered the kitchen. Her face was pale and there was a sense of disorientation about her.

"Mama, *odimma?* Are you all right?" I asked.

"Fine enough," she responded.

She walked up to the stove, lifted the lid of the pot.

"The relief lorry did not come," I said. "I'm making us yam."

She nodded.

"You will eat today?" I asked.

Mama was silent for some time, as if considering the food.

"We don't have anything else," I said. "No matter if you don't like it, you need to try and eat it."

"I'm not hungry," she said.

I was eleven years old, a couple of months shy of twelve, but I knew by then the ways in which worry dulled the appetite, the ways in which too much anxiety made it so that even the best-tasting food had the same appeal as a leaf of paper or a palmful of sand. But there were also those days when food was like consolation. And anyway, people had taken to saying all over Ojoto, "You better eat up now. You never know, one day there might be no food left to eat." Someone had said it again just the day before, and perhaps as a result, my hunger was full; my appetite must have been listening. I wished the same were true for Mama.

"Just a few spoonfuls," I said.

She stared blankly at me, shook her head, turned around, and left.

7

I WAS WATCHING FOR the relief lorry from just outside our front gate. A gentle morning breeze was blowing and the scent of earth was strong in the air. Not far from where I stood waiting, three soldiers were gathered, guns slung across their shoulders. Near them, an armored car, one of those with twelve thin, bicycle-looking wheels and a square cabin made entirely of metal. One of the soldiers was carrying a string of ammunition on his head. The ammunition appeared like a headpiece. The bullets, strung together as they were, fell in an almost decorative way, like a hat-turned-chain that extended to the front of his face.

Across the street, on the other side of the soldiers, a shirtless man was walking alongside his bicycle. On the back of the bicycle was a coffin, too small to fit the body inside, so that the feet of the deceased—perhaps his child or other family member—stuck out from the bottom end of the wooden box.

A toddler-aged boy was leaning against the cement wall near a gate down the road, as if to catch his breath.

Behind him several other children stood, a little older than the toddler, their bellies swollen like inflated balls from kwashiorkor, holding small plastic begging pans in their hands. If someone were to have snapped their picture, it could have been another one of Papa's newspaper front pages.

The soldier with the ammunition approached, his face sunken and sad-looking with mud stains all around. "Sista," he said. "Abeg, make I get wata."

I stared blankly at him, distracted, not really taking in his words.

"Make I get wata, abeg, *obere mmiri*," he said again, pleading.

The other two soldiers approached. The shorter of the two was holding a small, dirty white jerry can, empty, which he uncapped and then held out in my direction without saying a word.

A motorcycle sped by, sending dust like flames rising from the dry earth.

"Abeg, sista," the shorter soldier joined in. "Small wata."

They had captured my full attention by now.

From inside the compound Mama appeared, a wrapper tied around her chest, blinking with irritation at the men.

She looked at the jerry can and then back up at the faces of the men.

Unexpectedly, she snapped, "Don't you see that this is private property? Don't you know you can't go around begging like this?" She pointed her index finger at them as she spoke, brandishing it like a schoolteacher scolding a misbehaving child. She sucked in the air between her teeth and rolled her eyes, that combination of gestures that was a sign of a condescending sort of dismissal, of rejection. Before returning to the gate, she said, in pidgin this time, "Na who even tell you say I get wata?"

She stepped back into the compound, stopping only to call me to follow along.

I had not intended to disrespect Mama, but the soldier with the jerry can was now looking at me with eyes full of both longing and surrender.

"Abeg, sista," he said. His voice was weak, as if he were using his last ounce of strength to ask the favor.

I thought these things: What if he were on the verge of dying? What if he wound up dying right before my eyes? What if all he needed was water to be able to keep on living? Was he not, anyway, one of the soldiers fighting on our side, on Biafra's side? More than anything, it was the thought of his dying before me that terrified me.

There was a borehole in our backyard which connected to our water tank. I knew that there was still a good supply of water in the tank. Even if Mama was against it, I could give the men just a bit of water, not even half a jerry can.

I took the container from the man's hand.

In the backyard, on my way to the water tank, I saw Mama. She was seated at the side of the steps that led outside from the kitchen door. A swallow was hopscotching around near where she sat.

The bird sprang away, up to the top of our fence.

She had been watching the bird, but now her eyes fell on me.

There was a way in which Mama's lips had begun curling, followed by a widening, the top and bottom halves pressing into each other and becoming thinner that way. In that moment her lips did that very thing, followed by the question, "What do you think you are doing?"

Then she exhaled so that a soft whistling noise came from her nostrils. She shook her head slightly. Her eyes fell closed. Fatigue, I reasoned silently. It must be fatigue from hardly eating anymore.

But then she opened her eyes, and I saw a fury in them.

"Stupid girl," she shouted. As if to say, "What kind of child is it that goes against her own mother's word?" Or, "Did you not hear me say that we did not have any water?"

She reached out and slapped the jerry can from my hand. The can dropped at my feet. She pulled me by the ear, twisted my ear. "Disobedient child!"

She had become something outside of herself. Very different from the Mama I knew. She picked the jerry can up from the ground and stormed back to the gate. I followed her, out of shock and of not knowing what else to do.

Just outside the gate, the soldiers stood leaning on the fence, waiting. Mama tossed the empty container out to them. It landed lightly on the ground and tumbled halfway across the road.

"Did you not hear me say that we have no water?" she shouted at the soldiers. She closed the gate and locked it too.

I followed her again to the backyard. I crouched near the water tank, waiting. For what? I wasn't quite sure.

"What are you doing crouching here? Get up and find something to do," she said. It was not forceful, the way she spoke this time. She had calmed down by now. But the way the words came out — the tone of them, as if to say that I should just disappear from there (*Biko, comot from here!*) — and with everything that had come before, I knew well that Mama was somehow beginning to see me as a burden, the same way that she saw the soldiers as a burden, the same way the war was in fact a burden to us all. She was overwhelmed. No other explanation for it.

It must have been shortly after this incident that she began to make plans to get rid of me. In a warped, war-induced sort of way, it made sense that she should find ways to shed us all: the soldiers, me, and the house. To shed, if she could have, all memories of the war. To shed, and shed, and shed. Like an animal casting off old hair or skin. A lizard. A snake. A cat or a dog. Even chickens molt.

To shed us all like a bad habit. Or maybe, simply, the way one casts off a set of dirty, thorn-infested clothes.

8

AUGUST HAD COME and gone, and it was once again relief day, but morning had also come and gone with no sign of the Red Cross workers.

Usually by now there would have been a ruckus not far from our house, from those makeshift sheds where the village volunteers turned the relief packages into meals and portioned them out to the queue of villagers.

Rumors told of a blockade around Biafra by Gowon and the Nigerian forces that prevented the Red Cross from delivering us food. But rumors also had it that relief organizations were strategizing ways to break the blockade. It appeared there was still hope.

It was a school day, but the schools were by this time permanently closed.

I stood outside the gate, keeping an eye out for the relief lorry. Two older girls from school came strolling by, their hair in disarray, strands sticking out at odd angles. There was something in the manner of their movements that reminded me of old dishrags, worn and poked through with holes. But there was something beautiful about them too. Something about the way their bodies swayed as they walked.

Their skin was dark as cacao, which made me think of my own light skin, the kind of skin on which every scratch and bruise and scar showed, the kind of skin that people were always saying was so beautiful, but only because they didn't know, the way I did, that there was nothing beautiful about having marks like chicken pox scars all over your body.

But the girls, their skin would hardly have shown any marks, not with the way it was nice and brown and smooth in its brownness. Papa's skin was like mine, but a little darker. "The effect of age and the sun," he once said. As I looked at the girls, I found myself thinking that maybe in time, with age, the sun would darken my skin enough that I would be at least a shade closer to theirs.

Beyond their skin there was something else that made me think: their chests. They actually had chests. Mine, on the other hand, was hardly a chest at all, more like two tiny balls of pounded yam, flattened, each about the size of a tablespoon, not even enough to fill a palm.

Maybe it was a side effect of envy, or maybe it was a side effect of the awe I felt for them. Or maybe it was something else. Whatever the case, I felt suddenly shy and inadequate, and it would have required too much courage on my part to call out to them and let them know that the relief food had not yet come. I watched as they passed by in the direction of the relief center, only to watch again as they turned back around when they realized no one was there. Inside the house, Mama was likely still sitting in the parlor, on the mattress or on the sofa, praying fervently with her Bible, the way she had begun to do these days.

The streets were silent. Across from our gate, a pair of dogs lay sleepily on the dusty earth, dirty and sickly, corpses in the making. A light drizzle was falling, but the sun through the clouds was strong. Pink roses hung pitifully from their bushes, as if weakened or weighed down by the daylight. Before the war came, the land, where there were plants, was covered with lush green grass. On the grass grew weeds, and among the weeds, and from the bushes, grew flowers. The wind carried the dandelion clocks, and the hibiscus flowers painted the bushes red, and it was barely remarkable a thing, that deep redness of theirs. But now almost all the plants had withered, and the wind carried in it only traces of destruction. The hibiscus flowers all appeared to have lost their color.

I had gone back into our yard when I heard Mama calling my name.

By now she had moved from inside the house to a spot in the far corner of the veranda where the shrubs formed gaunt shadows on the outer walls of the house.

I joined her, taking a seat beside her on the orange and yellow bamboo mat where she sat.

"Did the relief lorry come today?" she asked.

I shook my head no.

She sighed. There was that now-familiar tired look on her face. She turned her gaze away from me.

After some time she spoke again. "There's no way we can remain here. If it's not enough that there is no more food, I'm also still having nightmares of your papa."

Smaller episodes now, she explained, not enough to wake me anymore, but still, they were there. To make matters worse, every once in a while, she said, she caught a whiff of him—of his death, something like the scent of blood. All the sights were a constant reminder that he was gone, she explained: the way gummy, oozing lesions sheathed the trees, cracks and cankers all over the bark. Dry brittle branches snapping at every turn of the wind. The way the petals of the hibiscus flowers had begun to dry out too. She imagined them choking—the trees and the flowers. She imagined them growing lifeless, no air, no breath, just like Papa.

The voices and all the sounds were also a reminder of his death. Not just the screaming and the war sounds, but now the floors of the house creaked, and each creak was something like the sound of his footsteps.

How could floors made of cement creak? I wondered, but I did not ask.

In the daytime she saw shadows, and each one was in the form of Papa. Sometimes she saw Papa's face jutting out of the walls, begging her to come with him.

"If we stay here any longer I will lose my mind!" Mama exclaimed.

Once upon a time, there was a girl who had an idea of the way the world should be: castles in the village, a papa and a mama who were alive and happy, and flowers and green grass that grew tall and bright.

Only, the girl's world was small, and not very representative of the real world, but she could not possibly have known this at the time. She was too small to know.

But she was older now, and she had begun to see the ways in which the world she had imagined was never going to be the world she would have. Of late, it seemed it was always one upheaval after another, one change and then the next. It was all overwhelming to her.

But she was old enough to know that not all change was bad. She was old enough, in fact, to have some awareness of the general tendency of things in life to change: night became day, the rainy season turned into the dry, today became tomorrow, and this year became the next.

She thought of church, and she thought that change was indeed a thing sanctioned by God, whether good change or bad change. Perhaps it was part of His aesthetic, part of His vision for the world. Perhaps everything was a reflection of that vision of change. Perhaps the nature of life was change. Wasn't creation the ultimate proof of this? The changing of something without form into something with form. Turning void into full. The division of light from darkness, of waters from waters, of sky from land. Maybe even death was a reflection of God's vision of change, the same way that birth was. Maybe it was the point of life, and of the Bible, that things had to change. Was this not what the pastor had said was the reason why the New Testament was created after the Old?

I was that girl, and even at eleven I reasoned it that way. Because a new change was looming, and I was finding myself forced to acknowledge that the limit of my imagination was by no means the limit of the world. I'd never known anywhere else but Ojoto. It was a scary thought to have to leave the only place I'd ever known. But if Mama was unhappy, then I wanted her to be happy. If leaving was what it would take her to feel better again, then leaving was what we should do. Maybe wherever it was that change took us would do us both some good.

When I was smaller and sulking for one reason or another, or having a tantrum, Mama used to make me dance with her, and she would say jokingly, "Dance your sadness away." Or if she was too angry with me to be jokeful, and if it happened to be mealtime, she would make me wait to eat, saying, "We must learn to fast our sadnesses away." Or if it was bedtime, she would pull me to her and begin praying, and afterward she would say, "It always helps to pray our sadnesses away."

I was thinking of the ways in which I could dance or fast or pray this sadness away when Mama spoke. In the distance voices were rising and falling, children shouting at one another.

"I've been thinking," Mama said. "Your grandparents — my parents — have that house in Aba. It's still there. If there's a place for me to go, that should be it."

There was a dull, faraway look in her eyes, and a quiet laziness to the way she spoke, as if at any moment her words would fade out. But she continued to speak; the words continued to come. She said, "No matter what happens, you must keep in mind that not a day will go by that I will not think of you."

Until now, I had been taking in her words as best as I could, digesting them without protest just as they came. They were the kinds of words that I had expected would come. But in this very moment my eyes snapped open. I looked at her, startled. "Not a day will go by that you will not think of me?" I asked.

She remained silent, her face very stoic.

She turned away so that she was no longer looking at me. Rather, she looked upward in the direction of the sky. The sun was high and bright, and she said, "I'll need to send you off."

I felt something sink inside my chest.

She turned so that she was again looking at me. She said, "They say Aba is not as bad as here, but who knows for sure."

And how could she know for sure? Aba was far enough away, no less than three hours south of Ojoto by automobile, a trip that she had not made since the war began.

"I won't know until I get there," she said.

She had yet to see for herself the consequences of the war on Aba. If the place was a disaster like Ojoto, she explained, then she might have to find another place to go, and what point was there in taking me with her until she figured it out? What if it turned out that the place was just as badly destroyed as Ojoto? And what if the food situation was just as bad as what we were now experiencing in Ojoto? "I'll have to send you off, at least until I get there and see how things are."

Her voice cracked as she spoke, and there was a hurriedness to her words, as if she were struggling to get them all out before she ran out of breath.

Already I knew what was causing her to hurry that way. Already I knew what was causing her to seem so out of breath. It was a problem with her words. Because she did *not* in fact *have to* send me off. And yet there were the words, flowing out of her mouth, all of them justification for what was essentially a lie, though an honest kind of lie, an unintentional sort of self-delusion. She could not possibly have believed what she was saying. I could see this in the movement of her mouth. The way one corner of her lips twitched a bit as she spoke. Unconvincing lips. As if even her lips did not believe the words. And her eyes. The way she could not quite hold my gaze.

She had hardly finished speaking when I began to plead with her. Already I had lost Papa. How could I bear to lose her too?

I shook my head. "Mama, please, no. I want to go with you."

But she was determined to follow through with the lie. "It has to be done," she said. "It will be for a short while, maybe just a few days, and I have found a place where you can stay in the meantime, a place I know you will be taken care of. Just until I'm able to come fetch you and take care of you myself. I'm thinking of your safety, Ijeoma. It would be terrible for me to take you with me to Aba. If I did, who knows what could befall you there?"

I struggled to hold back tears, but they came out anyway.

"Stop your crying," she said. "*Ebezina.*"

"But Mama—"

She pulled me close to her, held me tight in an embrace. "It has to be done," she said. "You will be in Nnewi with a former friend of your father's. The grammar school teacher and his wife. You will help them around their house, and in return they will look after you. Like I said, it will be just for a short while. Believe me, it's the best place that I can think of to send you right now."

"But Mama, please," I continued to beg.

Her mood changed. "You're not hearing me," she said, engaging with me now in a different manner than before: her eyes turned almost feral—biting eyes, like teeth severing flesh, teeth tearing into my insides. My insides could have bled.

She took me by the shoulders and, in a stern voice, she said, "Open your eyes, Ijeoma! Can't you see that all of this will be for your own good? For God's sake, I am doing this for your own good!"

No matter how much she tried to convince me of this, I knew the truth all the same: that she was doing it for *her* own good. At least, that it was more for her own good than it was for mine. That she was doing it because she was overwhelmed: by life, by the war, by the thought of having to try and make it without Papa. And she was overwhelmed even by me. Didn't matter that I myself was overwhelmed. My world had narrowed down to my mother, and now my mother was betraying me.

"What if the food situation in Aba is just as bad as it is here?" she repeated. "Then what will you eat? Are you ready to starve? Even more than you're already starving now? There are no miracles these days. Manna will not fall from the sky. Bombs, yes, enough to pierce our hearts, but manna, no."

I looked at her with all the pleading my eyes could muster. But even as I begged, I knew there was no way out. Plans had, clearly, already been made. How else would she have been so certain that the grammar school teacher would accept the proposal?

Still I begged. I looked around frantically, as if all potential arguments in my favor were particles in the air, as if I only had to land on the right one in order to be able to convince her why I should go with her. But I was unable to land on the right particle.

She smiled at me, a tired smile. Her voice low and gravelly. "Do you remember the grammar school teacher and his wife?"

I nodded, though it was only a skeleton of a memory, hardly there at all.

"I know for a fact that you will be fine in Nnewi," she said. "I have gone and seen it for myself." Nnewi was a much shorter distance from Ojoto, she explained; south like Aba, but only something between ten and twelve kilometers away, which was less than half an hour by automobile and could be walked in well under two hours. Unlike Aba, she had actually made the trip to Nnewi to see it with her own eyes, and to visit with the grammar school teacher and his wife. Only now did I recall that day. A day when she claimed that she had been going to "run errands." From those "errands," apparently, she had found out that Nnewi, though close in proximity to Ojoto, was indeed faring better than Ojoto, at least where food supply was concerned.

Not only was my face covered in tears by now, but my nose had also begun to run. Mama reached into the folds at the waist of her wrapper, grabbed a handkerchief from there, and gently dabbed away the moisture on my face. "No more crying," she said. But she herself was crying now. Soft crying, the kind that hardly had an effect on her breaths. But there were the tears for proof. In that brief moment, she appeared to be battling her own plan. She might have had a change of mind. In that moment, she might have sacrificed her own desires in exchange for mine. I held my breath and hoped. Moments passed, and then, instead of going back on her plan, as I was hoping, she took my hands in hers and prayed: *Dear God in heaven, I am placing my child in Your care. Please guide and protect her even as I cannot. There is power in the blood of Jesus. Amen.*

She wiped the tears off her own face with the palms of her hands, and she said, "I promise that the grammar school teacher and his wife will look after you."

9

ANOTHER RAID HAD come and demolished our church, torn a hole in it and then completely flattened out that holy construction of a place that was responsible for keeping our faith and hope intact. By the morning of the day before we left Ojoto, the church and everything inside it had disintegrated like cubes of sugar in water: none of the original structure was recognizable to the naked eye.

The Ejiofors arrived sometime between eleven o'clock and noon on that penultimate day. A bowl of garden eggs and groundnut paste sat on the center table, along with a jerry can of water and some drinking cups, to welcome them. This was as much as Mama could gather for their visit, which was not really a problem, as they would not be staying long.

Mama went out to the front yard to greet them. She embraced Mrs. Ejiofor first. I watched from the parlor window. "*Unu a biana! Nno nu!* Welcome o!" She stepped aside and did the same with Mr. Ejiofor. She had hardly finished exchanging greetings with Chibundu's parents when I watched Chibundu race to the front of the house, across the veranda, and through the front door.

"Ije!" he called out, his nickname for me.

He found me standing by the parlor window.

"Why can't you come stay with me and my mama and papa?" he burst out.

I turned to face him. The aroma of groundnut paste was strong in the parlor. "Mama says it's hard enough for any family to take care of their own child, let alone take care of someone else's child," I replied. She had said exactly that. The day after she had told me about sending me off, I had come up with a list of my school and church friends whose families I would rather have gone and stayed with, but she had given me this response as a reason why none of my friends' homes was a viable option for me.

"I don't know why both of you can't stay in Ojoto," Chibundu said.

"I want to stay," I replied simply.

Mr. and Mrs. Ejiofor entered the parlor along with Mama. On the wall between the parlor's two windows was a silver-trimmed mirror, all damaged and strewn with crack lines but still intact enough for us to see ourselves. Chibundu walked toward it, pulling me along with him.

We stood in front of the mirror together. His parents settled themselves on the sofa, getting ready to eat the garden eggs.

Chibundu said, "Look very closely into the mirror and see us standing together. Look really closely at us so that you never forget that we were friends."

"Are we not going to remain friends?" I asked.

He was staring at me now, and suddenly I remembered the time when he had loosened the thread from my plaited hair, pulled on the tip of the plait so that the knotted end came undone, so that the thread flowed out in one continuous and wave-like strand. When I had begun to shout at him — *Look what you've done to my hair!* — and when Mrs. Ejiofor had joined in scolding him for it, he put his hands in the air, as if this was some part of his Police game. He held his hands up, all innocent-like, saying he did not understand what the big deal was, that he only did it because he needed some thread for a project he was in the middle of out in the yard — a small toy lorry that he was trying to build out of some discarded pieces of wood.

Whatever became of the lorry I cannot now remember, but what I knew even then was that this Chibundu standing by my side in front of the mirror was certainly not the same one who had caused my hair to be undone. There was something pitiful about him, and I thought that perhaps this was the effect the war was having on him.

I smiled at him instinctively. He smiled awkwardly back, then looked away in the direction of the parlor where his parents were seated.

"You won't forget, will you?" he asked, but he did not wait for me to answer. Instead, he began walking to the center of the parlor near where the sofas were. I followed him. He went straight to the center table. There, he poured himself a cup of water and invited me to drink with him, saying, "Between true friends even water drunk together is sweet."

Our parents were chatting away, not paying us any mind. I felt more pity for him, the way he stood there, looking expectantly at me. I took the water from him and drank.

Outside, the air was heavy, and if you breathed deeply, you could smell the rainwater in it, as if it were about to pour from the sky. Chibundu and I made our way to the front yard and perched ourselves on a branch of the orange tree just outside the compound gate.

Down below, on the road, a woman was carrying a tray of groundnuts or cashews, and loaves of bread. A man in a bright white shirt went by on a bicycle, riding zigzaggedly and recklessly down the road. Chibundu and I sat together on the branch, just watching.

"He is going to jam her!" Chibundu said.

I pictured all the items on the tray falling, the poor woman struggling to gather her items back together again.

But the bicycle man stopped at the point just before he would have rammed into the woman. He got off his bicycle.

"Wetin be your problem? You dey blind?" the vendor woman shouted. She set her tray on the ground and then, positioning herself directly in front of the man, she stood with her hands on her hips.

It was always serious when people spoke this way in pidgin. Pidgin was the language of amusement and relaxation, but it was also the language of conflict.

We sat watching from our spot in the tree. We were close enough to see and hear, but far enough that we could not readily be seen by passersby.

The bicycle man spoke. "Sorry," he said, after which he made to move around the vendor woman, but each time he tried, she stepped in front of him, preventing him from passing.

"Biko make I pass," he said, impatient to be on his way.

"Ehn-ehn!" the vendor woman shouted, shaking her head from side to side. "Which kain sorry be that? You no fit say sorry proper?"

"I don say sorry already," the bicycle man said, and he tried once more to move around her.

By now people were beginning to gather. The man appeared to take a deep breath, and then he tried a third time, only to be met with the woman's thundering voice, and her body once more blocking his escape.

It was a bit comical the way the wide-hipped, rather large vendor woman was refusing to let the man pass. The man was rail-thin in comparison to her and looked like he could have used some of her fat.

Chibundu brought his hands to his mouth, began to laugh quietly at the silliness of the whole scene, soft chuckles that he made sure to contain with the cupping of his hands.

The bicycle man tried the vendor woman's left side, and then her right, and her left again, but no luck.

I started to laugh too. Little by little, Chibundu and I moved closer to each other on the branch, huddling together, trying to muffle each other's laughter. Soon we were no longer listening to the dispute on the road, and we were no longer laughing. Chibundu was staring at me, just staring at me.

"What?" I asked in a whisper.

He remained silent, but continued to stare.

I looked down at the road. The man and woman had somehow worked it out. They were walking their separate ways. I turned back around to see Chibundu's face close to mine, and soon the tip of his nose was nearly touching mine.

There on the branch, nose to nose with him, I knew I could not go on sitting there. I knew I should jump off the tree, and after I landed, I should put one foot in front of the other. One foot and then the next, and then the next. It was like taking a spoonful of chloroquine when you had malaria. There was hardly another option, so you just did it. The first spoonful and then the next, and then the next. If not, things would only get worse.

But I did nothing.

Some seconds went by. There was an awkwardness to it all. I knew Chibundu felt the awkwardness too. I knew that he bore the brunt of it. As well he should. He was, after all, responsible for it much more than I was.

But for some strange reason, I found myself feeling a need to equalize the awkwardness between us. I found myself feeling a need to relieve him of the burden of it. I felt distressed on his behalf — felt his distress as if it were my own.

And so, after no more than a few seconds, I leaned in and gave him the kiss I knew he sought.

10

Buses were few and far between, so we found ourselves in the back section of a small passenger lorry instead.

Before the war came, Papa drew plans: he was a drafter, on his way to becoming an architect. During the daytime he worked at his company's offices, but even in the evenings and on weekends, when he was not working in an office, he could be found at his desk at home, tracing the graphite tips of his pencils across fancy white and blue-tinted paper, carefully measuring the placement of vertical and horizontal lines. He used to talk with Mama and me while he worked, about when and where the next bungalow or two-story would be put up, about the size of it and all the rooms that it would have. Sometimes he would tease us, talking about how one day he would design a new house for us, one so big that it would be like a castle. "Can you imagine a castle right in the middle of Ojoto?" he'd ask. Mama would laugh and say that this was not England. Castles did not belong in Ojoto. But me, I'd tell Papa that I wanted one anyway, whether or not it belonged. I had my castle-in-the-village dreams, after all. Could he please design me one that was as wide as the sky and rose all the way up to it, as tall as the tallest of iroko trees? One that was the same color as our house: a bright shade of yellow.

Even when the sky grew dark, he continued to work, his kerosene lantern flickering and making a shadow of itself on the wall. He drew, and there was no indication that he'd ever cease to draw.

But now so many of the buildings in Ojoto had crumbled with each strike of the bombers. Now he himself was gone. Now there was not an iota of a dream of any kind of castle gracing the land of our dear little Ojoto.

Riding in the back of the gwon-gworo to Nnewi, I hardly thought of much other than how I would miss our Ojoto house, if for no other reason than for the memory of Papa in it, the way he used to sit and draw his designs at his desk. The way he used to lounge on the couch reading his newspapers.

In the back section of the lorry, benches stood in rows. In the spaces between the benches, people crowded together, hanging on to the ropes that dangled from the lorry's ceiling.

Mama and I sat on one of the benches at the opening of the lorry's back. We had come upon our seats just in time, which was lucky, Mama said, and even luckier that our position allowed us to look outside as the vehicle drove along. Through the open back, we watched the scene on the road. Biafran soldiers were marching, about a dozen young men in singlets and khaki shorts or trousers, axes and guns slung across their shoulders. They chanted as they marched:

> *Ojukwu bu eze Biafra nine*
> *Emere ya na Aburi,*
> *Na Aburi!*
> *Enahoro, Yakubu Gowon, ha enweghi ike imeri Biafra!*
>
> *Biafra win the war!*
> *Armored car, shelling machine,*
> *Fighter and bomber,*
> *Ha enweghi ike imeri Biafra!*

Corpses flanked the roads. Decapitated bodies. Bodies with missing limbs. All around was the persistent smell of decaying flesh. Even if I was no stranger to these sights and smells, Papa's case being the foremost in my mind, still I felt a lurching in my stomach.

I swallowed, rapid intakes of saliva, in order to settle myself back down again.

The marching soldiers crossed the road, now singing a new song:

> *Ayi na cho isi Gowon*
> *Ayi na cho isi Gowon*
> *Ayi na cho isi Gowon*
> *Ka egbu o ya,*
> *Ka egbu o ya, we gara ya Ojukwu.*

Our lorry continued to wait as they crossed.

"But why are they looking for Gowon's head?" I asked Mama.

"To kill him," Mama replied plainly.

"Why do they want to kill him?" I asked.

"Didn't you hear the last part of the song?" she replied. "They want to kill him so they can deliver his head to Ojukwu."

For the rest of the trip, it was more of the same thing: more corpses, more soldiers marching, more chanting, all of the typical sights and sounds of a nation at war.

The Nnewi lorry dropped us off on the main Ojoto–Nnewi road, not far from the big market, at the opening of the small dirt road leading to the neighborhood where the grammar school teacher and his wife lived. We set off on foot from there.

We had almost reached the grammar school teacher's gate when Mama stopped and said, "I'll let you go on from here. It's not a long or difficult distance; it's the first house you get to where this road crosses with the next. It has a red gate. You can't miss it. The grammar school teacher will be there waiting for you."

All this time she had been carrying her own bag along with mine. In my bag, a change of clothes, an extra pair of slippers, a small container of pomade, another of body cream, some chewing sticks for my teeth, a flask of water, a small blanket.

I looked at her face. There were wrinkles on her forehead. Her face as a whole reminded me of Papa, those moments before the raid took his life.

She handed my bag over to me so that she was carrying just her own bag in one hand. With her free hand she pulled me to her. We stayed that way, in an embrace, so that I felt the movement in her chest when she took a deep inhale. She held me for a moment longer before finally letting go of me.

She was wearing a multicolored adire gown, and on her head was a simple black scarf. Her feet, those areas not protected by her sandals, were covered in dust so that her toenails appeared the color of mud.

She said, "You will be better off this way. A mother always knows best."

I could have argued even that late, but I acknowledged to myself that there was no sense in arguing anymore. All my arguments before this had gotten me nowhere.

I nodded and then hung my head so that all I could see now were our feet, hers and mine both, covered to the ankles in dust.

Mama lifted my chin with her hand. I looked into her unsmiling face. "Cheer up," she said. "Remember what I said. I will think of you every minute that I am away from you. And I will send for you as soon as I can."

She stroked my hair, as if to put back any stray strands in place, like she used to do before the war came, early in the morning before she sent me off to school. It was as if she were once more getting me ready for school.

"*Nee anya*," she said. "You must be respectful, always do as they say. Are you hearing me?"

"Yes, Mama," I replied.

"They are your father's very close friends, almost family, so you can call them Aunty and Uncle. I'm sure they will like that. Are you hearing me?"

"Yes, Mama," I said.

She fumbled with her bag, searching for something in it. When she found what she was looking for, she pulled it out. It was Papa's old Bible, the one he used to read from every Sunday at church. She handed it to me, holding my hand in hers even as I held the book in my hand.

"If God dishes you rice in a basket . . . ," she said.

I knew the second half of the proverb. "Do not wish for soup," I finished.

She smiled. "*Ngwa,*" she said. "*Gawazie.* Go on. They are expecting you any minute, and I have to be off myself before the Aba lorry leaves me behind."

I turned around and began walking, forcing myself to hold back my tears, forcing myself not to look back, forcing myself to resist the temptation to run shamelessly back to her.

11

THE GRAMMAR SCHOOL teacher was corpulent, and he walked with the gait of a man who had always been so. His skin was almost as dark as his hair, which did not grow very high from his head — it was hard to tell where the hair stopped and his face began. His belly stuck out, rotund as an udu, the kind made from the roundest of calabash gourds. His body appeared to lean backward at the hips, as if it were a struggle for it to follow any forward movement of his feet.

His wife's skin was not exactly light, but neither was it as dark as her husband's. But her eyes were just like his, a dark shade of brown. She had long hair, straightened, not natural like mine. She held it up in a bun at the nape of her neck. Her brows were penciled in and formed perfect arcs above her eyes. Her lips were a dark shade of red. Where his body leaned backward, she was so full of chest in an otherwise small frame that it appeared she had no choice but to lean forward, in the direction of the weight.

They met me at their gate.

She had a handkerchief with her. "On account of my asthma," she explained, and began to cough. When she finished coughing, she asked, "How are you?"

"I'm well, Aunty," I said.

Her husband stood just watching me, then he said my name. "Ijeoma," he uttered enthusiastically. He repeated it, as if tasting it in his mouth.

I stared at the ground, my mind pondering the way he was saying my name. I hoped he would not taste it only to turn around and spit it out. By the sound of things, probably not. There was, after all, a warmth to his voice that reminded me of Papa's voice. But then he was not Papa. He was fat and awkward-moving where Papa was thin and lithe. Would he really be warm like Papa, or was this warmth in his voice just a trick? Would it melt away the way a candle melts away with fire?

I had been looking down while he uttered my name, but now I looked up to find him peering at me. He said my name again. "*Ijeoma, ke kwanu?* Welcome! How are you?"

My mouth felt dry, like I had somehow gotten a mouthful of sand. But I forced myself to speak. "Fine, Uncle," I said.

"It's been such a long time since we last saw you," his wife said.

"Yes, yes," he said, reaching out to pat me on the shoulder. "It's been a long time." In a more quiet voice he said, "I'm sorry about your father."

"Yes, we are both sorry about your father," his wife echoed.

I nodded, then looked around the front yard. It was a neat yard, but it was easy to see the effects of the war on it: A shattered dresser sat in front of the veranda. Next to it, some downfallen branches and what looked to be shattered glass. Their hedges were just as withered as ours had become in Ojoto, and the palm fronds they were using to camouflage their compound appeared to be losing their green, just like our Ojoto palm fronds.

He broke the silence. "*Ngwa,* let's go," he said in a spirited sort of way, as if he had suddenly remembered what he had been planning to do next.

"Yes, let's go," his wife repeated.

He led us from the gate to a small house-like structure in the yard behind the main home. The structure was something like a boys' quarters, only a bit too small to be one. And anyway, there was no indication that the grammar school teacher and his wife had ever had any household help. As he walked, he made his apologies. "We don't have extra room in the house, or else we would have . . ."

"Yes, we would have put you in the house with us if only we had the room," his wife said.

"Surely she understands," he said.

"I'm sure she does," she said.

"We've made the place as comfortable as possible," he said.

A padlock hung near the top of the door. He unlocked it with a key.

His wife and I remained outside as he took my bag in.

When he came back out, he said, "You'll be fine here."

She nodded and said, "Yes, you'll be fine here."

"You'll be a good girl for us," he said.

"Yes," she said. "A good girl indeed. Helping us around the house as needed. That sort of thing."

She appeared to be examining me. After a moment, she said, "Yellow skin, the color of a ripe pawpaw. That's very lucky for a girl. It should be easy for her mother to marry her off."

"There's still plenty of time before that," he said. "But, yes, I imagine. When the time comes for it."

She nodded.

They observed me a moment longer, very awkwardly, and then they were off.

I sat on the yellow foam mattress that was to be my new bed, taking in the place. Far from being a self-contained mini-home, it was a very basic, open one-room space. Just four cement walls patched with zinc pieces, a wooden floor, and a ceiling. Neither a kitchen nor a bathroom inside. Maybe they had used it for storage before my arrival. Whatever the case, it was a crude construction, more a hovel than a home. But it was sturdy enough.

After some time, I lay down and drifted into sleep. I did not wake up until much later, four or five hours it must have been, after having arrived. Evening had faded into a dark night. No one had come to call me or check on me. Or, if they had come, perhaps I simply had not heard.

On the table that formed my desk was a kerosene lantern and a pack of matches. I struck a match and lit the lantern.

Outside the hovel was a water tank. A pipe came down the side of the tank, leading to a silver tap. A bucket sat by the tap, and a bar of soap.

I removed my dress — my orange and brown adire gown. I filled up the bucket that sat nearby with water from the tap. Near the tank was a cement slab. I squatted on the slab. Fireflies, the moon and the stars, and the flame in my kerosene lantern were the only lights that shone on me. I flicked away insects and slapped the tingling spots where the flies perched on me. I crouched tightly, an attempt to cover myself, because though I should have felt veiled, concealed by the night, there was that other element of darkness, the one that left me feeling more vulnerable, more naked than in the light. And there was still the war — the possibility of an arbitrary night raid.

I bathed carefully and quickly, lathering up and rinsing away the suds, counting as I did to distract myself from all my fears. I was done bathing by the time my count reached fifteen.

Back in the hovel, I put on an old nightgown, one of Mama's ancient cotton frocks, passed down to me because, years ago, I had fallen in love with its floral design and begged her to give it to me. At one point it had been bursting with pinks and yellows and soft blues, but now, if you looked closely at it, you saw moth holes throughout the sleeves and bodice, and it was as if all the colors had reached a compromise and found a middle ground in the light and dark shades of beige.

Some months before the war came, Mama had insisted that the nightgown was too old to continue to be worn and that I should allow her to throw it out. But I had refused.

Now, as I slipped it on, it reminded me of Mama, and of Papa, and of Ojoto, and of peace and calm, and of our lives before the war. I was grateful to have it. What did it matter about the holes or the fading colors? My life had been turned upside down, so perhaps it was fitting that I should have such a nightgown — just the kind of thing that a castaway would wear. And I was indeed a castaway: no more the security of Papa or Mama. I might as well embrace and play the part of a derelict child.

I did not go back to sleep right away. Instead, I sat by the open door of the hovel, on the small steps that led out of it. The moon shone, and the air was only a little cold. The crickets sang. I held Papa's Bible in my hand and stared into the vast sky, and I wondered what Mama was doing at that very moment in time.

When I finally went back into the hovel, I stood by its door for some time, just to get a sense of the place, even in the darkness. I observed the room by the light of my kerosene lantern. There was a part of the zinc walling where the metal was clear and a little bright, so that it appeared like added light. I scanned with bewildered eyes. Again, the yellow foam mattress. The desk and table. The otherwise bareness of the place.

Would I survive here? If so, how long would I need to survive? Mama had said that I'd be with the grammar school teacher for only a short while, maybe just a few days. What were the chances that it would be just a few days? How long was a short while? A few weeks? A couple of months? Would she really send for me? What if she somehow forgot?

No matter, I decided. If this was the rice that God was putting in my basket . . . there was no point wishing for soup.

PART II

12

SOMETIMES I THINK back to the year 1970 — the year the lessons began — and it feels like I'm reliving it all over again in my mind: sitting rigidly at the kitchen table with Mama, or in the parlor, my heart racing inside of me, my mind struggling to digest the verses, turning them inside out and upside down and sideways, trying hard to understand.

Time and time again I've tried to bury the memory of those lessons, to act as if they were not part of my reality, because claiming them would be like continuing to remember that former version of Mama, the one who believed so much that there was a demon in me.

Still, I remember.

Speaking of Mama. By 1970, about a year and a half had gone by without my seeing her. I had spent the tail end of 1968, all of 1969, and the beginning of 1970 at the grammar school teacher's, during which time Mama never once sent for me. True that she had not known for how long we would be separated. True that a part of her really did imagine that my stay in Nnewi would be for a short while. But time went on, and the grammar school teacher and his wife grew comfortable in their use of me as a housegirl. My papa was, after all, gone, and no matter that he would not have tolerated my working as a housegirl, no matter that he would have frowned upon them using their friend's daughter as a housegirl. But he was gone, and as for Mama, she had convinced herself that she was only doing what she had to do. Anyway, the truth is, though we had been an upper-middle-class family before Papa's death, with his death, and with the war, we plummeted with full force to lower class. What Mama was doing was nothing different from what lower-class families sometimes did, sending their children off as housegirls and houseboys. It made sense. Some other family could then assume responsibility for the children — for their food, their shelter, and, more important, the cost of their education.

Mama has said many times that she had been just on her way to get me when she got the grammar school teacher's call. At first it struck me as dishonest. No way could she have sworn on a Bible. Hardly would she have laid her palms on it and the thing would have blasted up in flames. But then, with all those Bible lessons — all those times she held her Bible downright in her hands — she would very well have blasted up into flames if she had been lying, so chances are that she really had been getting ready to come collect me at the exact moment when I made it so that she *had* to come get me. Sometimes that's the way coincidences are.

In a way it all worked out. As I had been good for them — with the exception of that final incident — as I had worked hard for them around the house and mostly behaved myself, the grammar school teacher and his wife had, like upstanding ogas and madams, agreed to see to it that I got a proper education. Mama said, "Remember what I said a long time ago about using your brain? They will keep their end of the bargain. They will pay your school fees, buy your school uniforms, your textbooks, all your school supplies, so that you can study hard and make something of yourself. It is important to think of your future. I was only thinking of your future . . ."

The bungalow that I met with when I joined her in Aba was a beautiful little ivory-colored thing, but it had not always been so — neither beautiful nor ivory.

The way Mama tells it these days, it's a little like a Hollywood drama, or maybe a James Bond film — so many parts to it, and even some surprises. But I do believe her, down to the smallest details, because her memory of *those* days — even of the lessons — has remained very sharp and has been consistent throughout the years.

As she tells it, she had returned to Aba to find holes in the roof of the house, to find the grass overgrown, extending almost halfway the height of the walls of the bungalow. At first she had not recognized the place. She had gone past a field of green and yellow grass, and after six or so kilometers of trekking up the road, she reached an area where the land appeared to rise more abruptly than before. She thought that she had come close to where the house was, because she knew well that the house was on a bit of a knoll, almost overlooking the village. She continued to walk, ten more minutes of climbing the small incline, but the house was nowhere in sight.

She put down the bag that she was carrying and took a rest. She wiped her forehead with her handkerchief; she remembers this, she says, because the handkerchief was one of Papa's old ones, with the letter *U* embroidered on it. *U* for Uzo. She remembers thinking of Papa then.

A woman was passing by, carrying a bucket of water on her head, and though Mama knew it would be an inconvenience to interfere with the woman's errand, she did, out of a feeling of helplessness, of turned-upside-downness, of extreme disorientation, which was a little like a blow to the face, given the fact that she was in a town she thought she knew, a town she thought she would always know, because Aba was where she had been born and raised.

She had just opened her mouth to ask the question when her eyes fell on it. The house was there after all, barely visible on the slight incline ahead. It was a brittle box of worn cement and zinc, barely peeking out from the middle of some overgrown bushes.

She apologized to the woman for troubling her. As the woman proceeded on her way, Mama looked around the area again, taking it in more fully with her eyes. She had been aware that the war would change things for the worse, and so she reasoned that perhaps this was exactly what it should be: the windows broken; the orange and guava trees fruitless, their leaves dry and cracking, having the appearance of hunger. Some animals had been on the premises — grasscutters or bush squirrels, goats or stray dogs. She could see their paw marks on the earth.

She set her bag down at the entrance of the bungalow. She had just gone through the doorway when she saw the person, presumably a man, crouched on the floor to her right. She screamed, "*Chi m o!*"

He was almost all skeleton by now, if he was not beforehand already so. It appeared that his flesh had been eaten into, likely by the same animals whose tracks she had seen earlier outside.

She continued to scream, and several villagers came running in response. She felt their hands on her, their attempts to hold her, to calm her. "*Rapum aka!*" she screamed. Leave me alone! "*E metukwana m aka!*" Don't touch me!

She decided then and there that Aba was no better than Ojoto, at least not in the way she had hoped, this fact of her having once more been subjected to the vision of death.

What was the meaning of all of this? Wasn't the point of coming to Aba to escape all the reminders of what had happened to Papa? But here was this corpse in the house, soiling the energy of the place, making it so that her home was marked all over again with memories of death.

A feeling of faintness overcame her, and she broke out in a sweat. She crouched to the floor to steady herself. A woman nearby offered her a decanter of water. She gulped down the water, sprinkled a bit of it on her face. She returned the decanter to the woman when she was done. She looked around in order to further examine the place. On the ground not far from her, shards of glass.

She screamed some more.

"Madam," the woman next to her said in a mollifying voice. "Madam."

She turned to look at the woman. She wanted to explain that she had come so far only to find things just as bad as where she had come from. "I can't stay here either," she said. She shook her head and body so erratically that the woman had to hold her to calm her down. Several men prepared to move the corpse. Who had he been? people asked in hushed tones. But they did not stay long questioning. The men removed the body with the resignation and stale sorrow of people who had confronted death far too many times.

One of the men began picking up the shards of glass.

The woman comforting her recognized her then. "Aren't you Adaora of the late Kenneth and Flora Amaechi?"

Mama nodded.

The woman cried with excitement. "Welcome, Adaora," she said. "*Nno!*"

"This is no home to return —" Mama was saying.

The woman interrupted, saying, "Not to worry. Your father's land greets you. I tell you, don't worry. All will be well again. Together we will fix up the place. One person alone cannot move an elephant, but an entire village, that is a different story."

"I can't stay here," Mama shouted. "Just how am I to stay here?" But deep inside she knew already that she would stay. Because if not, where else was there to go? And anyway, she could not continue to run forever.

So it was that she remained in Aba. The villagers helped her rebuild the bungalow, its roof, its windows, its doors. They painted its walls ivory. They cut the overgrown grass with their machetes, and Mama irrigated the land with jerry cans full of water. For camouflage, they covered the place with palm fronds. Inside, they swept and washed the tile floors.

It was they who helped her plant a garden and trees in her front yard after the war ended. Another guava tree and an orange tree. A mango tree and a pawpaw tree. Pineapples, their crowns sticking up in spikes above the surface of the earth.

It was they who helped to put up the four walls of the little shop that stood in front of the bungalow, just behind the compound's gate.

All of this had taken some time. "Which is why I took so long to come for you," Mama says, like a defense, each time she tells the story. "I had not forgotten you. Things were very difficult for a long time."

It was a small bungalow with a large parlor and two bedrooms, one of which Mama had prepared for me. The other room was hers.

The first week I was back with Mama, she did not bother speaking to me. Every morning, I came out of my room, took my morning bath, and got dressed. I walked to the kitchen, found myself some food to eat, and went back to my room. For lunch and dinner I came back out. Each time I came out, she was not there. She either was already in the shop or doing something else around the house.

Nearly a full week passed and not a word between Mama and me.

Finally, when that first week came to an end, I found her in the kitchen as I entered to look for breakfast. She was wearing a black gown, as if in mourning. She also had a black cloth tied around her head.

I stopped at the kitchen doorway and fought a mental battle over whether to stay or leave. The thought occurred to me that whatever I decided to do, I must do it respectfully, which essentially meant that, whatever I did, I must first greet her.

"Mama, good morning," I said.

There was the kitchen table along with its two chairs where we should have already been sharing our meals. But the whole week, if we had not so much as spoken, then we had certainly not eaten together, so we had yet to sit at the table together.

This particular morning, she must have made it a point to be there waiting for me. She was sitting at the table, stirring a cup of tea with a spoon. She must have just eaten a tangerine, because the crisp citrus scent of freshly peeled tangerines filled the air.

The kitchen was a wide, well-lit room with two large louver windows. The panes of the windows were open, and sunlight was filtering through.

Mama looked up at me, responded to my greeting very solemnly. "Good morning, Ijeoma," she said, and returned to stirring her tea.

I remained at the doorway. I said, "I'm sorry for interrupting you. I'll come back when you're done."

She shook her head. Still looking down at her tea, she said, "You may stay. I was just thinking that today might be a good day to speak with you about things." She pointed at the empty chair at the table. "Come, take a seat," she said.

I moved toward the chair, pulled it out, sat.

Mama spoke again. "Now that you have had the week to settle in, we must make a schedule for you. There's nothing more important now than for us to begin working on cleansing your soul."

13

THOSE INITIAL SESSIONS, the lessons took place right there at the kitchen table, with the two of us seated across from each other. They took place in the evenings, after Mama had closed up the shop, but before supper.

That first session, Mama opened the pages of her Bible. Page one, chapter one, verse one. She began:

> *¹ Na mbu Chineke kere elu-igwe na uwa.*
> *² Uwa we buru ihe toboro nʼefu na ihe toboro nkiti; ochichiri di kwa nʼelu obu-miri: Mo Chineke nerughari kwa nʼelu miri.*

> *¹ In the beginning God created the heavens and the earth.*
> *² The earth was formless and void, and darkness was over the surface of the deep, and the Spirit of God was moving over the surface of the waters.*

Her voice was gentle and calm. There was a steady cadence to it as she went down the page and then back up to chapter two. I followed along with my own Bible, Papa's old one, as we made our way through.

> *²⁰ . . . but for Adam there was not found a helper suitable for him.*
> *²¹ So the Lord God caused a deep sleep to fall upon the man, and he slept; then He took one of his ribs and closed up the flesh at that place.*
> *²² The Lord God fashioned into a woman the rib which He had taken from the man, and brought her to the man.*
> *²³ The man said,*

"This is now bone of my bones,
And flesh of my flesh;
She shall be called Woman,
Because she was taken out of Man."
²⁴ *For this reason a man shall leave his father and his mother, and*
be joined to his wife; and they shall become one flesh.

She repeated that last part:

²⁴ *N'ihi nka ka nwoke garapu nna-ya na nne-ya, rapara n'aru nwu-*
nye-ya: ha ewe gho otu anu-aru.

She said, "*Nwoke na nwunye.* Man and wife. Adam *na* Eve. *I ne*
ghe nti? Are you listening?" She was shaking her finger, a reminder
and a warning.

I nodded.

She said it again: "*Nwoke na nwunye.* Adam *na* Eve. Man and
wife."

I nodded but remained quiet, keeping my eyes steady on her. The
look on her face was the look of a person watching a gradually sinking boat from afar. She seemed about ready to scream at the captain
of the boat, but she seemed also to understand that if she screamed,
the captain could not possibly hear. Not from so far away. So she
talked softly instead, as if in prayer, as if prayer might have the effect
that shouting could not.

I listened to her, watched her brow furrow, her lips tighten and
loosen, tighten and loosen again.

Before the session began, Mama had handed me a black prayer
scarf and instructed me to tie it on my head. "The mark of true
penitence," she had said. I tugged at the scarf now.

"*I ne ghe nti?*" she asked. "Are you listening?"

I nodded.

"*I na aghota?* Are you understanding?"

I nodded again.

She smiled at me, tugged at my headscarf, perhaps to pull it forward to cover more of my hair. She patted me on the head.

"The bottom line, Ijeoma, my dear," she said, "is that if God wanted it to be otherwise, would He not have included it that other way in the Bible?"

She closed her Bible and announced that we would stop there today. The session must have lasted all of fifteen minutes in total, but the discomfort of it made it feel as if it had lasted for much longer.

She rose from her chair. Over at the cupboards, she pulled out two plates and walked with them to the stove. She dished out the rice and stew at the stove and brought them back to the table for us.

We ate silently that evening. Afterward, we both retreated to our rooms.

14

THE NEXT MORNING, I met Mama again in the kitchen, at breakfast time. We sat together at the table, soaking our slices of bread in tea, when her eyes narrowed at me, and she said, "It's not easy getting set up in a place. You really must understand that it took me all this time to get it looking the way it does now."

I replied that I understood, and I thanked her, though at the time I had not yet understood, and was not yet to the level of gratitude, because I was still smarting from her desertion of me and the memory of all that time at the grammar school teacher's when my mind tortured itself with all the possible reasons for why my own mother had thought it best to abandon me.

"All that work and now here we are with our very own home. A new life with new memories to be made. I can tell you I'm no longer having those terrible nightmares."

There was something desperate and pleading in her face as she spoke. In that moment it was as if she were the child and I were the parent; she was seeking validation, trying to convince me of why I should be proud of her.

"That's good, Mama," I said. "I'm glad the nightmares are gone."

"It's unfortunate," she said, looking forlornly into her cup of tea. "If only I had finished setting things up a little earlier, I might have prevented . . ." Her voice tapered into silence.

I stared silently at her.

She lifted her head from her cup and, with a forced sprightliness in her voice, she said, "I was thinking of making okra soup for supper tonight. I don't sell okra at the shop. Would you mind picking up some okra at the market for me?"

I nodded.

"The market is not far from here," she said. "Out our own road, a right onto the main road, and you will see the church steeple. Walk in the direction of the steeple, and not a couple of kilometers beyond that you will start to see signs of the market—the open umbrellas and zinc sheds, the items hanging out of the vendor stands."

We were done with our tea and bread by now.

"*Oya*, I'm off to the shop," she said, rising from her seat. Her handbag was on the countertop near where we sat. She reached for it.

I stood up along with her and cleared the table, collecting our saucers and teacups and placing them in the sink.

I had not yet begun to wash the dishes when Mama said, "I meant to say earlier how sorry I am that I left you there for all that time."

I turned to face her. She was holding her handbag and fumbling in it for the okra money. When she found the money, she stood there holding her bag in one hand and the money in the other. Finally, instead of just giving me the money, she took some steps closer and pulled me into an embrace. "I'm really, really sorry," she said.

My first thought was that it was strange to be in Mama's arms like this. There was a distance between us that had not existed before, not even in her initial embrace when she had come to collect me from the grammar school teacher's. There was a strain. She was my mother, and I should have leaned into her embrace, should have relished it like I did the day she had come to pick me up from the grammar school teacher's—and like all the days before she sent me off there. But things were different now. In this moment, she felt more like another warden than my own mother, more like a husk —more an emblem of motherhood than motherhood itself.

Outside, in the distance, an engine was revving, and I thought I heard a goat bleating loudly. I circled my arm around her, but I could not get myself to fall into the embrace. I stood there, rigid as a post.

When she finally let go of me, she pulled out a handkerchief from the waist folds of her wrapper and dabbed her eyes with it. "If you need anything, I'll be at the shop. Don't be afraid to stop by. Just walk in."

I nodded.

She turned around and headed for the back door. There, she stopped, turned once more to face me, and appeared to study me for a moment.

She said, "Don't forget that this evening we will be continuing our Bible study."

I had already forgotten, but I said, "I won't forget, Mama."

On my way back from the market, I stopped by the church. It was a Friday; not a Sunday had passed since my return, so I had not yet been to the church for worship. It made sense to familiarize myself with the place, seeing that I was in the vicinity.

I entered and found a seat on one of the pews facing the altar, from where I could take in all the little decorations on the shelves that lined the wall behind: red and yellow flowers, clay and glass bottles, a pile of Bibles and books.

At the grammar school teacher's, Amina and I had only intermittently followed him and his wife to church. Our chores had always taken precedence over Sunday service.

Sitting in the Aba church that day, I couldn't help noting how much I had missed Sunday worship, how much I had missed just being in a church, even without worship.

There was no one else around. The place felt extra holy: a hollow sort of holiness, the kind of hollowness that caused me to think of an echoing voice. It brought to mind those Bible passages in which God was said to have spoken. I thought, If He were to speak to me now, what would He say?

Whatever it was He did say, His voice would surely echo. Perhaps that was the point of the hollowness of the church. So that it heightened the voice of God in our ears, and in us. So that His voice echoed in our hearts.

Suddenly I felt an urge to pray. I wanted to ask for forgiveness for the things I had done in Nnewi. Not a day had passed when I did not remember those things. Not a day had passed when I did not crave those things, when I did not find myself wanting to repeat them. But now, I sat in church and for the first time I felt an over-whelming sense of guilt. I wanted to ask God to help me turn my thoughts away from Amina, to turn me instead onto the path of righteousness. I wanted to ask Him to guide me, to allow His word to echo in my heart. I opened my mouth to pray, but somehow the words of prayer would not come. It was as if they had become stuck in my throat. I tried over and over again. Still no luck. After a while, I stood up and took myself back home.

That evening, we read the Bible as we had done the night before, Mama reading aloud and me following along in my own Bible.

We had not prayed the previous session, but this time, when we were done reading, Mama said, "Let us pray."

She rose from her seat and knelt in front of her chair. I followed her lead, knelt on the floor in front of my chair. She rested her el-bows on the chair seat, and I did the same.

"Almighty God in heaven," she began, "protect this my child from the devil that has come to take her innocent soul away. *Zoputa ya n'ajo ihe.* Protect her from the demons that are trying to send her to hell. Lead her not into temptation. *E kwela ka o kwenye na nlanye.* Give her the strength to resist and do Your will. May her heart re-member the lessons You have given, the lesson of our beginning, of Adam and of Eve."

I faded in and out of the prayer, my thoughts of what we had read, of Genesis and of Adam and Eve, and of me and Amina, dis-tracting me.

She continued on like that, pleading with God, asking for His mercy and His protection. Finally she said, "Your will be done on earth as it is in heaven. *Ka e mee uche Gi n'uwa ka e si eme ya n'eluigwe.*"

She exhaled. I exhaled with her.

"Amen!" she said, very firmly, like a vow.

In that moment, I felt a weakness come over me. I opened my mouth to say "Amen," but it was a struggle for me to speak, a strug-gle for me to utter that tiny word along with her.

15

DON'T YOU SEE?" Mama asked. "It's that same behavior
that led to the destruction of Sodom and Gomorrah, the
very same behavior that you and that girl—what's her name again?
—engaged in."

We were still in Genesis. Mama was lingering on the story of
Sodom and Gomorrah:

Two angels had come to visit Sodom, and Lot had persuaded
them to lodge with him. But then came the men of the city, knocking on Lot's door, demanding to see the guests. *Bring them out to
us, that we may know them.* But Lot refused. Instead, he offered the
men his two virgin daughters, for them to do to the daughters as
they wished, so long as they did not harm the guests, so long as they
did not do as they wished unto the guests.

"Lot was a good man," Mama said. "Hospitable. Was willing to
protect his guests from sin."

"But he offered up his own daughters to be done with as the Sod-
omites wished," I replied. "How did that make him a good man?"

"The point is that Lot protected his guests from being handled in
that terrible way that the Bible warns against."

"What terrible way?" I asked.

"Man lying with man," she said, sighing with irritation.

"And *that* is the lesson we are to take from the story?" I asked.

She rolled her eyes at me but remained silent.

"Maybe it was a lesson on hospitality," I said in a soft voice,
though she had clearly struck a nerve in me. Still, I did not want
to provoke her any more than I already had. "The idea that he was
willing to put in danger his own belongings, and that he was willing

to risk the welfare of his own family members in order to safeguard his guests. It could simply have been a lesson on hospitality," I said.

"It isn't," Mama said. "Everybody knows what lesson we should take from that story. Man must not lie with man, and if man does, man will be destroyed. Which is why God destroyed Sodom and Gomorrah."

"It couldn't have been because they were selfish and inhospitable and violent?" I asked. "It has to be that other thing?"

"Yes," Mama said. "It had to be that other thing. It couldn't have been anything other than that other thing."

16

LEVITICUS 18.

²² *Thou shalt not lie with mankind, as with womankind: it is abomination.*

OUR LESSONS HAD by now moved from the kitchen to the parlor. We were sitting on the floor between the pale green sofa and the short wooden center table, holding our Bibles in our hands.

"What is the meaning of 'abomination'?" I asked.

"Simple: something disgusting, disgraceful, a scandal."

"But what exactly is disgusting or disgraceful or scandalous about lying with mankind as with womankind? Does the Bible explain?"

"The fact that the Bible says it's bad is all the reason you need," Mama said. "Besides, how can people be fruitful and multiply if they carry on in that way? Even *that* is scandal enough — the fact that it does not allow for procreation."

I knew enough to know that the grammar school teacher and his wife could not have children. I knew enough to know that there were other men and women, husbands and wives like them, who also could not have children. "But even with a man and a woman, procreation is not always possible. Is that an abomination too?" I asked. "What if there's nothing they can do about it?"

"God intended for it to be man and woman. And God intended also for man and woman to bear children. It is the way it should be, so yes, it is an abomination if it is not man and woman. And it is an abomination if man and woman cannot bear a child."

My head felt as if it were about to explode. Did she not realize what she was saying about the grammar school teacher and his wife and couples like them? I felt a million questions churning in my mind, the sorts of questions that might only have exasperated Mama more. I could have gone ahead and asked them, but the questions were like tiny bubbles in my head. I could feel them floating around, but they were either too small to amount yet to anything or too busy floating this way and that; I could not quite settle on them.

Mama carried on. Leviticus 19.

19 Ye shall keep my statutes. Thou shalt not let thy cattle gender with a diverse kind: thou shalt not sow thy field with mingled seed: neither shall a garment mingled of linen and woolen come upon thee.

"Can you see how this applies to you and that girl?"

I shook my head.

"Okay. Why don't we read it one more time and see if you can't figure it out on your own."

She read it again.

"Any thoughts now?"

"Mama, I have no thoughts," I said.

"I'll give you a hint. You're Igbo. That girl is Hausa. Even if she were to be a boy, don't you see that Igbo and Hausa would mean the mingling of seeds? *Don't you see?* It would be against God's statutes." She paused. "Besides, are you forgetting what they did to us during the war? Have you forgotten what they did to Biafra? Have you forgotten that it was her people who killed your father?"

She placed her open Bible on the center table and stood up. She walked in the direction of the kitchen, entered.

I looked at her Bible as it lay open on the center table. There were notes written all over its margins, both in Igbo and in English. There were small sheets of paper tucked between the pages. I saw that she had also written notes on these tiny sheets of paper. The notes around the margins of her Bible might have been old notes, but I could tell that those notes on the pieces of paper were new notes, which were to serve as her guide. All of them for my benefit.

She returned from the kitchen holding two glasses of water. She placed them on the center table near where her Bible lay. She took a seat and then a sip from her glass and offered me my own.

17

BEFORE THE WAR came, Papa told candlelight stories, folktales about talking animals and old kingdoms. In his nighttime voice, gruff from hours of silence at his drawing table, he told of kings and queens, of magic drums, of scheming tortoises and hares.

Once when I asked about the tortoises and the hares — why they did not speak or appear to behave in real life the way they did in his stories — he slipped into a mellow state of consciousness; his face became meditative. But his eyes were sharp and lustrous, reflecting in them all the passion and energy that his face withheld. He spoke of allegories, and of the literal versus the figurative. He explained that certain things were symbols of other things, and that certain folktales were only allegories of certain situations in life.

"What is an allegory?" I asked.

The look on his face became even more reflective than before. He was a man who liked to wallow in his thoughts. Sometimes he seemed to get lost in the wanderings of his mind. That day, he said, "A dove can be quite literally just a bird. Or it can be a symbol of peace, and sometimes a symbol of more than peace. An allegory is a symbol. Something that represents something else. Maybe it is something small, a simple thing like the dove. But always, it is used to represent something very big, a larger idea, something so big that often we don't fully grasp the scope of its meaning."

We arrived at the book of Judges. Chapter 19.

Mama read the words quietly, as if God were physically there with us in the room, as if she were paying obeisance to Him:

¹ And it came to pass in those days, when there was no king in Israel, that there was a certain Levite sojourning on the side of mount E'phra-im, who took to him a concubine out of Beth-lehem-judah.
² And his concubine played the whore against him, and went away from him unto her father's house to Beth-lehem-judah, and was there four whole months.
³ And her husband arose, and went after her, to speak friendly unto her, and to bring her again, having his servant with him, and a couple of asses: and she brought him into her father's house: and when the father of the damsel saw him, he rejoiced to meet him.
⁴ And his father-in-law, the damsel's father, retained him; and he abode with him three days: so they did eat and drink, and lodged there.

The father and the Levite went on to bargain over a price for the damsel, and the damsel was forced to return with the Levite. On their way back to his home, they passed the town of Gibeah, where most of the citizens were up to no good. One of the noble townspeople, in order to protect the travelers, offered them shelter at his home. But before the night was over, the other men of the city showed up at the kind man's door and demanded to rape the Levite. The kind man pleaded with his fellow townspeople, even offering up his own daughter to be raped instead.

Rather than offer up himself to the townsmen, the Levite offered up the damsel to be raped. The men of the town defiled her all through the night before finally letting her go. When they were done, she collapsed in front of the door. In the morning the Levite came out, prodding her to get up so that they could be on their way. She did not respond. Annoyed, he threw her over his donkey and took her with him that way. Back at home he cut her into pieces, limb by limb, which he then sent out to all the territories of Israel.

We were in the parlor, settled on the floor around the center table.

"Think about it," Mama said when she was done reading.

It was a mess of a story. I was not sure what she wanted me to think about. "Think about what?" I asked.

"Don't you see how this applies to you?"

I did not, but just for the sake of trying to see things from her point of view, I forced myself to think deeper of it. I imagined the whole thing in my head. The terrible image of the rape, of the poor damsel lying unconscious at the doorstep, and then being flung over the donkey by the Levite. The terrible image of the Levite cutting up her body into twelve pieces. These were what came to my mind. What part of that could possibly apply to me?

I stretched out my legs under the center table and said, "Mama, I don't understand what you're asking. *A ghotaghi m.*"

"What is there not to understand?" she said. "Do you not see why the men offered up the women instead of the man?"

I said, "No, I don't see why."

After a moment I realized that I *did* know why. The reason was suddenly obvious to me. I said, "Actually, Mama, yes, I do see why. The men offered up the women because they were cowards and the worst kind of men possible. What kind of men offer up their daughters and wives to be raped in place of themselves?"

Mama stared wide-eyed at me, then, very calmly, she said, "Ijeoma, you're missing the point."

"What point?"

"Don't you see? If the men had offered themselves, it would have been an abomination. They offered up the girls so that things would be as God intended: man and woman instead of man and man. Do you see now?"

A headache was rising in my temples. My heart was racing from bewilderment at what Mama was saying. It was the same thing she had said with the story of Lot. It was as if she were obsessed with this issue of abomination. How could she really believe that *that* was the lesson to be taken out of this horrible story? What about all the violence and all the rape? Surely she realized that the story was even more complex than just violence and rape. To me, the story didn't make sense.

I thought, What if all of these stories were actually only allegories for something else, something more than we could easily put our fingers on?

In addition to our studies, I had now begun to accompany Mama to church on Sundays. Why was it that these questions never came up at church? Why was it that people never asked any questions at church? Instead, everyone nodded, and cried "Amen" after everything Father Godfrey said, and clapped, no one asking him to explain anything. I wished that Papa were here so that I could have asked him what he thought. I wondered what Father Godfrey would say if I confronted him with these questions. Would he even know the answers? How much did pastors pretend to know?

I looked at Mama and said, "Mama, the Bible is full of stories. Maybe they're all just allegories of something else."

"Hush," Mama said. "The Bible is the Bible and not to be questioned. What we read in it is what we are to take out of it."

Earlier, Mama had risen mid-lesson to fetch us glasses of water. The glasses were now on the table, one for me and the other for her. We had not yet touched them.

I opened my mouth again to ask her if she knew what an allegory was. But this time she must have seen the moment when my mouth opened. She reached out to the table, shifted one of the glasses to me. "Here," she said. "Drink some water."

It occurred to me that I was indeed thirsty. I picked up the water and drank.

She watched me drink. When I was done, she said, "Good. We have no time to stop. We must continue. *Osiso-osiso.*" She took a hurried sip out of her glass, turned the pages of her Bible, and continued to read.

18

BIBLE STORIES AND thoughts of their potential as allegories were beginning to invade my mind. One night I lay on my bed, alone in my room, and thought about everything. If my mind were one of those old-fashioned scales, the scales of justice, with one metal pan measuring right and the other wrong, both sides would have been dead even. It was turning out that all that studying was not actually doing any good; if anything, it was making it a case between what I felt in my heart and what Mama and the grammar school teacher felt. The Bible was beginning to feel almost negligible, as it was seeming to me more and more impossible to know exactly what God could really have meant.

But I wanted to know. I rose from my bed and knelt by its edge, because it also seemed to me, rather suddenly, that maybe I could arrive at the answers if I tried again to pray to God on my own. Perhaps God would speak to me. Perhaps He would allow His voice to echo in me, providing me with the answers.

I had just come out of another one of my studies with Mama. My headscarf, which I always wore during the sessions, had come completely undone by now, and my braids hung loose, aimless around my shoulders. I was in the middle of gathering the braids together, of tying the scarf around them, when my mind circled back to Adam and Eve.

The thought occurred to me: Yes, it had been Adam and Eve. But *so what* if it was only the story of Adam and Eve that we got in the Bible? Why did *that* have to exclude the possibility of a certain Adam and Adam or a certain Eve and Eve? Just because the story happened to focus on a certain Adam and Eve did not mean that all other possibilities were forbidden. Just because the Bible recorded one specific thread of events, one specific history, why did that have to invalidate or discredit all other threads, all other histories? Woman was created for man, yes. But why did that mean that woman could not also have been created for another woman? Or man for another man? Infinite possibilities, and each one of them perfectly viable.

I wondered about the Bible as a whole. Maybe the entire thing was just a history of a certain culture, specific to that particular time and place, which made it hard for us now to understand, and which maybe even made it not applicable for us today. Like Exodus. *Thou shalt not seethe a kid in its mother's milk.* Deuteronomy said it too. But what did it mean? What did it mean *back then?* Was the boiling of the young goat in its mother's milk a metaphor for insensitivity, for coldness of heart? Or did it refer to some ancient ritual that nobody performed anymore? But still, there it was in the Bible, open to whatever meaning people decided to give to it.

Also, what if Adam and Eve were merely symbols of companionship? And Eve, different from him, woman instead of man, was simply a tool by which God noted that companionship was something you got from a person outside of yourself? What if that was all it was? And why not? By now I knew enough that there were at least a few allegories in the Bible — those ones that were explicitly identified as such. So why should other stories in the Bible, like the story of Adam and Eve, not be conducive to allegorical treatment as well? After all, if it were to be taken so literally, whom, then, did Cain marry, if only Adam and Eve and Cain and Abel were in existence at the time? If it were to be read literally, whom, then, was God warning against taking vengeance on Cain? Who else would have been on earth to warn save Adam and Eve, Cain's own parents, who, from all signs, had no intention of killing their son? Surely there must have been other sets of mankind, other possibilities of human existence, Adam and Eve being only one instance, a symbolic representation of them all.

I was excited by my thoughts. From the time our Bible studies began, I'd had the feeling of a person wandering lost and aimless and thirsty in the desert. But now I had stumbled upon a tap of water. The joy of my discovery washed over me. My first instinct was to go to Mama and present my case to her. It might result in a fit of argument, but she needed to know that there was more to the Bible than her interpretation of it. I ran from the side of my bed toward the door.

I had just reached the door when I realized I'd be better off not trying to present these theories to Mama. What good would arguing over it do? She might decide that I was being insubordinate to her and to God, and then maybe she would increase the lessons to two times a day.

I stood at my door for a moment, then turned and headed back to my bed.

19

W E   H A D   A R R I V E D at the end of the Old Testament, the book of Malachi. Mama had just finished with the closing prayer. She was leaning on the center table, her elbows crossed above it. She was wearing an ugly expression on her face, like a frown, as if the sun, through the open panels of the louver windows, had somehow descended from the sky and was attacking her.

She looked away from me, all the while fiddling with the corners of her Bible. Finally she turned back to me and spoke. Her voice was a whisper, very calm. She said, "Do you still think of her?"

The question came as a surprise. I lowered my head, thinking of ways in which I could pretend not to have heard. But Mama would not let me pretend. She asked it again, and in more detail: "Do you still think of her *in that way?*"

The answer was simple: of course I still thought of Amina. And, yes, *in that way.* How could I force away memories of a person with whom I'd shared all that time? There were nights when I dreamed of her, dreams so vivid that when I woke it seemed that the waking was the dream, and the dream, my reality: Amina running errands with me, washing clothes and hanging them to dry, chopping wood, coming along with me to fetch kerosene.

Amina and I bathing together out by the tap, both of us looking into each other's faces. Amina and I on the mattress we shared, our warm breaths intermingling in the small space between.

I did not have the presence of mind to say anything but the truth. I looked Mama in the eyes and nodded. "Yes, I still think of her," I said. And, "Yes, I still think of her in that way."

Suddenly Mama was rising from the floor, flailing her hands in the air, shouting about prayer and forgiveness. She pulled me up by the collar of my dress.

She screamed, "Get on your knees now! I say, get on your knees!"

I got on my knees as she demanded, but I remained silent, unable to speak. My mind was too busy for words — too busy retracing steps and settling on and mulling over the moment that I had made the gaffe. I stewed over my foolishness, over why I had not been more clever — far less forthcoming — about the answer that I had given.

"Pray!" she screamed. "You must ask God for the forgiveness of all your sins, but especially for that one particular sin in you. Did I not just tell you to pray? Why do I not see your lips moving? Why do I not hear any sound coming out of your mouth? Pray, I say! No child of mine will carry those sick, sick desires. The mere existence of them is a terrible disrespect to God and to me!"

She continued to scream in that fashion, and all the while I could only get myself to look wide-eyed at her. Finally I made to rise up, but she shouted at me to kneel back down. "Kneel!" she screamed, panting as if out of breath.

I did as I was told.

She placed her hands on my head, put pressure on it so that I turned my face downward toward the center table.

"Only your own prayer will save you now. I have prayed all I can for you. Now you must pray for yourself! Only God can save you!"

I brought my hands to my face, shutting my eyes. I remained in that pose, still lost in my thoughts, still wishing that there were a way that I could go back in time and take back the answer that had led to this blowup.

"Pray!" she cried.

I could have prayed at this point. I *did* want to pray, even, if prayer would be what would calm things down. But my mind could not think up the words to begin. All of her screaming, all of her orders, were instead replaying themselves inside my head.

Kneel!

Pray!
Sinful!
Terrible disrespect!
Only God can save you!

It took me a while to register it when I was no longer hearing her voice. Only then did I open my eyes. Mama was nowhere to be seen.

I stayed kneeling for some time. I expected that she would soon return, but minutes passed, and when something like half an hour passed, I stood up, walked out the front door, across the veranda, around the house, and back into the kitchen through the back door. No sign of Mama.

I walked the path that led to the shop. The gate of the store was fastened with a metal chain. I knew that Mama could not be there.

I returned to the bungalow. I sat back on the floor where she had left me and waited.

Something like an hour went by.

The rattling came from the direction of the front door. The jingling of keys, the turning of the knob, smacks and whacks, objects bumping into the wall.

Mama entered with a decanter made of clay in her hand. It was a reddish flask with a dull finish, hand-painted in such a way that the red coloring appeared to drip in spots, something like trickling blood.

She approached until she towered above me. She got down on her knees. A scent of incense floated out of her. Her voice was weak, even a little apologetic, as she said: "I've been thinking. It's not you."

My head snapped up in her direction.

She continued. "No, it's not you at all. There's nothing wrong with you. It's the devil causing you to be this way."

She placed the items in her hand on the floor by the table.

"*Ngwa*, get down on your knees," she said in a far more composed manner than earlier.

I got down on my knees.

"Lower your head and close your eyes," she said, still calmly.

I lowered my head, and I closed my eyes.

She placed her open hands on my head.

"In the name of God the Almighty, I order you to come out of her," she said. Her voice was progressively louder each time she repeated it, but still controlled: "In the name of the Almighty God, I order you to leave my child alone."

I felt droplets of liquid on my neck and a little on my face.

Her voice came out piercing, almost like a wail, causing shivers down my back. "*Lagha chi azu! Lagha chi azu!*" she cried.

The droplets continued to wet the skin on my neck and face and even my arms. I felt lightheaded, as if the blood had drained out of me. She was speaking to the devil, crying for him to turn back and leave me alone. "I order you to leave. I order you to leave her alone. *Lagha chi azu! Lagha chi azu! Asi m gi, Lagha chi azu!*"

Finally she let out a lengthy sigh of exhaustion. Everything grew quiet. I no longer felt the droplets on me. I opened my eyes slowly. Mama was sitting on the floor by my side, her face tear-stained. Her hands dangled aimlessly at her sides. The decanter lay nearby, in the little space between her one hand and the couch.

"It's my fault," she said, weakly now. Her throat was hoarse.

I moved closer to her, leaned my head against her shoulder. "It's not your fault, Mama."

We stayed quiet.

"It's my fault," she repeated in a thin voice.

"No, Mama. It's not anybody's fault."

"Yes," she said. "Of course it's my fault." She went on to recount that day out on the veranda when I begged to follow her to Aba. Maybe she should have allowed me to go with her, she said. What kind of mother sent her daughter off to be a housegirl for someone else, and for all that time? And beyond that, to send off a child who had just seen her father's corpse lying in all that blood. To send off a child under those circumstances when she should have done anything to keep her close.

Up to this moment, I had still been holding a grudge against Mama for abandoning me at the grammar school teacher's. But now, hearing how much she herself had been thinking about it, how much she was still tormenting herself over it, all my grudge melted away. "Mama," I said, "you're not the only person who sent your daughter out to be a housegirl." I knew of other families who had also kept housegirls. The girls' parents must have been the ones who sent them to work in that way. I said, "You're not the only one. There are many others too."

She nodded. "It was for your own good," she said softly.

I nodded.

"For your safety, for your well-being."

I nodded again.

"He and his wife were kind to you the entire time?"

"Yes, Mama. They were nothing but kind to me."

"You know, some people leave just to have the benefit of coming back home."

"Yes, Mama," I said.

She placed her palms on my cheeks, held my face tightly. Her hands were wet. The air was stuffy, thick. "Don't you worry," she said. "There's no sin so bad that it can't be forgiven, no wrongdoing so terrible that it can't be repented of. You will repent and you will be forgiven by the glory and the power of God."

There was silence.

She said, "You will be cured by the glory and power of God."

I remained silent.

"Say it!"

"I will be cured by the glory and power of God."

She took the decanter from where it was sitting, tilted it until more water poured into her cupped hand. She sprinkled the water over my head.

"Amen," she said.

"Amen," I replied.

We moved on to the New Testament and made our way quickly to Revelation. Six months had passed since our studies began. It was approaching the time for me to start secondary school.

The last day of our Bible study, Mama called me to the parlor, and I appeared to find her holding a list, handwritten by her on posterboard. It was a summary — and a reminder — of what she decided were the important points, the highlights from the Old and the New Testaments. She stood in the front area of the parlor and asked me to sit on the couch. She began to read like a schoolteacher lecturing a class:

LEVITICUS 18:22
Thou shalt not lie with mankind, as with womankind: it is abomination.

LEVITICUS 19:19
Ye shall keep my statutes. Thou shalt not let thy cattle gender with a diverse kind: thou shalt not sow thy field with mingled seed: neither shall a garment mingled of linen and woolen come upon thee.

LEVITICUS 20:13
If a man also lie with mankind, as he lieth with a woman, both of them have committed an abomination: they shall surely be put to death; their blood shall be upon them.

MARK 10:6–9
But from the beginning of the creation God made them male and female. For this cause shall a man leave his father and mother, and cleave to his wife; And they twain shall be one flesh: so then they are no more twain, but one flesh. What therefore God hath joined together, let not man put asunder.

ROMANS 1:26–32
For this cause God gave them up unto vile affections: for even their women did change the natural use into that which is against nature: And likewise also the men, leaving the natural use of the woman, burned in their lust one toward another; men with men working that which is unseemly, and receiving in themselves that

recompense of their error which was meet. And even as they did not like to retain God in their knowledge, God gave them over to a reprobate mind, to do those things which are not convenient; Being filled with all unrighteousness, fornication, wickedness, covetousness, maliciousness; full of envy, murder, debate, deceit, malignity; whisperers, Backbiters, haters of God, despiteful, proud, boasters, inventors of evil things, disobedient to parents, Without understanding, covenant-breakers, without natural affection, implacable, unmerciful: Who knowing the judgment of God, that they which commit such things are worthy of death, not only do the same, but have pleasure in them that do them.

1 CORINTHIANS 6:9–11

Know ye not that the unrighteous shall not inherit the kingdom of God? Be not deceived: neither fornicators, nor idolaters, nor adulterers, nor effeminate, nor abusers of themselves with mankind, Nor thieves, nor covetous, nor drunkards, nor revilers, nor extortioners, shall inherit the kingdom of God. And such were some of you: but ye are washed, but ye are sanctified, but ye are justified in the name of the Lord Jesus, and by the Spirit of our God.

1 CORINTHIANS 7:2

Nevertheless, to avoid fornication, let every man have his own wife, and let every woman have her own husband.

1 TIMOTHY 1:10–11

For whoremongers, for them that defile themselves with mankind, for men-stealers, for liars, for perjured persons, and if there be any other thing that is contrary to sound doctrine; According to the glorious gospel of the blessed God, which was committed to my trust.

JUDE 1:7

Even as Sodom and Gomorrah, and the cities about them in like manner, giving themselves over to fornication, and going after strange flesh, are set forth for an example, suffering the vengeance of eternal fire.

REVELATION 21:8

> *But the fearful, and unbelieving, and the abominable, and murder-*
> *ers, and whoremongers, and sorcerers, and idolaters, and all liars,*
> *shall have their part in the lake which burneth with fire and brim-*
> *stone: which is the second death.*

(Here, she double-underlined the words "the abominable" for me.)

After reading aloud the contents of the posterboard, Mama said, "You really must understand that that kind of behavior between you and that girl is the influence of demonic spirits. *I ne ghe nti?* Are you listening?"

I nodded.

"Satan finds a way to influence us all the way from hell," she said. "But I will continue to pray for you, and you must continue to pray for yourself. There's nothing that can't be conquered when we receive Jesus as our Lord and our Savior."

By the end of all those lessons, all that praying, if anyone had asked how I felt, I would have told them that I was exhausted. Not angry, not confused, not even penitent. Just exhausted.

A week before I was to leave to board at the secondary school, two or three days after that last Bible study session, Mama turned to me again and asked, "Do you still think of her in that way?"

I looked into her eyes, knowing better than to tell the truth, but I could not get myself to speak the lie. I shook my head. I forced myself to shake it with authority, making sure not to blink. It was the first time that I had lied to Mama. I comforted myself with the thought that at least I had not *spoken* the lie.

Mama smiled, patted me on the shoulder. "Very good, my child. Very, very good." She sighed, then she said, "The power of God! The wonderful power of our glorious and Almighty God!"

Part III

20

I T TURNS OUT that I became the businesswoman Mama thought I might, seeing that I wound up taking over the business end of things for her. Of course, I didn't go to any special schooling for it beyond secondary school, so maybe it also turns out that all that talk by Mama about eating protein and using my brain actually was valid, schooling or not.

In any case, sometimes as I'm going about my life outside of working with Mama at the store, my eyes land on something that causes me to think back to those days at the grammar school teacher's. A heap of sand, for instance. Or the deep brown seeds of an udala fruit. Sometimes just seeing a pail of dirty laundry reminds me of those days. Doesn't matter the kind of clothes in the pail. Doesn't matter that they are nothing like the grammar school teacher's or his wife's. Suddenly my mind is back there, and I can't help recalling all those years ago: the rat-tap-tapping of the grammar school teacher's knocks on my hovel's door, the flame of the kerosene lantern flickering on the desk. Amina and I cowering from fear.

The day I met Amina, it was still my first month at the grammar school teacher's, and we had run out of kerosene. A heavy rain had fallen that morning. The sky was gray. Then morning turned to afternoon and the sun came out. I finished my morning chores and set off to fetch the kerosene just as the sun was starting to shine.

That whole first month at the grammar school teacher's place, it was as if we were always running in and out of the bunker. Even on my way back from the market, I would hear the bombers appear above and would have to run and hide in the bushes. There was usually no way to tell if they were enemy planes or not, so we all hid in the bushes to be safe. We stayed there until we could no longer hear the bombers up above.

Once, I had been so turned around after hiding in the bushes that the sun was beginning to set by the time I got back to the grammar school teacher's. This was the latest that I had ever returned. He and his wife had been so upset that he threatened to flog me, thirteen strokes to my backside—because I was almost thirteen years old—to teach me a lesson on not ever coming back late again.

When I went to fetch the kerosene that day, I ran at first, not wanting to risk being late. The roads were muddy from the morning rain, with puddles like creeks accumulating intermittently through-out. Even so, I ran. I could not have been running very long when I got winded. I stopped to catch my breath.

Just past a grove of withering palm trees some puppies lay in crescent-shaped mounds, fetal-like, nipping at the dusty earth as if to bury themselves within. Not too far from the dogs were several kwashiorkor children, carrying their begging bowls.

In a field right next to the road, a policeman was moving through a row of corpses, using a long cane to prod them or mark them as he went. He was a stone-faced officer, with a crinkly sort of nose and a mouth that appeared permanently upturned so that his lips seemed to cover his nostrils. Perhaps he carried his face this way deliber-ately, owing to the odor that the job required him to endure.

Maybe he was counting the bodies, or maybe he was inspecting them for something. I watched as he went about prodding them one by one.

Up till now, I had seen so many images of death—Papa's corpse, for one. For another, all those decapitated bodies that Mama and I had seen flanking the road on our way to Nnewi. Death was all over the place. But in this moment I observed its opposite.

More people had gathered near the field: A singlet-wearing, shoeless man in khaki trousers, who seemed unable to stop scratch-ing his head. A stick-thin woman holding a small girl's hand. A boy who looked to have been not much older than me, carrying another, smaller, wounded boy on his back. A gray-haired old woman with a tree branch walking stick, breathing hard.

They all stood watching as a body — a boy's, naked — proceeded to rise from the field of corpses, like a resurrection. As the boy rose, all the people around me gasped, one perfectly synchronized, collective intake of breath.

The boy wore a startled expression. Perhaps he had fallen asleep among the corpses, or perhaps somehow he had been stunned into imagining himself dead. The policeman, who had jumped back as the boy rose, quickly recovered from his shock, raised his cane, and began whipping it into the air like a warning. The boy recoiled, taking backward steps, tripping over the corpses among which he had been sleeping. The policeman raised his cane over and over again, using both of his hands, raising the whip and bringing it down with such force that it made a sound like the shot of a gun, and as it did, the boy ran off into the distance, naked as the day he was born.

Okeke was a tall man whose wiry thin face drooped on one side, as if half his face was always sad. The rest of his body was like his face: altogether wiry thin and a little sad-looking.

Everyone knew him by that name, and everyone called him by it: Okeke. It made no difference if it was a child or an adult referring to him. They all called him Okeke.

I also had begun referring to him as Okeke, but never to his face. It was a thing I had been trained not to do as far back as I could remember, never to refer to an adult by his or her first name. Each time I went to Okeke, I simply called him "Sir."

Everyone must have been out of kerosene that day, because the line was long, circling out of the doorway of the small cement-walled shop and meandering out onto the tip of the main road. After over an hour of waiting, I finally neared the front of the line, third in line. The kerosene was stored in large translucent plastic jerry cans through which the liquid line was visible. From where I stood, I could see that all of the large jerry cans holding the kerosene behind where Okeke stood were empty, no liquid to speak of.

He had different sizes of funnels that he used to transfer the kerosene from the larger jerry cans into his customers' containers. Now he was gathering all the funnels together, as if to pack them up.

Another tall wiry man at the head of the line called out, "Brother, abeg-o! Make say we get kerosene-o!"

Okeke continued to pack up the funnels. Not bothering to respond to the man, he set the funnels on the countertop near where the jerry cans sat.

"Nawa-o! E don finish?" a woman behind me asked. The way she said "finish," it was as if she were saying "dead," as if she were lamenting the death of a family member. "What am I to do now?" she asked. "How am I to cook my food? How am I to light my lanterns?"

A sliver of panic blossomed in me. What was I also to do now? I could go back home and report to the grammar school teacher and his wife that there was no kerosene, but it meant that there would be at least one more day without any real food to eat, not having any oil with which to light up the cooking fire. There was garri, which we could soak in cold water and eat, but not much of anything else, not even some groundnuts to mix into the garri. At this point there was not even bread.

The man who was first in line raised his hands in the air, in a gesture of both frustration and resignation, then turned to leave. The second man turned and left as well.

I looked behind me. All the people who had been standing behind me were now leaving. Okeke was moving the empty jerry cans, taking them one at a time through the door at the rear of the shed. After the second trip outside, he came back and simply regarded the open area of the shop. There was no one left but me. He looked at me.

My hands were clenched in tight fists. I was holding, crinkled up in my palms, the Biafran pounds that the grammar school teacher had given to me to buy the kerosene.

"Still standing here," Okeke said to me, not quite a question.

Papa used to say, whenever I began pleading or whining or complaining about something, that the hunter who makes too much noise goes home empty-handed. And anyway, I already knew, just from the experience of being a child, that the children who got what they wanted were, more often than not, the ones who were quiet and behaved the best. I remained silent and tried to be on my best behavior, which wasn't very hard to do, seeing as how there was not much else I could have done.

The last time I had come, about two weeks earlier, I had been sent for bread and a can of Titus sardines, along with kerosene. I had not come with enough money for the sardines, and yet Okeke had given me the sardines anyway. "On credit," he had said. "Next time you come, just bring me the sardine money."

I realized that I had forgotten about the owed money. In fact, not only had I forgotten to bring it, I had even forgotten to mention it to the grammar school teacher in the first place, those two weeks ago. Perhaps it was just as well, then, I thought to myself, that the kerosene had run out, because what money would I have used for the kerosene after paying back the sardine money?

Okeke looked at me as if inspecting me. His eyes went down to the empty bottle in my hand.

I knew by now, from snippets of talk between the grammar school teacher and his wife, as well as from talk around the village, that Okeke had a family of his own — a wife, three daughters, a son. The son, Dubem, had, some months ago, joined the Biafran army. There were whispers that he might not make it back home, that Okeke might soon find himself without a son.

Somehow it occurred to me to tell him about the scene I had just witnessed, the one of the dead boy rising. The whole thing was still fresh in my mind.

I would have told it to him to give him hope about his son. To say that perhaps his son would be like that one boy, the one resurrected boy in a field of dead people. Because maybe this was what war was about: the dying of the masses in exchange for the resurrection of one.

Before I could open my mouth to speak, my mind began to wander. Inside my head it was as if a grasshopper were hopping about, this way and that, not knowing where it wanted to land. Or maybe as if my mind was playing hopscotch in the sand, the ground all marked up with a stick, deep depressions forming boxes, each numbered from one to ten. My mind was hopping from one box to the next, trying to make it to the ten.

I'm not sure if it ever made it to the ten, and even if it did, I'm not sure what that ten would have been, but where it finally landed was on the story of Ogbuogu, one of the old folktales Papa used to tell me. Perhaps that was the ten.

Once upon a time, two neighboring villages were at war with each other in a relentless struggle over land. The first village had an army of mighty warriors, intimidating warriors, all equipped with fancy spears and with fancy bows and arrows. The second village had none of the mighty warriors; neither did it have any of the fancy weapons. What it did have was a boy by the name of Ogbuogu, whom the gods had endowed with mighty powers so that he always knew the best way to organize his people in order to win every battle that came their way. The neighboring villagers knew this, and it aggravated them to no end to have this boy as their obstacle, in the face of whom they would surely lose all battles.

Whenever the opponents were about to come battle Ogbuogu's village, the town crier went around announcing that *ndi iro abiawana*, that the enemies were coming. He blew his opi in that specific way that was Ogbuogu's signal to report for battle. Along with the blowing of his flute, the town crier sang:

> *Ogbuogu nwa, Ogbuogu nwa,*
> *Anyi agbarana ogu oso*
>
> *Ogbuogu nwa, Ogbuogu nwa,*
> *Anyi agbarana ogu oso*
>
> *Ima na ofu nwa n'egbu ora nine!*
> *Anyi agbarana ogu oso.*

Fighting child, Fighting child,
Let's not run away from fighting

Fighting child, Fighting child,
Let's not run away from fighting

Imagine, one child can kill an entire village!
Let's not run away from fighting.

One day, as Ogbuogu's village was nearing the point of securing all the land belonging to them, the opposing village found out the secret of the town crier's call. They brought their own opi and blew it in the same fashion as Ogbuogu's village's town crier. Of course, Ogbuogu responded.

He came out, prepared with his bow and arrow, not knowing that it was the opponent playing a trick on him. He arrived at the battle-field only to find that none of his fellow warriors were there with him. Rather, he was all alone on the battlefield surrounded by the enemy warriors.

The battle began. Ogbuogu fought, and he fought. One would hardly have believed that he was one single man on that field. One would hardly have known just how outnumbered he was. But eventually he grew exhausted. It was too late by the time his fellow warriors got wind of what had happened. They arrived at the battlefield only to see that Ogbuogu was dead. There was nothing they could do but carry Ogbuogu's body back to the village. And as they did, they wailed and shed tears. Not only had they lost a kinsman, but this particular loss, they knew, would leave them vulnerable to attack. This particular loss might even lead to the end of their village as they knew it, because the conquering village might go so far as to force them off their land.

They were still in the middle of mourning Ogbuogu when the town crier announced that the neighboring village was approaching for another battle. This news sent them into a panic, of course. How could they possibly fight any battle without Ogbuogu? What hope did they have of making it out alive?

They held a quick meeting where they considered their options. When the time of battle arrived, they gathered themselves and prepared, bows and arrows in place. As luck or cleverness would have it, they came up with the idea of tying Ogbuogu's body on a horse. They set a plank of wood at his back, to hold him up so that it looked as if he was alive and sitting on the horse. They put a small colony of ants in his mouth so that from a distance it appeared that his mouth sometimes moved, that he was the one doing the moving, the way the living do.

They arrived at the battlefield that way, with Ogbuogu in their midst, riding high and looking very proud on his horse.

Upon seeing Ogbuogu on the horse, the enemies fell into disarray, scattering about, exclaiming that here was Ogbuogu's spirit returning to deal with them. Surely, they said, if they were to so much as attempt to do battle with him, as with any member of the spirit world, there was a good chance that they themselves would soon die and be sent to the most terrible part of the spirit world.

So it was that Ogbuogu's village remained undefeated.

The sound of my stomach growling snapped me out of my thoughts. That morning, I had been so busy with chores, trying to finish them early, that I had completely missed breakfast. And, the night before, I had eaten only a piece of bread for supper —the last remaining bread, a very small piece, almost a morsel, hardly enough to fill an ant.

I felt the stabbing ache of hunger in my stomach. Reflexively, I brought my hand to my belly, as if to assuage the pain that way.

Okeke's eyes followed my hand, settling with it on my belly. Then his eyes traveled back up to my face.

"When was the last time you ate?" he asked.

"Yesterday, Sir," I replied. "We have no kerosene to cook."

"What about bread?"

"I ate the last piece of bread last night, Sir," I said.

There appeared a frown on his face, but it was hard to tell if it was really there or just the effect of the drooping half.

He looked at the container in my hand, the glass one that I had come to fill. "Hand me your bottle," he said.

I did as I was told.

He took the bottle, headed to the cabinet beneath the countertop on which he had set the funnels. He took out a small container of what must have been his personal stock of kerosene and set it on the counter near the funnels. He chose the smallest funnel, stuck it into my bottle, and began pouring the kerosene from his container into mine.

When he was finished, he brought the filled-up bottle to me.

"Thank you, Sir," I said, extending my hand and collecting it from him.

I turned to leave, but he stopped me. "Wait," he said. "One more thing."

He went back to a different cupboard. The loaf of bread that he took out of the cupboard was wrapped in a polythene bag, so he first had to unwrap it before tearing it in two, dividing it in an uneven half. He gave the larger piece to me, kept the smaller piece for himself.

He walked to the place where a tall stool sat, took a seat on the stool, began to eat his portion of the bread right there before me. He bit hungrily into it, catching the crumbs as they fell and eating them too. I remained standing where I was but followed his lead and began eating my portion as well.

A few moments later, it seemed he was about to speak, but suddenly there was a loud crashing sound outside. I startled, stared wide-eyed at Okeke.

He furrowed his brow, a look of concern, but then a thought appeared to occur to him. "Don't worry," he said. "I remember now. This one is just the Biafran army. Practice rounds. They'll be finished within the hour."

When he was through with his bread, he wiped his hands brusquely on his thighs. As I took the last bite of my bread, I realized that I had not yet thanked him for it. Hardly had I gotten out the thank-you when he said to me, "What are you waiting for?" His voice was soft. "Go on, you can go now. This is it. I don't have anything else to give. Go on. You may go now."

I said, "But I have money for the kerosene."

He shook his head, waved me away. "Just go," he said. "Save it. Use it to buy something for yourself the next time you run out of kerosene to cook. Your oga won't know any better unless you tell him."

I nodded. Thanked him. Turned around and left.

Heading back from Okeke's, the trees glistened, both the bare trees and those that had managed to retain their leaves. Sometimes when a leaf dangled low enough to fall within my reach, I turned my face upward and tapped it, and the water on it, left over from the earlier rain, sprinkled forth on me like a blessing.

I wasn't far into my return when I felt a shadow following me, a shadow other than my own. It crossed the roads with me, hopped over the puddles with me. It appeared to tap the leaves with me, or at least it stood close behind me as I did.

I stopped in order to allow the shadow to pass me. I found a large rock near where an udala tree stood and sat down there. I waited on the rock, hoping that the shadow would continue along, but it did not. Instead, it sat across from me, on another rock, eyes bright, like a pair of light bulbs. She was no longer a shadow.

She had skin as light as mine. Yellow, like a ripe pawpaw. She wore a tattered green pinafore that was bare at the sides. Her hair hung in long clumps around her face, like those images of Mami Wata, hair writhing like serpents. But there were no serpents on her. She looked too dazed or disoriented, or simply too exhausted, to speak.

Someone had discarded udala seeds near where I sat, forming a tiny mound on the ground. Ants had paved themselves a path to the mound. I watched the ants for some time, the way they lined up, one after the other, the way they gathered in circles around the seeds.

There were crushed leaves all around. The sun hovered above, watchful over us.

We moved our plastic-slippered feet around the muddy earth. We looked down at the ground as we did, but I sneaked peeks at her, and I'm sure she did at me. A bird flew from the udala tree, its wings beating hard through the air. We tilted our heads and watched. Finally we gathered the courage to look into each other's faces. The moment our eyes locked, I knew I would not be leaving without her.

I arrived home, but later this time than ever before. I sensed deep inside that I would get a flogging. I resigned myself to it.

I lifted the metal latch to unlock the gate, pushed it open to let myself and her in. We cut through the backyard and walked the path leading to the house. We stopped outside the kitchen door.

The grammar school teacher and his wife stood leaning on opposite sides of the kitchen counter. There was a coolness about the kitchen, and a coldness in their faces. His eyes were very stern, hers even sterner.

She held her handkerchief to her chest. Her breathing suddenly became loud and labored. "Do you know what time it is?" she asked angrily.

"What possibly could have taken you this long?" he asked.

"There's really no excuse for it," she interjected.

"No, there really is no excuse for it," he agreed.

She cleared her throat and said, "And now it's well past dinnertime, and here we are with nothing to eat." She began to cough lightly. Three little coughs.

By now it was clear to me that her asthma was just a manifestation of her aversion to doing housework.

"I could really flog you for this," he said. "Twelve strokes for each of your twelve years. Or is it now thirteen? Whatever it is, I could even multiply it by two. Twenty-six strokes for good measure."

"Yes, we really could flog you for this," she said. "Twenty-six strokes for good measure," she repeated.

I hung my head. "I'm very sorry," I said.

"You are lucky," he said. "Very lucky, for the simple fact that I'm too tired to do any flogging today. Anyway, I'm sure you can already see how upset you've made us. That should be enough punishment for you this time. But as long as you live under our roof, you are never, ever again to return this late."

I nodded and told them again how very sorry I was.

"Luckily, in the time that you were gone, your oga did manage to find some yams from the vendor down the road," she said. "The tubers are there in the cupboard. Take them out, peel them, cut them up, and boil them. *Osiso-osiso.* Quick, quick. Any longer and I'm sure I'll die of hunger."

She turned, began walking in the direction of the dining room. At first he followed along, but then he stopped. She stopped with him. Almost simultaneously they turned around and looked at the girl next to me. They appeared to study her intensely before turning back to me.

"Who is she?" the grammar school teacher's wife asked.

A minute went by while I thought of how to answer. I cleared my throat and replied simply, "Aunty, a friend."

"She looks like a street urchin, a homeless little imp," the grammar school teacher said.

"A friend?" she asked. Her voice was raspy and harsh.

Now the grammar school teacher's wife's face was more than mildly thoughtful. "Well, street urchin or homeless imp, never mind that for now," she said. "Boil the yams. She can help you. The more help we have for dinner, the faster it will be done."

He appeared to think about what she had said. "Yes, I suppose that's true. Yes, you certainly have a point."

Finally there was the tap-tapping of their feet, and then the increasing distance between us and their words.

That evening, Amina and I peeled the yams together, rinsed them together, our fingers brushing against each other's in the bowl. I doused the wood with the kerosene and lit the cooking fire, and she set the pot of yams on top to boil.

After the grammar school teacher and his wife had eaten, after we ourselves had eaten, and after we had washed the dishes and cleaned the kitchen, I filled the bucket at the tap outside my hovel. We rinsed ourselves off together on the cement slab. The crickets sang their usual night songs, and the mosquitoes perched on us, and the fireflies glowed green, like luminous droplets of grass.

At the end of it all, I carried my lantern and led Amina into my hovel, where I offered half of my mattress to her.

21

THE WEEK FOLLOWING her arrival, the grammar school teacher and his wife made remarks about throwing Amina out. "What are you still doing here?" he asked. "You must go back to where you came from. Better find your way before I make you find it."

I knew why the grammar school teacher was so ill at ease with her. I was not oblivious to the rifts between the tribes, especially between the Hausas and the Igbos. Chances were that had Amina been an Igbo girl, or even from Cross River State, he would not have been so agitated by her presence. Maybe even if she had been Yoruba, he would have been more at ease with her. But there she was, a Hausa girl, an enemy of the Igbo people.

It was the first time that I was befriending a Hausa person. Until then, I'd seen them only as they walked along the roads and in the markets where they sold their goods. This was my first time getting to know one in an intimate way.

It made sense that the grammar school teacher and his wife would be worried. Given how relentlessly they were killing us Igbos, to keep a Hausa was a safety hazard. If she had any relatives, they might come find her and kill us in the process.

Amina always responded by looking blankly at him.

One afternoon, he came out to the veranda, his face looking very cross. Amina and I were chopping wood at the left side of the front yard. The sky was overcast, but the rain had not yet come.

He stood watching us, just watching and looking very annoyed. Half an hour must have passed by while he simply stood and watched. Finally he called her to him.

She walked from the side of the front yard where the pile of firewood sat in small clumps to the side of the veranda where he stood.

"Is it that you don't have somewhere else you can go?" he asked.

She shook her head and said, "No, Sir."

"Uncles? Aunties? Cousins?"

She shook her head again and said no.

The grammar school teacher remained silent for a while. Amina stood before him, her head facing the ground.

His wife came out of the house at that moment, joined her husband in looking at Amina.

"She has no family," the grammar school teacher said to his wife.

They stood there for a full minute, staring some more at Amina.

"When you think of it, she's not exactly that much Hausa-looking," the grammar school teacher's wife said to him. "Actually, she is more Fulani-looking than Hausa-looking. Which means she could pass for Igbo."

The grammar school teacher considered his wife's words. "It's true," he said. "Some Igbos and Fulanis do have a certain similarity in their features. Their complexion, for one thing."

"And she appears to be a hard worker," the grammar school teacher's wife said.

Her husband nodded.

"In the grand scheme of things, she'll probably be doing more good than harm by staying."

"Yes," he said, nodding.

"We could always use an extra set of hands," she said.

"I suppose that's true," he said. "But at the first sign of trouble, I'm sending her off."

"Makes sense," she said.

"Good," he said.

. . .

The way things worked out, Amina was not exactly in the habit of talking much, so there was little or no risk of her revealing herself or being found out as Hausa. All the time that we went about our errands, no one ever raised the issue. With time, it must have settled on the grammar school teacher and his wife that she was no threat, at least not in the way that they had feared she would be.

22

LATE ONE EVENING, Amina and I, having finished our chores for the day, took our evening baths, then sat together in our nightgowns on the stoop of our hovel while I plaited her hair with thread.

Out of the blue, she said, "Did you used to go to school?"

She was sitting one step lower than me, and I was holding a lock of her hair in my hands, combing it out the way one does before wrapping it with thread. I held the thread between my lips as I combed.

By now I had learned that the reason she could not find her other family was that most everyone outside her immediate family was up north. The war being what it was, they might all have thought her dead. No one had come for her, and she had not gone to them. She would not have known a way to go finding them on her own anyway. She did not know where exactly they lived.

"Tell me," she said. "Did you used to go to school?"

I took the thread out of my lips. "I used to go until the schools closed," I said. "Until just a little before Mama sent me here to stay."

She said, "Oga says that he will send me to school when the war finishes."

I nodded and told her that he had also agreed to do the same for me.

"What was it like—your school?"

I was in the middle of plaiting, but she pulled out of my grasp and turned to face me.

I slapped her on the shoulder, more like a hard tap. "Look what you've gone and done! You've messed up this one and now I'll have to do it all over again!"

"Sorry," she replied in a very aloof way.

"Well, sorry is fine and all, but it doesn't fix anything." I exhaled exasperatedly, then said, "You need to turn around so I can get back to it."

"Okay," she said nonchalantly, ignoring my irritation. "But first, what was it like?"

"What was *what* like?"

"School!"

"What do you mean, what was school like? Don't you already know what school is like?"

"I do," she said. "But tell me anyway."

There must have been a confused look on my face, because she chuckled softly and said, "Stop making that face. Are you going to tell me or not?"

"You sound like a person who has never been to school," I said.

She said, "Of course I've been to school. Yes, I have." Slowly, her face turned thoughtful, then she added, as if to clarify, "I've been to school, but only off and on. Not long enough to really know." She stretched out the word. *Reeeaaallly.* Very plaintively, like a sigh.

"Oh," I said.

"My mother needed me at home, for trading, for running errands, for hawking. That kind of thing."

I said, "So, do you know how to read?"

She laughed. "Of course I know how to read. I used to read the Koran every day. But I know more than just Arabic. My mother used to let me read English books at home. *Aladdin* and *Ali Baba and the Forty Thieves.* Those kinds of books."

"Maybe one day you can teach me Arabic," I said.

She laughed. "Maybe one day."

We were silent for a while, and then she said, "You know, I could have been married by now."

I looked at her, startled. "But you're barely thirteen."

She laughed. "I had my dowry, marriage pots and bowls, plenty of gifts already. Just a little bit more and I would have been married and entered purdah, secluded, no longer able to come out. If things had gone like that, I probably would never have met you."

I said, "It's good that things happened the way they did, so we could meet."

She scowled at me, and immediately I knew that I had misspoken.

"You're happy that they set fire to my family's house?" she shouted. "You're happy that my father and mother died? You're happy that my brother is somewhere in the war, or probably dead too?"

I shook my head. "I didn't mean it that way."

"How else could you have meant it?" she shouted. "You weren't there. You didn't see it. I leave to buy some kosai. Not more than thirty minutes later, I come back and the house is gone and everyone in it is gone."

Now all I could see in my mind was her house burning down and her arriving to find it so. I saw her screaming, running toward the burning house, all the while pleading for help.

She was crying now.

"I'm sorry," I said. "I'm really sorry. I really didn't mean it that way."

23

W E COULD NOT have known it for sure at the time, but by early January 1970 the war was nearing its end. All the radios were hissing with news about an operation. Operation Tail-Wind, they called it. The final Nigerian offensive. First there was talk that Owerri had fallen once again to the Nigerians. And there was talk that Uli had fallen as well. Then one day we heard the announcement.

Amina and I had just returned from the market. We were both in the kitchen. I was pounding yam; she was at the sink washing plates.

Earlier, outside the compound, there had been an unusual flurry of action, a sort of commotion. Several men were conversing vehemently while pushing their wheelbarrows down the road. A couple of women were chatting loudly as they peeled corn in front of their gates. A third woman was speaking forcefully to another woman while feeding her small child tidbits from a fist-sized roll of bread. Several girls were carrying buckets of water on their heads, and the way they talked, their voices surged, and with their arms they gesticulated as widely as the buckets on their heads would allow.

Now, as I stood in the kitchen, Amina out by the sink, the grammar school teacher's radio came on. It started off softly, but soon he turned it up so high that even from the kitchen we could hear clearly when the Radio Biafra announcer said that Ojukwu had fled, that he had gone off on a plane to Ivory Coast. Something about his going for the sake of exploring possibilities for peace.

But we all knew what it meant. Ojukwu had surrendered.

The grammar school teacher shouted, "Traitor!" It came out like an expletive.

"Coward that he is," his wife said, "he would have killed us all if we had given him the chance."

The radio broadcast continued.

The yam that I had been in the middle of pounding was still sitting in the mortar, the pestle idle in my hands. I stayed staring at the cubes of yam and listening, thinking of all that it would mean now that the war was over. For example, it was over, but even the fact of that could not bring Papa back. It was over, but nothing could be done to bring Amina's family back. The dead would not suddenly leap out of the grave. Chances were that not a single one of them would rise the way Jesus rose from the dead. No resurrection for them.

At the sink, Amina stood, looking very alert, listening to the fading voice of the Radio Biafra announcer.

I imagined Ojukwu riding in the sky on that plane. I imagined him landing in an open space, a quiet and peaceful space, a land full of white sand, gray sand, brown sand. Where he landed there was no war. There, elephants roamed lazily about, those elephants from whose tusks, I'd read, ivory somehow came.

"To be on a plane headed somewhere else," I finally said to Amina, leaning into the pestle, which was propped up by the mortar.

"What for?" she asked. She turned from the sink to face me. Her eyebrows scrunched together and her eyes narrowed. "What would be the point of leaving now that the war is over? If you wanted to leave, wouldn't it have been while the war was going on?"

"I know, I know," I said. "But what if you could go anywhere in the world? Even to *Obodo ndi ocha!* Do they even have wars in the white man's land? Just think about it! Anywhere in the world!"

She shook her head as if to erase the question from her consciousness.

The grammar school teacher entered the kitchen then, clearing his throat loudly to announce his presence. I returned to the yam that I should already have been done pounding. I heard Amina sigh as she walked out the door.

• • •

Some days later, Gowon declared the official end of the war. Again we listened to it on the radio, from the kitchen. Outside, the sun was high in the sky, and Gowon said:

Citizens of Nigeria,

It is with a heart full of gratitude to God that I announce to you that today marks the formal end of the civil war . . . The so-called Rising Sun of Biafra is set forever. It will be a great disservice for anyone to continue to use the word "Biafra" to refer to any part of the East Central State of Nigeria . . .

Gowon had not finished when the grammar school teacher said, "That imbecile!" His wife joined in: "Murderer!"

. . . The tragic chapter of violence is just ended. We are at the dawn of national reconciliation. Once again we have an opportunity to build a new nation . . .

Gowon went on like that.

That evening, we were outside by the gate when the soldiers came, Nigerian army men, Hausa soldiers, marching in a parade along the road.

"One Nigeria! One Nigeria!" they called out. They lifted their legs high as they marched, all dressed up in green uniforms, berets on their heads, their guns held firmly across their chests.

24

T HE SAYING GOES that wood already touched by fire isn't
hard to set alight.

We had finished our dinner, some garri and vegetable soup. Then
we'd stepped out to the backyard, onto the slab of cement at the side
of our hovel, to take our night baths.

Near the bucket, on the corner of the cement slab, was a stool that
we'd left there from early in the morning. On the stool, the comb we
shared, some hairpins, our body cream, and a small mirror. We had
just dried ourselves with our towels when Amina lifted the mirror. Our towels were tied around our chests, extending down to our
thighs. She leaned so that her face came close to the kerosene lantern. Its rays illuminated her face. She tugged at the loose braids on
her head. "Does it look all right?" she asked.

I went closer to her, ran my fingers through her braids. Those
were the braids that I had plaited for her just that morning. I held
her face in the palms of my hands and pretended to inspect her hair.
I nodded and smiled. She smiled back.

There were the usual night sounds: grasshoppers hopping, fireflies buzzing, crickets singing their songs, leaves rustling in the
breeze. I ran my hands up and down Amina's braids some more, up
and down her arms. And Amina did the same to me.

Back in the hovel, our towels fell to the floor.

In the near darkness, our hands moved across our bodies. We
took in with our fingers the curves of our flesh, the grooves. Our
hands, rather than our voices, seemed to do the speaking. Our
breaths mingled with the night sounds. Eventually our lips met.
This was the beginning, our bodies being touched by the fire that
was each other's flesh.

25

W E MIGHT AS well be married," Amina said one day.
A moment passed and a thought occurred to me. I
asked, "You mean to each other? Or do you mean to other people?"

She rolled her eyes at me. "Of course I mean to each other. I mean
that it would be nice to be married to you."

"It would be nice to be married to you too," I said.

Silence.

"But that's not the way marriage works, you know," I said. "Besides, we're still too young yet for it."

Another silence.

"Have you kissed anyone before?" I asked.

She shook her head. "No. Not at all. Where would I ever have
kissed anyone before?" She looked skeptically at me. "What about
you? Have you ever kissed anyone before?"

It had been on my mind, which was why I had brought it up. All
this time it had been troubling me, feeling a little like a betrayal.
Perhaps she would hate me for it, for having done this thing we did,
this thing that was supposed to be special and only between us, with
somebody else. But I owed her the truth.

I said, "Someone kissed me once before. My best friend from
Ojoto. It didn't feel the way it feels with you."

"Your best friend?" she asked.

"Yes," I said.

"What kind of best friend is that?"

"Just a friend," I said.

"It happened just once?"

"It happened just once."

"You promise it didn't feel as good as with me?"

It was a funny question, its answer being so obvious to me, so I laughed a little. Then, very honestly, I said, "I promise it didn't feel as good as with you."

After some time she asked, "How exactly does it feel with me?"

I thought about it. How could I describe it? I could not think of the words. Eventually I simply said, "Tingly and good and like everything is perfect in the world."

She smiled. "But maybe you were just too young to feel it with your best friend," she said.

"Maybe," I said.

"Do you think you could have married him?"

"No," I said. "Anyway, if I'm too young to be married now, then I was really too young to be married back then."

"You're always talking about being too young to marry," she said.

"I suppose I am," I said.

26

IT HAPPENED AT the beginning of August, the end of the rainy season, the day of the New Yam Festival.

Boutique shops had begun to open along the margins of the roads, small shops inside narrowly built zinc sheds. The items they carried were different from those sold at the old vendor stands. They included lipstick, perfume, and soap in green, red, blue, and purple packages — all colors — wrapped so delicately in their fancy boxes that they seemed like precious gifts. They included toothpaste in plastic tubes for those people who were ready to switch back from chewing sticks to toothbrushes.

That particular day, we had eaten yam porridge for breakfast, boiled yam with palm oil for lunch, and pounded yam with soup for dinner. By now the war had been over for about seven months. Schools had not yet reopened, but the palm fronds were regaining their green. Yam was not exactly abundant, but people celebrated the festival all the same.

It must have happened on a Saturday, because Saturdays were when the grammar school teacher brought his dirty shirts and trousers, along with his wife's dirty blouses and wrappers and gowns, in a pail for us to wash. He always made sure to bring the pail early in the day, usually in the morning. Never later than two or three in the afternoon.

But that Saturday, he brought it late.

If only he had remembered to bring the pail just a couple of hours before he did. Then we would still have been outside running our errands, or in the kitchen cooking or cleaning, or just sitting on the steps of our hovel, waiting for him to arrive.

If he'd remembered, there would have been nothing to be discovered: we would simply have collected the pail, set out immediately to wash the clothes, and then hung the items out in the sun to dry.

Papa used to talk a lot about infinity. He used to harp on how there were infinite possibilities for the way anything in life could turn out. Even with a limited number of building blocks, he said, the possibilities were endless.

These days, when I think of that particular Saturday, I think of Papa and of his infinite possibilities, of the way they applied even in the framework of something as routine as the handing over of a pail of dirty clothes.

It was long after supper, and Amina and I had by then finished cleaning up the kitchen.

Out at the tap, we had taken our night baths and had returned to the hovel to sleep.

It was dark inside but for the kerosene lantern that sat on the table next to Papa's old Bible. We settled ourselves in our usual positions on the mattress: she by the wall, and me on the side nearer the door.

We lay facing each other, ready to fall into sleep, but sleep refused to come. By the light of the lantern, I watched the blinking of her eyes. For a long time we said nothing. Finally she said, "Every morning while we ate breakfast, my mother used to ask me what I dreamed at night."

Mama used to talk a lot about dreams too. I told Amina as much. Maybe that was a trait shared by all mothers, we decided.

I thought about my dreams that night. The first one that came to mind was not the one where I was getting stuck in the dream, but rather the one where my teeth were all aching, all falling out.

Amina said, "Did you ever have the one where you continued to rise from the ground for no reason at all, like a balloon floating in the air, higher and higher, and all you wanted to do was come back down, but you were unable to do so?"

"Yes, those were my scariest dreams," I said. "What do you imagine a dream like that means?"

She said, "My mother told me once that it means you will continue to rise, but eventually you will fall. Good things will happen to you for some time, and then the bad will follow."

I almost wished I had not asked.

I tried to remember the last time I had had that dream. I could not remember. Well, maybe I had already fallen. Maybe being here, working as a housegirl for the grammar school teacher, maybe that was my falling.

"The day before the house burned down, I dreamed of a yellow flower growing alone in a field," Amina said. "I would have told it to my mother when I returned from fetching the kosai, but I never got the chance."

"I'm sorry," I said.

The sheet was pulled up to our chests, but now she pulled her side higher, up to her shoulders. We lay there quietly. Neither one of us spoke.

Finally I said, "Dreams are not always sad. Or at least they don't have to be. Not even the scary ones have to mean something bad."

I shifted my body, lifted myself, and turned so that I was no longer facing her.

The flame in the kerosene lantern shivered. Papa's Bible lay next to the lantern. I tried to think of some Bible stories in which there were mentions of dreams. Almost immediately the story of Joseph came to me. I turned back to Amina. "Did you ever hear of Joseph and his dreams?"

"Who is Joseph?" she asked.

"You know, Joseph from the Old Testament."

She shook her head, told me that she did not know who Joseph was.

I filled her in on him. How God had given him a sign by way of his dreams. How, in one dream, Joseph and his brothers were tying wheat into bundles when suddenly Joseph's bundle of wheat stood up straight, nice and tall. Meanwhile, his brothers' bundles of wheat folded over, bowing to Joseph's bundle of wheat. In another dream, the sun and the moon and the stars all bowed down to Joseph.

I said, "At first when Joseph told his brothers of the dream, they were angry with him because they thought Joseph was trying to say that he was better than them. It seemed at first that the dream would only end up causing trouble. His brothers sold him into slavery because they were so angry with him. But many years later, it all worked out. Joseph was reunited with his brothers. In the end they found out that the dreams, and everything that came from the dreams, were part of God's plan for them. Imagine, all of it was part of the plan all along. Because from them came the twelve tribes of Israel."

She sighed and pressed herself against me. "I don't understand why God made them to first have to go through all that wahala. Why have his brothers sell him off as a slave for all those years? It's like going around in a circle instead of taking a straight line home. Doesn't make any sense to me."

I said, "Maybe sometimes it's worth it to go around in circles. Maybe you learn more lessons that way."

"I don't know," she said. "But I suppose that could be true too."

Amina was so close to me now that I felt an urge to lean in and kiss her. I began with her forehead. I took a stop at her nose. Soon I was at her lips, then at the crook of her neck, which was exposed by her loose nightgown.

She rose so that she was above me, straddling me at the waist, on her knees. There was a sadness to the way she moved, to the way her lips lingered in the crook of my neck. She might have stopped out of all that sadness, but she continued, as if she were determined to fight off the sadness this way.

Slowly she made her way to my chest. We'd never gone farther than the chest. But now she gently removed my nightgown, and then removed hers. She cupped her hands around my breasts, took turns with them, fondling and stroking and caressing them with her tongue. I felt the soft tug of her teeth on the peaks of my chest. Euphoria washed over me.

She continued along, leaving a trail of kisses on her way down to my belly. She traveled farther, beyond the belly, farther than we had ever gone. I moaned and surrendered myself to her. I did not until then know that a mouth could make me feel that way when placed in that part of the body where I had never imagined a mouth to belong.

The knock snapped us back to reality. The grammar school teacher had knocked like that many times before. But always he'd waited for permission to enter. Only when we answered the knock did he walk in to find us just lounging about — chatting, or plaiting hair, or maybe eating a snack.

The door opened before we were able to pull our nightgowns back on. He walked in in a bustle, talking about how he had lost track of time. Explaining that he would leave the pail for us right outside the door and we should see about washing the clothes first thing in the morning.

And then his eyes settled on us. Amina had been lying on the mattress, flat on her back, my head hovering in the space above her legs. We had done our best to scramble away from each other as he entered the room. But we had not managed to get very far apart. I had only succeeded in lifting my head, and Amina had only managed to pull together her legs.

The sight of us must have startled him, because he gasped like a dying man taking his final breath.

He went immediately for the lantern on the table, lifted it in our direction, leaned closer, his eyes peering, as if to make sure that what he was seeing was indeed what was before his eyes.

The sight of us startled him all over again, and he gasped once more.

The whole incident was startling to me too, and must have been startling to Amina as well, not only for our having to endure the discomfort of his looking at us in this way, but also for our having to endure the misfortune of being forced to see ourselves through his eyes.

He walked over, pulled us off the mattress one at a time, slapped us on our cheeks. Over a year with him, sometimes the threat of a beating, but never an actual beating, until then.

He must have noticed the Bible on the table when he grabbed the lantern, because he turned back to the table, set the lantern back down, and grabbed the Bible. Pointing to it, he cried, "An abomination!"

The word reverberated in my head.

He looked directly at me. He shouted, "That is what it is, if a name is to be given to it! That is what the Bible calls it!"

Now he turned to Amina. He shouted at her too. "The Koran condemns it as well. I don't know much of Islam, but I know enough to know that the Koran and the Bible see eye to eye on this matter!"

He paced back and forth as he spoke, made frantic gestures with his hands as he told us that we would be held accountable for our actions. He had heard of such cases, in which the accused were stoned all the way to the river. Stoned even as they drowned in the waters of the river. Of course, it was rare that such cases were spoken of. So taboo the whole thing was, anathema, unmentionable, not even deserving a name.

Amina and I began to cry, deep cries that made our shoulders heave. Our clothes lay scattered on the floor, dispersed like discarded seeds. We were naked, and we felt our nakedness as Adam and Eve must have felt it in the garden, at the time of that evening breeze. Our eyes had become open, and we too sought to hide ourselves. But first we had to endure the grammar school teacher's lecturing. There he went, pacing back and forth in our little hovel, going on and on about our shame, his eyes furious, his mouth opening wider and wider.

He lectured and he lectured, and he lectured. As God must have lectured Eve.

27

THAT WAS THE way in which Mama came back to me. Nearly two years gone by, and then that incident, and at last she found herself coming back for me.

The first thing I did when I saw her was run up and embrace her. I did so just as she was entering the gate. Despite the unfortunate circumstances under which she had sent me off, and despite the unfortunate circumstance under which we were all now gathering, I was genuinely glad to see her. So much time had passed, and I had missed her.

Mama had never been a buxom woman, but she appeared even less so now, a little withered.

When I came out of the embrace, we stood there face to face, taking each other in with our eyes.

Even today, I remember the way her clothes draped over her body with no discernible shape, the way she smelled of stale sweat — not terribly unfamiliar, but a little off-putting.

I remained with her, standing and tugging gently at her clothes in the mindless way that people who know each other well sometimes do. I tugged at the flap of her top wrapper.

Finally I moved from the wrapper and slid my hand into hers. The skin of her hand was wrinkled, as if from too many washes. Or from overuse. Or from age. I felt the quivering, what seemed to be tremors in her palm. My eyes had been lowered all along, but now I raised my head and saw in my mother's eyes a wetness: tears glistening before me like those silvery raindrops of the rainy season. Her cheeks appeared sunken. In that moment I wished that I could crawl back into her womb, if only to thicken her out, to put flesh upon her hips, into her breasts, to put life back into her sunken cheeks.

She began humming, as if unaware of herself, and as she hummed, she laughed at nothing at all, a soft laugh, a smooth sound. I leaned in close to her and fastened my arms around her legs, praying that the day did not come when she would slip completely away from me: shrinking, shrinking, shrinking until there was nothing of her left on this earth.

The grammar school teacher must have been watching the whole time. After Mama and I had come out of our last embrace, he cleared his throat, signaling that it was time for the meeting to begin.

Stools were set up in the backyard of the grammar school teacher's house, in the area of land near where lush green grass carpeted the earth, the area between the bungalow and the hovel. It was late morning, and we sat in a circle, like a village council meeting except without all the flourishes and jubilant greetings that marked the beginning of one.

The sun was shining brightly. I felt the weight of its rays on my shoulders. On the cement wall that formed the fence of the compound, lizards scurried about.

"So, tell me what this is all about," Mama said.

The grammar school teacher replied, "I will allow Ijeoma to tell it to you herself. Tell her," he said, turning to me. "Go on. Tell her."

I remained silent, my throat numb.

The grammar school teacher's wife had been silent up till this point, but now she spoke. "The day waits for no one," she said sternly.

Mama glared at me. "Ijeoma," she said. "What is it that you have done?"

Amina had been seated with us from the start, and Mama had paid her no mind the entire time, but now she seemed to notice her.

Mama smiled and spoke to her in Igbo, a series of rambling questions: How are you? Who are you? What exactly are you doing here?

To which Amina responded with silence, because though she

had picked up some basic Igbo greetings, which came to the rescue with passersby and such, she did not know enough Igbo to understand all that Mama had rambled, let alone know how to go about responding to her.

The grammar school teacher piped in then and explained who Amina was, to which Mama scowled and expressed her dissatisfaction with the fact that he had allowed a Hausa into his home, and not only that, but had allowed her to share living quarters with me, her child. Did he not see how dangerous it was? Did he not already know that it was the Hausa army that had killed her husband, the very same Hausa people who had destroyed Biafra?

He replied that Amina had not once been a problem until now, and that, anyway, she was just a harmless little girl.

Still, Mama did not hold back her dissatisfaction. She continued to scowl.

The whole situation was very stressful for me and was causing my stomach to do frightful somersaults. I found myself fading into my thoughts. I imagined myself removed from time and place. Or rather, I imagined myself in a place where nothing had happened in the past and nothing was happening now, and in the future nothing would be the consequence of all the nothings that had come before.

I woke up to Mama's voice. "Ijeoma, do you hear me?" Her words were shrill with irritation. "Do you hear me, or am I talking to the air?"

I responded, "Yes, Mama. I hear you."

"So, go ahead. Tell me what it is that has happened."

I sputtered, my tongue tumbling over a string of words, before something coherent came out. "Amina and I, we didn't think anything of it," I began.

"You didn't think anything of what?" she asked.

"Of what we were doing," I said.

"And what exactly were you doing?"

"Our clothes," I said.

"Your clothes?"

I nodded, but I could not go on.

Suddenly there was a look in her face that seemed to say that she was now understanding. Her eyes and mouth opened wide. "*Chi m o!*" she exclaimed in a whisper. My God! She was still sitting on her stool, but she was flailing her hands and then wringing them the way a thief who has been caught in the act sometimes does.

"We didn't think anything of it, Mama," I said again.

Mama was making soft wailing sounds now.

"Mama, I'm sorry," I said, going to her, kneeling before her, wrapping my arms around her knees. When I rose back up, I saw that Amina was standing by my side, her face coated in tears. She said, "Madam, I'm sorry too. Please don't be angry with us."

Mama appeared even tinier now, smaller than before. She shook her head slowly at us. Then she lifted her hands slowly to her mouth, covering it, a feeble attempt to stop herself from weeping.

I stood there watching her weep, and I imagined the punishment that the grammar school teacher had described: all the villagers gathered together at the mouth of the river, Amina and I being dragged into the river, stones thrown at us until we were sore and bruised and weak from all that pelting. I imagined us being left there to drown.

That was the way in which I finally left the grammar school teacher's place. As for Amina, since she had no family, nowhere to be sent, she remained at the grammar school teacher's. He and his wife would do their part in straightening her out, and Mama would do her part in straightening me out.

Mama led me down the road to the bus stop without uttering a single word. She simply maintained her grasp on my hand. In that stiff, unnerving silence we boarded the bus. Her grasp was tight, painful even. *Loosen up,* I imagined saying to her, to her fingers. *Loosen up.* And I imagined the reply something like this: *This is anger. It does as it pleases.*

PART IV

28

THE SECONDARY SCHOOL, Obodoañuli Girls' Academy — Land of Joy Girls' Academy — ironically had a humble and subdued look to it, almost austere, like a place where girls went to become nuns. Based on appearances alone, there was nothing joyful about it.

The school was not in Nnewi proper, but rather outside of it and to the west, in the nearby community of Oraifite, where the Ekulo River bisected the land. Near the river, and also at some points in it, mangroves grew, leaning in the water like old men and old women permanently bent at the waist, cowering as if to eschew the sun.

It was a small enclave of a school, hemmed in by bushes and trees, mostly plantain and palm trees. The only road clear of the bushes and trees was the road one took to get to the school. It was a muddy and potholed road at the tip of which was a gate that led into the school compound.

The compound was large, with several buildings in it — between twelve and fifteen — all smallish in size, like oversized huts. The classrooms were the smallest of the buildings, each one decked with a meager pair of windows, open spaces with only wooden shutters for coverings, most of which remained flung wide.

The other buildings — those larger than the classrooms — served as dormitories, lavatories and washrooms, a library, and offices for the teachers and headmistress. Sometimes the senior students hung around in the offices with the teachers — in the evenings especially, but never on weekends. On weekends there was hardly anyone around. Many of the teachers and students went home.

Outside the front entrance of each dormitory building was a veranda. Fluorescent lights hung from the veranda ceilings; they came on at night. On the inside, the dorms consisted of open rooms lined with cots, with equal spaces between the cots. Each dorm held six beds, two or three girls to a room. Beside each bed was a small table and chair on which we sat to read and complete school assignments. On each desk was a lantern. There was not much else in the dorm rooms aside from what each girl brought for herself.

"No more of that nonsense between you and that girl," Mama had said before sending me off to the school. "Remember, you're a new person now. And lucky for you that the grammar school teacher is still willing to live up to his end of the bargain by sending you to school, despite the shameful way that you behaved under his care. Now, look here. *Nee anya.* No matter what you do, stay away from that girl!"

"If you're so worried that I'll do it again, why send us to the same school?" I asked.

"It's the only school that the grammar school teacher can afford to send both of you to. If not, believe me, I would have seen to it that you two were sent to schools as far apart from each other as heaven and hell."

The school was made up primarily of Igbo girls. There were a couple of Efik girls, no Yoruba girls, and aside from Amina, there was only one other Hausa girl, who was as good as Igbo because she had grown up entirely in Igboland and, as unlikely as the match was, one of her parents was Igbo.

We all stuck to our kind. The Efiks stuck to the Efiks, the Igbos to the Igbos. And, especially during those first weeks of school, every time I saw Amina around the compound, she was either by herself or with the other Hausa/Igbo girl.

The third day or so after I had arrived at the school, I had run into Amina on the way to class. She was by herself, and I had hugged her and attempted to make conversation, asking her how she was find-ing the school and how she was settling in. But Amina was stiff in my embrace, and afterward she barely looked my way, not even as I walked by her side. She gave only one-word answers to my ques-tions.

We had been going to two separate classes. Eventually I left her and walked in the direction of my class. I tried again after my class session was over, waiting for Amina outside her own classroom. Just as she walked out of the door, I went up to her, but upon seeing me, she mumbled something about having to go, and off she went, her steps hurried, as if to get quickly away from me.

In the days that followed, no matter how hard I tried to get close to her, she continued to keep her distance from me. Those were days when I wondered if everything that had happened between us at the grammar school teacher's place had been a figment of my imagination. How was it that she could be so cold to me?

After several attempts, with no luck in getting her to return to her old self, I made it a point to keep away from her. There were close encounters, of course, those moments when we could not help but be in the same vicinity — morning assemblies, physical educa-tion classes, mealtimes in the school cafeteria — but for the most part we kept out of each other's way. Ugochi, my roommate, became the person whom I began to rely on for company.

Ugochi was sitting on her bed.

She was a dark-skinned Igbo girl whom we called *panla,* or stock fish, because she was very thin, and the way her body looked, it was as if all her flesh was so dried up that it clung to her bones. Even on her face, either the bones were too prominent or the skin was so tight around the bones that upon first glance she seemed to have a grave, almost angry look about her.

But at least she was endowed with a beautiful figure — a nice chest, curvy hips, very good proportions. Together with her rich, dark skin color, she wasn't altogether unattractive.

She was folding her scarf. I watched her from where I sat on my own bed. It was a soft beige scarf, embroidered with flower petals scattered across its surface.

Unlike the rest of us, who came to the school with very few personal items, all of which we used on a daily basis, Ugochi kept things she rarely used: a fancy, pastel pink hairpin which I had not yet seen her wear, a spool of satin ribbons which I'd not yet seen tied to her hair, a pair of yellow sandals with a big gold bow at the front. And the scarf. Every once in a while, she'd sit and admire it, then fold it back up and put it away. Sometimes I saw her packing the items into a bag and leaving with them. But aside from those times when she packed them up, her belongings remained in their little corners on her side of our room.

It was afternoon, just after morning classes. "I like your scarf," I said. "Can I see?"

She seemed to think about it, then waved me over. "Yes, come see. But remember, you can see it, but you can't have it. It's my special scarf."

"What makes it special?" I asked.

She placed it in my open hands, allowed me to hold and examine it. The petals were outlined in pink. The cloth was smooth and soft to the touch, like silk.

"Special means it's for special occasions."

"What special occasions?" I asked, staring questioningly at her.

She giggled. "Come on," she said. "You mean you really don't know?"

I shook my head.

She spoke in pidgin now. "You sef, you no dey know these things. Which kain girl you be? Yellow sissy like you, you no get special man friend?"

I couldn't help myself: a laugh escaped my mouth. A special man friend was the last thing on my mind. I shook my head and told her that I did not have a special man friend.

Now Ugochi looked at me with what seemed to be a mixture of

bafflement and pity. "Ah, well," she said, "maybe one day you'll find yourself one. But anyway, the point is, men like these things. They want *ocho mma, nwa nlecha, asa mma, asa mpete.*" She laughed a brief, womanly laugh, almost a mockery of herself. "You know, beautiful, beautiful. No be small thing o! I save my pretty things for when I spend time with my special man friends. Special things for special people. You know?"

The whistle blew, calling us for afternoon classes. Outside, the sounds of feet and the rising of voices. "Time to go," she said, and she reached out and collected the scarf.

29

EARLY ONE MORNING, I sat at my desk dressed in my school uniform, a green-and-white-checkered blouse and the matching dark green pencil skirt that went with it. I was studying, and in the gaps between my studying, I thought of Amina and heard Mama's voice in my head saying, "*Nee anya.* No matter what you do, stay away from that girl!" If Mama only knew that there had not been a need for her warning, I mused.

All night and morning long, I had not seen Ugochi, but now she flung open the door and entered with her usual bravado.

I turned around and watched her walk in. Her makeup and clothes were disheveled. Her hair was pinned up with one of her ribbons, but it was disheveled too. All of that mess and still she was wearing a big smile on her face.

"What are you doing there at your desk?" she asked.

"Studying," I said.

"Studying?"

"We have our history test today. Have you forgotten?"

She looked blankly at me, as if she were going through a stack of notecards in her mind. Finally she said, "Ah, that's right. Well, I'm sure it's not really something that needs studying for. I'm sure I'll do well enough even without studying."

"And how will you manage that?" I asked.

She was untying the ribbon from her hair. She stuttered a bit, then said, "Well, you know. Most of those things we learned this time around have those songs to go with them." She began singing: "There are seven rivers in Africa: Nile, Niger, Senegal, Congo, Orange, Limpopo, Zambezi. Azikiwe, Awolowo, Tafawa Balewa. *Onye ocha, sepu aka n'opu eze.*

"And there you have it," she said, stretching her arms wide open as if to say, Ta-da! "All in one song, you have the seven rivers and the first three founding fathers."

"Good job," I said. "But, you know, *that* will only get you so far. There's not a song for everything. And anyway, what if one of the questions is why the song ends with that last part: 'White man, take your hand off the chief's hat'? Do you know that answer?"

She laughed. "Nobody's hand should ever be on anyone's hat. Not without permission, anyway. But my point with the song is, I will know *some* of the answers on the exam. Even a little is better than nothing at all, *abi?*"

"What about *Things Fall Apart?* Have you read it yet? We will probably have to write an essay on it."

She waved her hand at me as if to brush the question away. As she did, she kicked off her skirt and said, "Everyone knows the story of Okonkwo."

I had been looking at her as she spoke, following her movements with my eyes, but as her skirt came off, I turned around to keep from watching. "I will manage just fine with that one," she was saying, and from the corner of my eye I could tell that she was now unbuttoning her blouse.

I continued to avert my eyes out of a feeling of self-consciousness, also out of a desire to be respectful to her. I looked up only when I was sure I had given her enough time to finish undressing and finish putting on her school uniform. But when I looked back at her she had still not managed to put on her uniform. Instead, she was wrapped in her towel and was holding her bathing bucket and bowl. She said, "I'm going to get a quick bath. Wait for me. Don't leave without me, okay?"

I nodded.

"As for studying," she said, in a mixture of proper English and pidgin, "really, no be big problem. I go manage. See you in a few minutes."

Her voice trailed off, and moments later the door was closing behind her.

30

CLASSES REALLY DO get in the way of living," Ugochi was saying as she bent to put some clothes in her bag again. "Imagine, the inconvenience of having to come back only to pack up and leave again!"

I laughed.

"But seriously," she said, "I can't help looking forward to the weekend. Nothing like being able to have unlimited time with my" — she winked at me before continuing — "with my special man friends."

"How many special man friends are you even talking about? And if there are so many of them, how can they all be special?"

"Daaaarling," she said, dragging out the word. She had recently started calling me "darling" because she could just tell, she said, that I was the kind of close friend she'd always wished for. Now she was calling me it again, saying, in a mawkish voice, "Daaaarling, that's for me to know and for you — not to find out."

Laughter sneaked out of my lips. "One of these days you'll get caught," I teased. "Sneaking in and out of campus like you're always doing. Don't be surprised when you finally get caught."

She shook her head. "Ye of little faith," she said. "Don't you worry about me. I know what I'm doing. I've got these things covered."

When the knock came, she had just finished packing her bag. She zipped the bag up and went to answer.

Through the window by my bed, I could see by the swooshing of leaves that a breeze was blowing.

The door swung open from the force of the breeze. Someone took a step inside. At first all I saw was the silhouette of a girl in a long dark dress. I could not make out her features, and if she had hair on her head, I could not have said. She took a few more steps into the dorm room. "I'm looking for Ijeoma," she said. It was the last voice that I had expected to hear.

Ugochi stepped aside and pointed the girl in my direction, and then she went back to her bed, picked up her bag, slung it across her shoulder. "See you later, daaaarling," she said teasingly. "I have some important business to take care of, as you know, but I shall be back." She winked.

I waved at her, but I was startled by the sudden awareness of myself and of everything around me. For one thing, I felt an urge to explain, even to apologize, to Amina for Ugochi's use of "darling," because what if Amina thought that it meant something more than just the word? I didn't want her to get the wrong impression, whatever that impression might be.

Amina glanced around the room, not saying a word. Finally she said, very timidly, "How are you?"

By now, some weeks had passed since my initial attempts to get back with her.

Her hair was braided loosely, and the braids fell down her shoulders. I thought back to the times when I used to braid it for her.

"I'm fine," I said. "And you?"

"I'm fine too," she said. After a brief silence she said, "I've missed you."

I felt a flutter in my chest, and I replied, very truthfully, "I've missed you too."

That evening, we headed off together on a walk on the campus grounds. We walked slowly, zigzagging and weaving circles across the lawn.

When we spoke, it was only about school, about the strict methods of the headmistress, the way she made us hold out our hands during morning assemblies, the way she walked around inspecting them for dirt, inspecting our uniforms for tears and wrinkles and stains. Have you ever been caned on the palm with the headmistress's ruler for not having clean enough nails? we asked each other. We walked separately. We did not hold hands or even allow our bodies to touch. We talked about our schoolmates, which of them we liked and which we didn't. We talked about the books we were reading and how we were finding our classes.

In the time that we had been separated, she had held on to the hope that perhaps some family member of hers would appear and reclaim her. It was not that the grammar school teacher and his wife were cruel to her, but that she had been craving her own family more than ever. Owing to this, the grammar school teacher and his wife had even made efforts to see if they could locate any of her extended family members. But word of mouth was only so effective. Anyway, perhaps her extended family, like her immediate family, had also been casualties of the war.

We did not talk about what happened in Nnewi. Not about getting caught, or the scolding that followed, or the meeting with Mama, or of our separate Bible studies.

By the look of things, she was still the same Amina I remembered, quiet and serious, only a little more contemplative than before.

31

THE FIRST HOLIDAY of the semester arrived. Many students packed their bags and headed home. Amina and I were among the few remaining.

One day during that holiday, with permission from the gate prefects we walked out of the campus and down the road beyond the school.

The Ekulo River, at the tip of the road where we met it, was narrow, but from where we stood, a point slightly elevated from the water, it appeared to grow increasingly wide. Weak waves crept up now and then, bathing the reddish-brown earth that flanked the river at its sides.

We walked farther and made ourselves seats on a tiny patch of grass under one of the palm trees. The earth was warm underneath us, having soaked up the sun's rays. Off and on, a cool breeze blew, and the palm leaves made whipping sounds as they thrashed against one another. Those leaves that had previously fallen tumbled on the sand.

At a distance, a woman washed her clothes. Sparrows flew. The air smelled of earth and river water.

At first there was some space between us, but I moved closer to her. We sat silently like that for a while, and then after some time I reached from behind, covered her eyes with my hands. "Hear it?" I asked.

"Hear what?"

"The water. Calming, no?"

"No," she said. She turned to face me. Wrinkles formed on her forehead. "Restless," she said. "It makes me restless."

My Bible lessons with Mama came flooding back in my head. Restless, I thought. Images of cattle and of creeping things and of wild animals and of the birds. God created them all, and on the seventh day He rested. Even God rested. But here was Amina, claiming to be restless — to be without rest.

I saw a stick on the ground near where we sat. I picked it up and mindlessly began clearing the sand in front of us of the larger pebbles.

"Why are you restless?" I asked.

"I don't know," she said. But she appeared to think about it for a moment, then she said, "For all sorts of reasons."

"What would it take to make you no longer feel restless?" I asked.

"I don't know," she said.

Above us, birds were chirping. With the stick I sketched a bird in the sand. "Birds are happy and free," I said. "Listen to them — don't they make you feel happy and free? We could come here as often as possible just to listen to the birds."

Amina drew her thighs up to her chest and wrapped her arms around her legs.

I scattered the sand, erasing the sketch of the bird. I put down the drawing stick.

To my surprise, she picked it up and began drawing in the sand. She drew two figures who stood holding hands. Clouds made of circles hung above them.

She smiled when she was done, a half-smile.

"It's a nice picture," I said, looking at her.

She reached over and placed her hand above mine. "Maybe just holding hands will be all it takes," she said. "Maybe just holding hands will be enough."

She was cupping handfuls of sand with her free hand now, letting the grains trickle out between her fingers. I replied, "Yes, maybe just holding hands will be enough."

The next morning, very early, she knocked on my door, and I answered.

Across her shoulders was a small blanket. She held the blanket tight. Underneath the blanket she was already dressed for the day in a periwinkle gown that I had never before seen on her. Her braids were gathered loosely into a bun at the nape of her neck. She looked worn-out.

"Didn't you sleep last night?" I asked.

She shook her head. "My mind was thinking so hard I couldn't sleep. I get worried sometimes."

"What are you so worried about?"

"I don't know," she said. "Everything." She paused. "Us."

"Don't be worried," I said. "There's nothing to worry about."

She stayed just looking at me a moment, then she said, "Anyway, I came because I was wondering if you'd like to go again to the river. I'd like it if you could."

"Of course," I replied. There was nothing I would have loved more to do.

32

SCHOOL HAD NOT yet resumed. It had been an ordinary day, and now Amina and I sat on the steps of the veranda of her dorm building, about to eat. There was an ashy smell coming out of the bowls of rice and beans.

"It's too burnt," I said.

She was the one who had prepared the meal. But as she cooked, she had been reading *The Drummer Boy*, which, before the holidays came, she had borrowed from the school library. The beans had sat on the fire while she got carried away with the book. As she was the one who was in charge of making the food, I had been blissfully tuned out, or else I would have gone and checked on it for her. Now it was too late.

She sat across from me, looking very apologetic.

"It's like eating ashes," I teased, lifting a spoonful of the beans to my mouth.

She hung her head a little. "I don't think it's that bad."

I teased some more. "Even worse than eating ashes. I don't know, this might very well poison us, char up our insides like burnt toast and leave us hacking our lungs out."

She rose angrily and began to gather the plates of food and the spoons, everything clanging with everything else. Ruckus here, ruckus there.

"I was just joking," I said, reaching out to stop her.

She paused in the middle of her gathering.

"I was just joking," I said again.

It was late in the evening. The sky was dark. With so many of the students still gone, there was no one nearby. I moved close to her, took the plates from her hands, set them down on the floor. I took her by the hand and led her to the far corner of the veranda, by the wall. I pushed her gently until her back was against the wall. We found ourselves in a tangle, our hands all around us, then settling on our waists. I placed my lips on the crook of her neck, and she moaned, holding me tighter by the waist. When our lips finally met, she kissed me hungrily, as if she'd been waiting for this all along. I breathed in the scent of her, deeply, as if to take in an excess of it, as if to build a reserve for that one day when she would be gone.

33

AT FIRST MAMA had come at least every other weekend to visit me at the school, as if to keep an eye out that I was not falling back into temptation with Amina. The school was a three-hour trip from her bungalow in Aba, and given that she was now running her shop, which was open every day of the week, locking up and coming to the school was a sacrifice where income was concerned, but she did it anyway.

Whenever she visited, she brought provisions for me: Cabin biscuits, tinned Titus sardines, garri, sugar, Peak milk, a can of Milo, a loaf of bread, and some cooked rice and stew. She and I would sit on the veranda of my dorm building and eat the rice and stew.

She'd stay with me for several hours. Amina knew to keep away during these times.

This was the way it went:

Me, taking one spoon for every five of Mama's.

"Eat more," she'd say.

"Mama, I'm not hungry," I'd reply.

"How can it be afternoon, you haven't eaten any lunch, and you tell me you're not hungry?"

I'd simply shrug.

When she could no longer persuade me to eat more, she'd shake her head and say something to the effect of, "This child, I don't know what I will do with you!"

We always sat around for a while afterward as Mama drilled me on my courses and general welfare. Sometimes we'd take a stroll outside the school compound before she then prepared to leave.

"You make sure you eat the remaining food," she'd say. "Don't let me hear that you threw it away or let it go to waste. Remember Biafra." Almost always, the same reminder of the war and how hard food was to come by during those days.

"I won't throw it away or let it go to waste," I always responded. Which was the truth, because after I had walked Mama to the school gate and seen her off, I returned to my room only to pick up the remaining food and take it to Amina's dorm. She was the reason that I was careful not to eat too much with Mama. Amina was the one I looked forward to sharing my meals with.

34

T HE DEVIL HAS returned again to cast his net on you," Mama would surely say of what I was doing. Or "Adam and Eve, not Eve and Eve." But even with those words in my head, I could not help myself.

I continued to see Amina. On evenings after classes, we ate our meals together, if not in the cafeteria, then on the veranda steps or inside our dorms, at our desks.

On weekends when we were allowed, or when more holidays rolled around, those holidays during which we did not go home, we strolled over to the river together. Sometimes we held hands as we walked, as inconspicuously as we could, making sure to present ourselves in a manner more like that of regular schoolgirls than that of two girls in love.

But we were in love, or at least I believed myself completely to be. I craved Amina's presence for no other reason than to have it. It was certainly friendship too, this intimate companionship with someone who knew me in a way that no one else did: it was a heightened state of friendship. Maybe it was also a bit of infatuation. But what I knew for sure was that it was also love. Maybe love was some combination of friendship and infatuation. A deeply felt affection accompanied by a certain sort of awe. And by gratitude. And by a desire for a lifetime of togetherness.

35

T HE DISCOVERY BEGAN with just a rumor and occurred well into our second year at the school.

On visiting days, which usually fell on Saturdays, students from the neighboring boys' school came. The teachers would walk around carrying their canes in their hands, chaperoning their visit. All over the campus, girls and boys gathered on the verandas in front of the buildings. No one was allowed to take a boy inside the dorm. But by the Monday following one Saturday visit from the boys, rumors began to spread.

The story had it that long before this last visiting day, a boy had been sneaking onto the campus and even inside a girl's dorm — or maybe the girl had been sneaking out to his dorm to be with him. Either way, now she was pregnant, and the rumors implied that she'd been pregnant for some time.

Ugochi's name was the first to pop into my mind. How long had I been watching her sneaking in and out of campus at night, meeting this man friend and that. It made sense to me that it must be her.

Monday morning and afternoon came and went, and I did not see or hear from Ugochi. She did not come to the dorm room at all.

Then, Monday evening, the whistle shrieked as one of the prefects came around announcing that morning assembly the following day would be earlier than usual. "Do not come a minute late or there will be consequences!" the prefect warned.

I thought of poor Ugochi. Where was she now? How was she handling all that was befalling her? How terrible it must be for her to have people whispering about her behind her back.

Tuesday morning came. We stood in rows, in our green and white uniforms, on the assembly grounds.

"Many of you know Ozioma," the headmistress began. "And by now many of you have heard that she is pregnant with a certain Nonso's child." There was a collective gasp at the revelation of the names. I sighed with relief that it was not Ugochi, and then it was a moment before I wrapped my brain around the fact that quiet Ozioma, whom everyone knew to be the headmistress's pet, had somehow slipped up and, in the process, wound up pregnant.

"Hush with your surprise," the headmistress was saying. "Now, I ask you all before me, why are you surprised? Is it a surprise? Is it not true that bad company corrupts good character?

"But let it be known that this was not the result of any negligence on the part of your teachers or on my part. Between assemblies and Sunday services and revivals, you certainly have been taught right from wrong. Those of you who have made a habit of sneaking out of school grounds, take note."

She finished: "A word is enough for the wise. Let this be a warning. Be wary of becoming like Ozioma, of allowing your good character to be soiled by bad company."

It was in this vein that Tuesday turned to Wednesday, and Wednesday to Thursday, and so on until the weekend rolled around. Many of the students packed their bags and went home for the weekend. Amina and I remained again, only this time with the headmistress's warning in mind.

36

BECAUSE IT WAS primarily an Igbo school, it was also a
Christian school, and because it was a Christian school, all
of the students were required to go to Sunday services and Sunday
revivals, as well as Wednesday-evening devotionals. This was a re-
quirement even on holidays, for those who stayed behind. If Amina
had not taken issue with the grammar school teacher's decision to
conduct Bible studies on her behalf — there was no indication that
she had remonstrated — she was not now taking issue with having
to attend services and practice the Christian faith. She attended and
participated just like any of the other girls, the Hausa/Igbo girl included.

Early on a Sunday Amina and I had gone to the service with all
the girls who had not gone home. Then we had whiled away time
reading at the library.

Now we were once again at the river, sitting in our usual spot,
observing as the sky changed from bright blue to gray. After a while,
the sun appeared to dissolve, and we watched as the sky turned a
deeper shade of gray.

Amina took my hand and pulled me up, smiling all the while. She
held my hand that way for a few moments, then stepped back from
where I stood, letting go of my hand. She twirled then, so fast that
her pleated skirt rose flat around her, like an upside-down plate. She
giggled, as if embarrassed that her skirt should come up so far. She
pushed it back down with her hands, looking into my eyes, searching, as if to find out exactly how much I had seen.

I twirled back in defiance, twirled so fast that the flared skirt of my dress came up as high as hers had, only I made no move to push it back down. Soon she was twirling with me. I heard her laugh, and I laughed with her, and soon we were falling down with all that laughter, at a joke that neither of us could quite have explained.

We sat on the ground to catch our breath, just looking at each other. The straps of her dress had fallen down her shoulders. I tugged at them, pulled them lower, looked longingly at her.

"Will you—" she began in a whisper.

"Will I?"

She moved closer to me.

"This?" I asked, pulling her straps lower.

She sighed, like a gasp, but she moved closer, her eyes steady on me.

I allowed my fingers to trace the upper part of her dress, its bodice, where the lace hem met her skin. She pulled my hand lower, just above her breast. I felt the thumping of her heart. She leaned into me and sighed again. We stayed a moment like that. Suddenly she turned her eyes from me, looked downward, as if suddenly self-conscious. Her dress still covered her body, everything but her shoulders, but she must have felt more naked than that, because she proceeded to wrap her arms over her shoulders.

We returned to campus in the dark, not saying a word, walking along the roads lined with palm and plantain trees, her yellow dress and my cream-colored one billowing in the breeze.

Back on school grounds, I started to go in the direction of my dorm, but she grasped my hand and we both walked in the direction of hers.

In her dorm room, we kicked off our shoes and sat on opposite ends of the bed. Her roommate had gone home for the weekend. My heart raced, a mixture of terror and excitement at the possibility of finally arriving at something that I had for some time begun to think of as a hopeless dream.

She rose from her end of the bed and moved so that she was next to me. After a while we stretched ourselves flat on the mattress. The room was dark, but the moon, through the horizontal slits of the shutters, shone through.

We watched each other by the light of the moon. We fell asleep that way.

It must have been sometime in the middle of the night that she woke up with a start, asking me if I had seen it, if I had heard it. "Hailstones," she blurted out, "and fire, pouring down and forming craters where they landed." Her body shook as she spoke, almost as if she were shivering from a fever.

She described the dream, something about a carriage in the sky pulled by golden horses with no horseman. People were lining up, marching toward the bright light that encircled the carriage in the sky.

I hadn't meant to do so, but I found myself laughing in her face. "I see you've been reading your Bible," I said. "Sounds to me like the book of Revelation." I laughed some more.

"The children," she cried, her voice shaky now. "Small children, sweat dripping from their heads. So much sweat that their clothes were soaking wet." With all that marching, she said, those poor children must have been achy, on the brink of exhaustion, some of them probably even beyond that, because every once in a while one fell to the ground, and the others simply stepped over him.

Maybe it was a sign, she said. Maybe we were the fallen children, the sinful ones without the strength to continue in the path of righteousness.

"No," I replied, taking her dream more seriously now. I shook my head, told her that it was all just a dream. I pulled her close to me and held her, my face in the crook of her neck. Was it her scent that gave me a feeling of joyful deliriousness? I kissed her, from her neck to her jawline and then to her lips. Her dress had come unbuttoned at the front, and I ran my hands across her chest, caressed her breasts. "We are far from fallen children," I said. "It's only a dream."

Her hand was moist on my lap. She leaned into me, stroked my face, returned my kiss with one full of yearning, deeper and more longing than mine. But I had already lost her. As soon as she parted from the kiss, she rose from the bed. She buttoned up her dress, found her sandals, and strapped them on. She walked over to the door and opened it. Cold air came in from outside. She stood there in the doorframe, her body faltering a little, like a shadow on the verge of fading. After some time just standing there, she walked out of the room, closing the door gently behind her.

37

FOR A COUPLE of weeks after that dream incident, Amina and I did not eat together, did not meet to go to the river, barely spoke to each other on our way to and from classes.

About the third Saturday after the dream, I was getting fed up with the way things were, fed up that everything between us should suddenly change again, and all on account of a stupid dream.

All day that Saturday, I had stayed in the library, hoping that Amina would stop in, but she didn't.

Now the sun was setting, and though I was not outside with the rest of the students, I knew that the teachers were announcing the end of visiting hours. From the open windows near where I sat, I could see that one by one the boys were sauntering away. Cardinal Rex's highlife music, *Ibi Na Bo*, was playing, coming from a veranda near the library building. Some people hummed along to it as they walked by on their way to let themselves out through the school gate.

I made up my mind then that I would get to the bottom of things. I closed the book I was reading and stood up. It was as if there was a fire at my feet, propelling me to move, to do something.

At her door, I knocked, three firm taps that I knew she would hear, if she was inside to hear. There was no answer.

In the distance, I could hear that *Ibi Na Bo* had finished playing, and now *Love Mu Adure* had taken over.

I knocked again. *Tap. Tap. Tap.* Still nothing.

Just as I turned to walk away, I heard the rattling of the doorknob.

She came out, closed the door behind her. "My roommate is sleeping," she said in a low voice. "She's not feeling well today."

"Oh," I said. "I'm sorry she's sick."

"It's okay," she said. "Just a stomachache. I picked some lemongrass and boiled it for her to drink."

"That was nice of you to do," I said. "I hope it helps."

She nodded.

I said, "I haven't seen you in a while."

"I know," she said. "Things have been busy."

"What's making them so busy?"

"I don't know," she said. "School. Reading. Sick roommate."

We were standing face to face. I moved closer to her, took her hand in mine. "We missed all the music and the dancing today," I said.

"I know," she said, pulling her hand out of mine. "Maybe next time."

I said, "We don't have to wait till next time. We can hear the music all the way from here." I took her hand in mine again, pulled her close to me. She did not pull away this time; instead she held on tightly. But she was wide-eyed and unsmiling. I moved closer, raised my hands to hold her by the waist. My hands had hardly touched her waist when she cried out, "Please stop!"

She said it again, more quietly this time, "*Please. Stop.*"

I let go of her.

She brought her hand to her forehead and said, "You know, actually, I have a headache. I think I need to sleep myself. I hope you have a good rest of the day. I'll see you around."

She turned and stepped into the room, shutting the door behind her, not bothering to wait for my response.

38

B Y THE END of that second year, no amount of persuasion or cajoling or flat-out rationalizing had managed to take away the standoffishness that Amina had acquired as a result of that dream.

If I said, "God loves us all the same," she said, "Not the thieves and the liars and the cheats, not the murderers, not the disobedient. He couldn't possibly love us all the same."

Once, I went so far as to quote her John 3:16: "For God so loved the world, that He gave His only begotten Son, that whosoever believeth in Him should not perish, but have everlasting life." And I said, "You see, God loves us all the same. He gave His only son to save us all. All of us, even the thieves and liars and cheats, even the murderers and the disobedient. Even those of us accused of abominations." By this time, a large part of me did not believe I had committed any type of abomination, but I said it anyway. Just to point out to her that God loved us all. Just to point out to her that He didn't put any qualifiers on His love. Not even when He said to love your neighbor as yourself. He didn't say don't love the thieving neighbors, or don't love the adulterers, or don't love the liars or the cheats or the disobedient children. He simply said, "Love your neighbor as yourself."

All of this explaining. Still, Amina would not budge.

By our third year, it was as if she had become a secondary-school-aged, Nigerian version of Margaret Thatcher, iron lady through and through.

Then one day, as if by a miracle, on a Sunday around the middle of our third year, the headmistress announced the upcoming visit of an *onye ocha* minister, who promised to perform wonders through prayer. I was all ears.

He would be the special guest at our revival ceremony the following Sunday, the headmistress said.

During the war, some of the villagers in Ojoto had gone around saying that the Red Cross *ndi ocha* workers had been sent to Biafra by God to save us. Once, I watched as several of the villagers threw their hands above their heads and exclaimed, "Glory be to God! The *ndi ochas* can even bring back the dead!" I have no idea what led them to say that—maybe one of the Red Cross nurses had successfully treated a dying person, returning him to health. Whatever the case, the idea of an *onye ocha* minister coming to our school to perform miracles instantly reminded me of what the villagers had been saying during the war, so that, for me, the impending visit took on the feel of medicine. In my mind, it was as if all I'd have to do was show up at the revival, take a full Sunday regimen of *onye ocha* prayer tablets, and just like that, everything would be fixed.

The Sunday of the minister's revival, it rained. The senior prefects led the way. We followed, all of us trudging along through the pouring rain, through swampy marshlands and mud-caked trails.

We reached an open field several kilometers from our campus, gathered in a large circle around the minister and his small crew of *ndi ochas,* the rain beating down on us.

The minister wore a short-sleeved white oxford shirt and a pair of brown trousers, both of which, soaked, clung to his body. He was pale, like any other white man, but he was dark too, tanned from the sun, so much so that the skin on his face and on his arms reminded me of a belt, or a cattle hide, owing to that leathery look of it.

By his side, a gray-haired *onye ocha* woman sat in a silver and black wheelchair. She was a cripple, the minister explained, speaking in his rambling, *onye ocha* way, one word melting into the next.

Another *onye ocha* man stood by the crippled woman, holding a long stick. "Look upon him and bear witness to the power of God!"

the minister announced. "Look and marvel at a man who has spent all his life deprived of sight. But today, my brothers and sisters in Christ, today he shall see!"

All around I heard the collective "Amen" of fellow students.

The minister began with the crippled woman. He wheeled her to the very middle of the crowd and asked us to position ourselves in the field so that we could properly see. The praying began:

"Dear Almighty Lord in heaven, we are gathered here today to ask Your mercies. We come to You to ask You to strengthen us and lead us into the light, so that we might not, through our weaknesses, remain in the dark. O font of life and blood and water, we acknowledge that we exist in this world only in order to allow You to exercise Your admirable grace and divine power on us. Eternal Father, we beg You to shower on us Your tender love so that we might see on our persons the changes we seek . . ."

He went on that way for some time when, abruptly, his words morphed from English into something I could not understand. He continued along the lines of: "Devetium nahalesh divium namaha selelehakim danashanka levan balaton zaphan alatay fakani . . ." He flailed his arms as he spoke. His eyes fell closed.

"Ushku bilani arakesh rushki rohush ekeleledu skuda wudswia . . ." On and on he went, so much jibberish that by the time I finally wrapped my head around what was happening, he was already coming to an end. The ending at least was sprinkled with words I could recognize. For whatever reason, he finished with the words "Shadrach, Meshach, and Abednego."

He leaned over the woman in the wheelchair, helped her up so that she appeared to stand in an upright position. He proceeded to pull her wheelchair away slowly. The woman continued to stand after the wheelchair was a few feet away. A minute went by during which she appeared to stabilize herself on her two feet. She steadied herself some more, and then, quite unexpectedly, she began to walk.

The crowd roared, raising their hands high toward the sky. "Praise the Lord!" All over the field, the collective rise of voices, thanking God and the Lord Jesus for the miracle before our eyes.

"Are you ready for what God has in store for you next?" the minister cried.

"We are ready!" the crowd screamed.

"Are you ready to witness God's next miracle before your very eyes?"

"Yes, minister, we are ready to witness the next miracle of God!"

The minister went over to the blind man, held him by the arm. The rain had stopped. Briefly the minister prayed again, distorted and unnatural-sounding words falling out hard from his mouth, words as hard as rocks.

He picked up a small decanter from the ground, poured its contents into the palm of his hand. He sprinkled the liquid on the blind man's head, on his shoulders, on his face. Finally he sprayed the liquid in the direction of the blind man's eyes.

"Now, brothers and sisters, bear witness to yet another miracle!"

The crowd cheered.

The minister held up two fingers. "How many fingers?" he asked the blind man.

"Two!" the blind man cried.

The minister held up his fingers once more, four fingers this time. "How many fingers?"

"Four!" the blind man cried.

"By the glory of God, this man has been healed! By the divine glory of God, he can see again!"

Once more, the collective raising of hands high toward the sky, and the collective cry of "Praise the Lord!"

Our voices were like eagles, and our amens soared.

Later, we lined up to get our own personal miracles, everybody in a straight line behind a gray metal bucket where the minister stood. But first the donation, without which the miracle could not be performed. The minister oversaw as we dropped our money into the bucket, the coins clinking as they piled in heaps, one on top of the other.

The naira notes he took himself, folded them, placed them carefully in the fanny pack he wore around his waist.

I had come with some naira bills, money that was supposed to be for my meals and school supplies. I took a couple out of my pocket and handed them to the minister. I explained to him that my ailment pertained to the heart. He nodded sympathetically, his lips curving downward to demonstrate his empathy. Next came the sprinkles of holy water on my head and all over my face, over my shoulders. He began again to pray, a hurried prayer, his voice like a murmur, but somehow still quite loud.

Finally he said, "Go in peace, my child." He seemed to be panting a little, struggling a bit for air. What hard work, performing miracles, his panting seemed to say.

"How long before my prayers are answered?" I asked.

He looked taken aback by the question, but he quickly replied, "By the time you return to the school compound, you should start to see changes." For a moment he looked at me with scrutinizing eyes, and then he said, "Don't worry. As an emissary of God, I can tell you that your prayers will be answered. Your heart will be just fine."

Until now, Amina and I had managed to stay out of each other's paths. But at that moment I looked up to find that she was standing next in line. As she walked up to the minister she hardly looked my way. Her face was somber, and though at the time I did not have the slightest clue what miracle she was asking the *onye ocha* to perform for her, sometimes these days I think I know. Sometimes I speculate that she must have gotten exactly what she asked for. But at the time, it appeared that it was I who would get my wish. Maybe this is the way it goes when people approach God with contrary requests. How does God choose whose request to fulfill? Does God fight a battle of wills on their behalf? Does God play favorites? Humans double-deal. If it is true that we are made in His likeness, then does God double-deal?

39

UGOCHI WAS IN her nightgown, sitting on the chair by her bed. On her desk, the flame of her lantern flickered, casting shadows like wandering scars on her face. She had not been at her desk long, because earlier she was out on the river, in a canoe with a boy. All evening, too, she had been with the boy. They had simply drifted on the river, she said, drinking Fanta and Coke and watching the flocks of swallows fly around in the blue skies.

"Just drifting and drinking soft drinks and watching the birds?" I asked. "Just how much drifting could you both have possibly done on that river, being that the river is not all that big, more like a narrow stream flanked at the sides by the jagged earth? Was there even room in it for a canoe?"

"*Na wa-oh,*" she said, rolling her eyes accusingly, as if to declare me the guilty one for daring to ask the question. "Little Miss Innocent, what do you even know of these things? You must know more than I think you do." She pursed her lips so that they formed a tight circle with only a bit of an opening between. She sucked air into her mouth so that out came a sound somewhere between a shush and a whistle.

I rolled my eyes back at her. "I know enough to know that you weren't just drifting and drinking soft drinks," I said.

Slowly her lips relaxed themselves into a naughty smile. "*Ngwa,* I will tell you," she said. "But, *nee anya,* you cannot tell anybody. Not a soul, you hear me? I don't want to become the subject of gossip-gossip like Ozioma."

"If you're not careful, that's exactly what will happen, only worse than Ozioma—you won't even know which man is the father of your child."

She laughed and said, "You know, sha, I have decided to do away with all those man friends and try a few younger boys. You know, secondary school boys my age. The men are good for money, but they are not looking to marry. All they want is a sweetheart on the side. I have to begin thinking of my future sooner or later."

"So you were with one of the younger boys today?"

Out of the blue there was a timid look on her face.

"Since when are you shy?" I asked.

She giggled. "The young ones do have their pluses. He's a really good one, you know," she said quietly. I'd never seen her act like this before. If she had been light-complexioned, her face would have glowed a shade of red.

"You like him that much?" I asked.

She nodded. "I really like am o."

"Enough to marry him if he asked?"

She laughed. "Marriage is still a long way off. Didn't you hear me? I said 'try a few younger boys.' Boys. Plural. Why must I choose one, and so early?"

There was a faraway look in her eyes. She said, "Anyway, boys and men do it all the time—they have many girls on the side. Why can't I?"

She stayed sitting on her chair but her arms were now folded at the elbows and resting on her desk. "And even if I must choose, it's not as if I would know where to begin. I like this one, yes. But there are others too. The one who hardly talks, or the one who talks a bit too much? The very tall one, or the one not quite my height? She wore a look of mock confusion. "Tough decisions. This kain life. E no easy o!"

"Well, if worse comes to worst," I said, "you can just line them up in a row and sing *tumboko tumboko beskelebe ti ti alaba bust*. If your finger lands on him, you eliminate him. Simple. You marry the last man standing."

She laughed deeply now, her shoulders heaving. "Tomorrow sef,

I will be with another boy. Maybe we will go to the river and borrow the same canoe from today, or maybe we will try something else. The possibilities are endless. But I will say that it's been very nice spending time with today's boy. Some secondary school boys really do know how to treat a girl well. It's too bad so many of them wind up turning into cheating, two-timing men."

I would have said that she was well on her way to becoming just like the men she was condemning. But I held my tongue, and instead I pictured her at the river with the secondary school boy. In my mind's eye, I watched as they climbed into the canoe, as the sunlight caught their bare arms and legs. In my mind's eye, they had gone prepared with fishing gear, and they were getting ready to cast their lines after some fish — maybe for okpo isiukwu, the big-headed catfish, or afor, the moonfish, or croaker or red snapper. Not that there was any indication that the river had any of these. I pictured it anyway. At last evening would come, and, tired, she and the boy would fall into those things that boys and girls did when alone and in the dark. By the end of it all he would reach into his pocket and pull out a beautiful bracelet for her. I imagined it all this way.

I kept a journal that year, at first writing on loose leaves of paper, which I folded into fourths and then again into eighths and stored in the wooden chest where I kept my pens and pencils. Eventually I found a small notebook. I kept the notebook also in the chest.

That night, I took out the notebook, and as Ugochi rambled on about boys, I wrote to Amina in it. Just a pledge of a note. Nothing that I actually intended to give to Amina, not in that moment at least. It was simply for purposes of catharsis.

I wrote:

All the things the boy will do, I promise to do better.
    In all the ways he can love you, I promise to love you better.

40

ONE DAY, STILL our third year, I went beyond the river, where rocks rose like hills and where the plantain trees grew high. Beyond the rocks was a narrow path. A rope bridge led to more plantain trees, and some banana plants in between. I stood at the entrance of the bridge, in the part of the forest where banana hearts hung, purple flowers dangling from stocky stems. In the distance, grasscutters and other bush animals stirred. A few steps in front of me, the ground plunged. The gorge it formed was deep and narrow and very rocky. I stood there and thought, If I should plummet to my death, would she come for me?

That day was again a visiting day. The sun had begun to set by the time I returned to the school grounds, and when I got back to my dorm I found that the party I had tried to avoid earlier was still going on on the veranda. Music was playing as it usually did on these days. The boys and girls were moving to the music, their arms and hips swaying like extensions of the beat.

I squeezed through the first set of students I met with, those standing a few steps in front of the veranda. I cut across the veranda, walked hastily toward the door. There, by the door, I found her. I'd never seen her with makeup on, but now her lips were painted red, her eyes lined in black. Ugochi and a group of other girls stood not far away from her. There she was, Amina in an off-the-shoulder blouse made of a lacy material. Amina in a tight skirt and sequined sandals. Amina with earrings I'd never seen on her before. They dangled like teardrops, bottom side heavy. One had only to turn them upside down and the thin, tapered ends would have been something sharp, like the tip of a knife. There she was, Amina trying to be beautiful, even if she already was.

I moved closer to her. She was unaware that I was there. I watched as she put her arms around the shoulders of one of the boys. His own arms came around her waist.

I tapped her on the shoulder. It must have been too light a tap, because she only leaned into the boy, and soon their heads were meeting. Afraid that their lips would soon follow, I wrapped my arms around her waist and pulled her to me. There was a fragrance coming from her, something sweet and floral, like the scent of a rosebush.

She looked me in the face, very shocked. The boy's arms came around her waist again, as if he had not noticed that I was standing there. She turned to him.

"Amina," I said, my voice flat and dry.

She turned back to me. "I'm sorry," she said. Her voice was a little more apologetic than the look in her eyes. She repeated it: "Sorry." And again, she repeated it. If sorry was meat, I could have cooked a pot of soup with it.

Whether they finally kissed or not, I did not stay to see.

41

BY OUR FOURTH and fifth years, Amina and I had drifted
even farther apart. We sat in the same classroom for our
mock WAECs, not saying a word to each other, not before or after
the exams. By the time the real WAECs rolled around, I had resigned myself to hopelessness. The possibility of any kind of relationship between us now felt like a lost cause.

The grammar school teacher and his wife had continued to remain in contact with Mama, and, through them, I received small,
infrequent updates on Amina, nothing significant enough to have
held my interest. But then our final year came to an end, and with it,
the big announcement.

It happened on the very last day that it could have happened, at
the conclusion of our senior send-off party, when the parents had
already arrived to collect their children. Out on the school fields,
chairs still stood in rows. But no one was sitting. Instead, parents
swarmed around their children like ants around morsels of sweets.
Some of them stood along the perimeter of the chairs, swaying
alongside their children to the rhythm of some invisible, inaudible
drum. Others simply stood around conversing.

Mama and I had managed to find the grammar school teacher
and his wife in the crowd. As Amina was still under their care, she
was with them when Mama and I approached.

The grammar school teacher was smiling mischievously. There
was hardly a greeting before he blurted out, "Amina has wonderful
news. Have you heard?"

By his side, his wife stood unsmiling. If she knew the news, it was failing to have the same effect on her as it was having on him.

He turned to Amina. "Go on," he said. "Tell them."

Amina cleared her throat. She looked at me as she spoke. It was a simple declaration: "There is a Hausa boy who wants to marry me."

It was not at all characteristic of me, but in that moment, I burst out with one quick *ha,* the vocalization of my shock.

Mama glared at me, then turned back to Amina. "Congrats, dear," she said, but in a way that came off, if not spiteful, then resentful. "He's Hausa, you say?"

"Yes, Hausa," Amina replied.

"Okay. Very good, then," Mama said. And now she seemed appeased that Amina had at least known to marry into her own tribe. "You'll be with your own kind, back where you belong, learn a little about your people. Keep to yourselves."

The grammar school teacher nodded with the overenthusiastic effort of a person trying hard to keep things jovial. "Indeed. With her own kind. It couldn't be better," he said.

"So tell me about him," Mama said to Amina. "Is he a student?"

Amina nodded. "Yes," she said. "He finished secondary school last year and passed the JAMB with flying colors. He'll be entering university up north this year. He wants to study civil engineering."

Mama's eyes had been widening, little by little, as Amina spoke. Now her hands came together, as if to clap, and she turned to look at me. "Did you hear that, Ijeoma? An educated young man! Please-o, better hurry up and find yourself someone like that before you wind up getting left behind. But," she added, "Igbo, of course."

I stood glaring at Amina. She appeared to avoid my gaze.

"Of course, he'll do it the proper way, not so?" Mama was asking. "He'll come to make the formal request?"

Amina nodded. The grammar school teacher was all smiles still. All the while his wife remained unsmiling.

"It's always a good idea to go the traditional way," Mama said. "Traditional wedding is a must. By that I mean Hausa, of course. White wedding, you can take or leave." She reached out her hand and patted Amina on the back. "Ah! The lost sheep of the shepherd, strayed from the group, now finding her way back to her people, to her very own pack of sheep."

The grammar school teacher nodded. "A true miracle. Certainly a cause for celebration."

His wife had been silent this whole time, but now she turned to me. Mama and the teacher were still going on and on about Amina. His wife looked at me. There was something sympathetic in her eyes, and when she spoke, she spoke softly. "It's just the way things are done," she said. "You understand, don't you?"

My head was a little downturned, but she reached for my chin, lifted my face so that I was looking into her eyes. She said, "Don't worry. Somehow it all works out."

Not long after, while the adults stood chatting among themselves, I found Amina off by herself, leaning on an udala tree behind one of the school buildings.

I approached her under the tree.

She was holding her head down, refusing to look at me.

At first neither of us said a word, but after some time I cleared my throat and asked, "Will you really marry him?"

She nodded, still not looking at me.

"You really want to marry him?"

Again she nodded, still averting her eyes.

"You and I both know it's not what you want," I said.

She looked at me now, her eyes narrowed. "It is," she said.

At this point we seemed to be staring each other down. When I could no longer hold her gaze, I looked away at the ground. There were yellowing weeds growing from the brown earth that circled the trunk of the tree. On the grass around that brown patch, a grasshopper was skipping about. Off in the distance I heard the grammar school teacher's voice, calling Amina's name, then Mama's name, then mine.

"I want to marry him. I really do," Amina said.

A breeze rustled the leaves above us just as the grammar school teacher, his wife, and Mama made their way to us.

PART V

42

ALL AROUND WAS an assortment of colors: bright reds and blues and greens. Oranges and purples. Shades in between. All the storefronts—and all the items in them—sparkled. Colors and more colors, dancing harmoniously under the glow of the brisk afternoon sun. But the roads were still wet from an early morning rain, poto poto everywhere.

A girl with a tray on her head called out, "*Akara oku! Hot akara! Akara oku!*"

There was the heavy scent of fufu and ground crayfish in the air. Above the haggling voices of the market people, radios played music and spouted out news. Some simply hissed with static.

A shirtless old man, with skin so loose that it appeared to be melting down his body, said: "Fine girl, look how say even sun dey follow you! Even sun sabi say you dey fine! Beauty-beauty. Omalicha! Carry go!"

"Mineral! Mineral! Come get your mineral," a hawker cried.

A middle-aged woman sang, "*Agidi, Agidi, Agidi, Agidi jollof!*"

I walked up the road until I arrived at the bole stand, where the vendor girl—Nnenna was her name—stood slicing the peels off some plantains.

"Two plantains," I said to her. "The usual."

Nnenna just stood there, slicing a plantain in the slowest possible way. As she sliced it, she sang out loudly, "*Onye ihe m n'ewiwe, ya biko wegbuo ya, osukosu nwa mpi, ya biko sugbuo ya, selense.*" Each time she got to *selense*, she moved her hips sharply from side to side, jutting her face in a pose, as if getting ready for her picture to be taken.

There was something mocking about the way she did all of it. She had recently begun teasing me about the stupid catcalls of some of the men vendors. "It must be nice to be so beautiful!" If she only knew that all the beauty in the world did not amount to much where many things in life were concerned. All those men shouting out their love as if tossing loose change into a beggar's can, professing to want to marry me in that careless way that people often tossed out trash. The way life often defied its own logic, the way it often threw us for a loop, a beautiful girl might as well be as ugly as the ugliest of ojuju masks.

Mama was waiting for me back at the shop. "Biko, make so I fit go!" I said to Nnenna. Did she not realize that if she made me wait any longer, she could altogether lose my business?

I had just turned nineteen, and Nnenna was a couple of years younger.

"Ehn-ehn," she said, shaking her head from side to side. "So you think se you be the only *selense* around here? I go show you o!" She sang even louder now and did the thing with her face and hips again. The way she held her face, she reminded me of a duck, and so I burst out laughing. But she was so carried away with her dancing that it took her a while to register the sound of my laughter. When she finally did, she put on a look of mock sadness, and immediately her laughter mixed in with mine.

"*Oya,* biko, give me plantain make I fit go," I said.

Business was booming at Mama's shop now that it stocked more than the basics. In addition to loaves of bread and meat pies, palm oil and a few crops, we sold wafers, chewing gum, peppermints. Toothpaste and toothbrushes, matchsticks, candles, newspapers, thread. Now there were beverages beyond palm wine. The shop carried crates of soft drinks neatly stacked along the walls. Glass bottles of Fanta and Coke and Sprite, of Guinness and Gulder, Heineken and Star.

Mama had relegated the stocking and dusting of shelves to me. There was quite a bit of stocking still to be done that day, and so I was in a hurry to get back.

Finally Nnenna stopped with her playing and she reached for two already roasted plantains. She sliced them open and proceeded to pour palm oil into them, proceeded to sprinkle ground pepper over the palm oil.

It was a steaming-hot afternoon, and the heat from the coal grill, combined with the mob of people, only made it feel hotter.

I collected the wrapped-up plantains and rushed back to the store.

That was the way things played themselves out earlier that afternoon. The whole business with Nnenna — the surprise teasing followed by our shared laughter. And then, not long after, that same day, there would be another surprise.

It started with Mama and I munching into our bole. Mama sat in her usual seat, on a stool along the back wall of the store. The cash register sat on the counter in front of her. We had barely begun eating — barely taken three bites — when a customer entered. She was a tall girl, taller than me by several centimeters. She looked to be my age, certainly no more than one or two years older. Her hair was packed high atop her head in a big round puff. A set of bright yellow gold circular links dangled down from her earlobes. She looked somewhat like Amina, the way her face was long and serious-looking, but her skin was darker, something between the color of a brown carton and the color of Guinness. Her lips were red, in a way that reminded me a little of the grammar school teacher's wife's, or of Amina's on that tragic day out on the veranda with the boy. But this girl's lips were a lighter shade of red. She was wearing an Ankara romper whose bottom came down to mid-calf. Its neckline angled down on one side, revealing a shoulder. On her feet she wore a strappy, flat pair of sandals.

She walked up to the register. Her eyes seemed to scan my face.

"Do you carry Mentholatum?" she asked.

It was the rainy season, and quite a number of people had been coming in asking for Mentholatum, and we had run out. I shook my head. "Sorry," I said. "We should be getting more in a few days, maybe even by next tomorrow."

Mama was now standing beside me, very close to the counter. "If you need something immediately, we have Rub," she said. "It's the same thing, maybe a little stronger than Mentholatum. Should work even better."

The girl shook her head. "Thanks, but I prefer Mentholatum."

My roasted plantain was out on the countertop, on the aluminum foil from which I was eating it. The girl looked down at it and then back up at me. "Mmmm. Bole. I was just on my way to get some."

I said, "Nobody roasts them as well as Nnenna."

She nodded, and for a moment she stood there smiling at me. It crossed my mind that maybe she was waiting for me to offer her some of my bole, which would have been awkward, this random customer just standing there looking with longthroat at my food.

I was wearing a navy-blue polka-dotted dress that formed a V-line at the junction between my breasts, and I saw the moment when her eyes flickered down to that area, and paused, before darting back up to meet my eyes.

She smiled an embarrassed, almost apologetic smile when her eyes met mine.

"I'll just come back for the Mentholatum in a few days," she said.

I nodded.

She scanned my face once more, very quickly, before turning around to leave.

43

L ATE AFTERNOON ON a Saturday, almost evening. In an
hour Mama and I would be getting ready to close up the
shop. Mama was reading the newspaper behind the counter. Fela
Kuti was playing on the radio.

I was still counting change from a previous sale when I looked
up to see the grammar school teacher and his wife walk in. I tugged
Mama by the arm. She looked up and saw them too, and exclaimed
with surprise, "Oga! Madam! What brings you here today?"

She went out from behind the counter to greet him and his wife
in an embrace.

I finished with the counting, placed the money into the register,
followed her out from behind the counter to greet them as well.

"Uncle and Aunty, good afternoon. Welcome," I said.

Mama turned to me. "Ijeoma, bring out the folding chairs," she
said.

I went to the stock room, pulled out two folding chairs and set
them up in the front corner of the store.

When they were seated, he said, "Ah. Long time no see. How you
dey?"

"We dey fine o, we thank God," Mama said very cheerfully. She
had by now pulled out her stool from behind the counter to join
them. "So what brings you two to Aba?"

"We were on our way to visit family," the grammar school teacher
said.

His wife said, "My sister moved here with her husband about
a month ago. We decided it was time we come see the new place.

While we were at it, we thought to stop by and see you. Kill two birds with one stone."

"Welcome!" Mama said. She called me. "*Oya,* Ijeoma, fetch our guests some beer and soft drinks." Turning back to them, she said, "We have Guinness, Coke, Fanta, Sprite—"

His wife requested a Coke. The grammar school teacher requested a bottle of Guinness.

When they had been sitting, drinking the soft drink and beer, and making small talk for about twenty minutes, the topic of Amina came up. I felt my stomach churn.

"It went just as you would expect," the grammar school teacher said. "The groom's family came down and took permission from us. I think they called it *Na gani ina so.* It didn't take much time before we arrived at the *Sa rana*—the setting of the date, that is."

"Look at you!" Mama laughed. "You've become a proper Hausa man, using their words even!"

"I try," the grammar school teacher said, laughing too. His wife joined in the laughter.

"So how was it?" Mama asked when the laughter subsided.

"It was a beautiful wedding," the grammar school teacher's wife said. "Very simple and intimate—just family—but beautiful. You should have seen her, with paint decoration all over her hands, up her arms, flower designs. Very pretty."

"How wonderful," Mama said.

The whole time I had been standing behind the counter, listening to their conversation, struggling to contain my anger. I wanted to scream out "Traitor!" for the way Amina had betrayed me. The last thing I wanted to hear now was talk about her wedding. I felt an urge to walk out, but it would have been rude to walk out with the guests there, and what if a customer came while Mama was still visiting with them?

The next thing the grammar school teacher said sent a wave of sadness that totally obliterated all the anger that I had previously been feeling.

He said, "They have since moved up north."

Up until then, it had been a bit of comfort to think of her as not being too far away. Sometimes I liked to fantasize about us accidentally running into each other. I would imagine the age-old lovers-reunion cliché: arms wrapping around each other, kisses, declarations of love.

But truthfully, the announcement should not have come as a surprise. Back at our send-off party, she had mentioned that the groom would be going to school up north.

"Where exactly up north did they wind up?" Mama asked.

"She mentioned it, but I can never keep those northern states straight." He turned to his wife. "Do you remember?"

"I think it's either Kano or Kaduna, I can't remember myself," she said. "He had mentioned Ahmadu Bello University in Zaria, but he had also mentioned that new federal university in Kano."

He said, "Yes o. Kano or Kaduna. Definitely not as far up north as Sokoto, but north enough that there will be an abundance of her people, just the thing a girl like her needs."

That evening, after the grammar school teacher and his wife left, Mama gave me a talking-to. We were together in the kitchen. She was sitting on her stool, her legs wrapped around the mortar, about to begin pounding the cubes of yam for dinner.

It came out as a chant. She said, "A woman without a man is hardly a woman at all. You won't stay young forever. Even that girl has gone and found herself a husband. Why won't you do the same?"

I was standing by the sink, cutting up okra for soup. I paused with the okra and turned to look at her.

A candle was burning on a tin can that sat on the countertop. It was nearly all used up, though some of its wax had congealed on the sides of the can.

Mama rose from where she was sitting to grab a new candle from the cupboard. As she did, she said, "*Gee nti.* Listen, and listen well. *Oge na gakwa.* Time is passing. You need to get out there and find yourself a husband. Time waits for no one."

She took what remained of the old candle and tossed it into

the dustbin. Under her breath, she muttered, "If you're not careful, you'll find yourself like that candle, all burnt up and nothing to show for it."

She picked up the pestle, held it, but she did not in fact pound. Instead, she looked at the cubes of yam and said, "Marriage has a shape. Its shape is that of a bicycle. Doesn't matter the size or color of the bicycle. All that matters is that the bicycle is complete, that the bicycle has two wheels.

"The man is one wheel," she continued, "the woman the other. One wheel must come before the other, and the other wheel has no choice but to follow. What is certain, though, is that neither wheel is able to function fully without the other. And what use is it to exist in the world as a partially functioning human being?"

Under her breath, she said, "A woman without a man is hardly a woman at all." There was something self-deprecating about the way she said it.

She began to pound the yam, one loud thump after another. The soft yam cubes did not do much to muffle the hard sounds of wood smacking against wood, of the pestle smacking against the mortar. A couple of more thumps and then silence.

I turned around at the sink, to go back to the okra I had been cutting. But Mama was not done with me yet. She said, "A word to the wise: go out, make some friends, socialize. How will the young men even know that you are available if you spend all your time moping around at home?"

It was true. Other than church and work at the shop, and some errands to and from the market, I spent all my time at home. Even in church I sat alone, at the very back of the room, and I'd be gone the minute the final benediction was said.

"Some people, you wonder if God was sleeping when He made them. But you, you are beautiful. God was definitely not sleeping when He made you. A girl as beautiful as you! You are nineteen, almost twenty, and yet no young man has so much as come for you. *Chineke bi n'elu!* God in heaven! How can this even be?"

44

T HE MENTHOLATUM GIRL came back early one morning, only not for Mentholatum. Mama was away arranging the purchases and deliveries for the store.

The girl walked in carrying a stack of composition books, her face perfectly made up, her navy-blue A-line skirt and white cotton blouse crisply ironed. She was wearing a pair of black medium-heeled shoes.

She dumped the composition books on the counter. "I don't know why I continue to give these children writing assignments. It's self-torture having to carry all these composition books home, read them, mark them, only to have to lug them back to school."

Back in Obodoañuli Academy, the social studies teacher Mr. Aderemi sometimes used to make us read our essays to him aloud. I said to the Mentholatum girl, "You could give them oral presentations instead. Just have them read aloud what they've written, and mark them that way."

"Something to consider," she said, nodding thoughtfully, as if she were weighing the pros and cons of the suggestion right then and there.

"By the way, I'm Ndidi," she said.

"Ijeoma," I replied. "So where exactly do you teach? What school?"

"The secondary school a few roads down. You can't miss it. Yellow buildings with green roofs. The only school in the area with that color combination. If you pass by when school is beginning or letting out, you might see me out on the grounds, overseeing the children."

She looked down at the pile of composition books on the counter. She said, "I'd love to say I stopped in to chat, but—"

One second I was fidgeting with my hands, out of nervousness, then the next second I was accidentally twisting a finger, turning it the wrong way so that I felt a sharp, unexpected pain. My gasp came out just as she was saying that last bit about leaving, so she stopped speaking and laughed. "You sound as if I've disappointed you," she said.

"No," I said. "Not at all. Just my finger." I began to explain, but I was suddenly more self-conscious, which meant that I might only end up stumbling over my words and sounding like a bumbling fool. I decided to hold the explanation.

"Actually," she said, bringing me back out of my thoughts, "I have a small admission to make. The reason I stopped by was that the bag I was using to carry all these books broke along the way. I don't know how I will carry them all the way to school without a bag. Do you happen to have anything I can use?"

I pulled out a small cloth bag from behind the counter and handed it to her. Our fingers brushed slightly as I did, and my eyes darted up instinctively, to see if she had noticed. It didn't seem she had noticed. She said, "Wonderful. Thank you. I'll have it back to you as soon as I can."

"You can keep it," I said. "We have many of them. We can spare that one."

"As you wish," she said. She paused, then added, "But you know, it will be a good excuse for me to come back."

If there were any confusion on my part as to what the connection was between us, at this point all of the confusion disappeared. And with its disappearance, I was feeling more confident. "It's a shop," I said, a little smugly. "We sell at least a hundred different things. You have at least a hundred different reasons to come back."

She smiled and nodded.

She was wearing a watch on her wrist. She looked at it. "I better be on my way. The headmaster will scream off my head if I'm late. He doesn't tolerate lateness one bit."

My hands were resting on the counter. She reached out and placed her free hand over my right hand before turning to leave.

She stopped by the shop again on her way back from school. "There's a place that makes really good jollof rice close to my flat. I know you like plantains. Their dodo is very good too. Do you want to come?"

Mama had been asking me to socialize and meet people for some time now, so going out with Ndidi seemed a good middle ground between what I wanted and what Mama wanted for me. At least, I reasoned it that way.

Her place was a small flat with postcards decorating the walls in neat squares and rectangles. Postcards of places she wanted to go.

As soon as we entered, and as soon as she had put down the bag she was carrying, she stepped behind the folding wall that separated the bedroom from the parlor. After some minutes she came out no longer wearing her A-line skirt and cotton blouse, but instead a colorful adire gown. Her black medium-heeled shoes had been replaced by a pair of brown flat sandals.

She joined me where I stood in the parlor, looking at a postcard of Venice with its canals and gondolas. She stood by my side. "Imagine, a city that is entirely car-free!" she said.

"No cars at all?" I asked.

"None."

"I never thought that was even possible," I said. "Not these days."

"I know," she said. "Neither would I have, if I didn't know. But there it is — riverboats, gondolas, water taxis, that sort of thing. But no cars."

I moved on to the next postcard. "That's Turkey," I said. "Istanbul."

"Yes," she said. "A very special city. The only city in the world on two continents. What I would give to go there and see its art and architecture: the Blue Mosque, the Basilica Cistern, and especially the Hagia Sophia!"

There were many other postcards, of Barcelona and Budapest,

Rome and Paris, Cairo and Cape Town. I moved from one to the next, ending with London and Paris.

"It would be great to find myself in front of Big Ben," she said. "You know, the big clock in London. Or imagine being able to watch the changing of the guard at Buckingham Palace. Or to be in Paris, climbing the Eiffel Tower."

She looked thoughtful for a moment before continuing: "The changing of the guard at Buckingham Palace. It's interesting, the way a place can have certain customs, passed down for ages. Somehow the ritual continues, even if there's no longer any real significance behind it. Go figure."

"Go figure," I replied.

That evening, we had some wine, a cabernet that she said was just the thing she liked to drink in order to relax.

I'd never had wine before. It left a full taste in my mouth, nothing like I'd ever drunk before. A little acidic, the way I imagined the color brown to taste, or ground-up bark from a tree mixed with perfume.

She'd been looking at me.

I said, "This must be for the aristos, upper-class people with their sophisticated palates."

She laughed.

I took a second sip. "I'm just a village girl, not used to fancy things like this."

She laughed again and said, "I'm not much different from you, and anyway, village girl or not, I'm happy to be here with you, just sitting and sipping wine with you."

"Thank you," I said, feeling a stirring in my heart. In a small voice, I added, "I'm happy to be here with you too."

Back at home, Mama was on the sofa in the parlor, hemming a skirt. "So how was it?" she asked, looking up at me as I entered.

"It was fine, Mama," I said.

"Just fine?"

I nodded.

"Did you meet any of her friends? Any handsome young men? There must be several young men at that school. I've seen some the few times I've passed that way."

"No, Mama," I said. "I didn't meet any handsome young men."

There was a disappointed look on her face. What I said next was far from the truth, because Ndidi had not in fact brought up any of her male coworkers. But I said it anyway: "Ndidi talked about some of the young men teachers though. Maybe next time we will all meet and we can go from there."

Mama's disappointed face transformed into a broad smile. "Very good," she said. "Very, very good. That girl Ndidi seems to have a good head on her shoulders. I'm glad she came along. You're still young. It's important for you to have friends like her. She might teach you a thing or two about the way things should be. With any luck, there might be hope for you after all."

45

NDIDI BEGAN INVITING me over to her place in the evenings, and I accepted, stopping by as soon as Mama and I closed up the shop. For the initial hour or two, she was busy with schoolwork. Still, she insisted that I come over, that she enjoyed my company, even my silent company.

She had a record player, which sat on a table beside her box TV. I would sit on her sofa, listening to her records playing softly while I watched her brows furrow and her lips constrict as she marked her students' papers. In between, I read books from her shelf. That was a period during which I read many books, many months of consistent reading, at least two hours every evening: Agatha Christie's crime novels, Amos Tutuola's *The Palm-Wine Drinkard. Efuru,* by Flora Nwapa. Charlotte Brontë's *Jane Eyre.* Emily Brontë's *Wuthering Heights.* I had already read *Things Fall Apart,* but as it was on her shelf, I read it again.

Ndidi took small breaks while marking her students' papers. Sometimes she'd go to the fridge and come back with two bottles of Fanta, one for me and the other for her. We'd drink together, not really talking, just staring and giggling at each other like small girls.

One Friday, as we drank our Fanta, she said, "There's a place I'd like to take you to. I think you'll like it very much."

"What kind of place?"

"It's a surprise," she said. "Let's just say there'll be good music and dancing."

"Okay," I said. "When would you like us to go?"

She answered with a naughty smile. "Tonight, if you want."

It was nearing eight o'clock. I said, "Mama will not like it if I stay out too late." I put on a stern face and mimicked Mama: "'A self-respecting young lady does not roam around at night.'"

Ndidi chuckled. "You make it sound like I'm proposing prostitution."

"Maybe not as bad as prostitution, but—"

"We won't stay out that late," she said. "Just a couple of hours or so."

We were seated together on her sofa. She reached out and slid her fingers up and down my arm. There was a clear attraction by now between us, and therein lay my struggle. My mind was a mess. First there was the issue of Amina. Each time I allowed myself to acknowledge my attraction to Ndidi, I felt wretched about the fact that she was not Amina, and that by beginning to have feelings for someone other than Amina, I was somehow betraying her. Never mind that she was the one who betrayed me. I felt it all the same.

And then there was the matter of Mama. To be living so close to her while carrying on an affair with Ndidi was not something I could quite stomach. There's a way in which distance represses one's sense of obligation, or rather, a way in which closeness intensifies one's sense of duty. Now that I was living with Mama, I felt—in a way I never felt while I was away at Obodoañuli Academy—a strong obligation to meet her expectations of me. Especially after the thing with Amina had anyway gone and backfired on me. Would this one backfire too? Would I go through all that emotional investment just for Ndidi to end up betraying me the way that Amina had done?

"So, what do you think?" Ndidi asked. "Shall we go?" The look on her face told me that she already knew my answer, but I replied anyway. "Yes," I said. "I'd like to go with you." Despite my inner turmoil about the whole situation, it was the truth. Wherever it was she was going to take me, I wanted still to be with her.

"Good," she said. Her bottle of Fanta was in her hand, at her lips. She held it there as she scrutinized my face. "You're sure?"

I nodded and said that I was sure.

As we freshened up, brushed our hair, and retouched our makeup, Ndidi said to me, "Now, there's one more thing I have to tell you."

"What?" I asked.

"It's about the place where we're going."

"What about it?"

"It's not the kind of place you want to go around talking about. In fact, you have to promise me that you won't go talking to anyone about it."

"Why not?" I asked. "What kind of place is it??"

"You'll find out. But for now you'll have to promise me that you won't. You can't let your mother know of it. No mentioning it to her. I can't take you to it if you don't promise."

"I wasn't planning on mentioning it to Mama," I said.

"Good," she replied. "Because mentioning it to anyone can cost some of us, if not all of us, our lives."

I laughed at the gravity of what she was saying. "Now you're being ridiculous," I said. "What kind of place is it you're taking me to that can result in people dying?"

She laughed back. "It sounds more serious than I meant it to sound. But it is serious still. So, like I said, just promise me that you will not breathe a word about any of it to anyone at all."

"I promise you," I said.

The place was a small, dimly lit church-like structure at the end of a dirt road, which we got to from the main Aba road. To the side of it, above a giant white cross, hung a sign that read FRIEND IN JESUS CHURCH OF GOD. Another sign, a banner stretched across the blue and white columns that led to the carved wooden door, announced, in deep purple print, FOUNTAIN OF LOVE.

"You brought me to church?" I whispered to Ndidi as we stood beneath the awning at the entrance, about to enter.

"Wait and be surprised," she said.

We entered. Inside, strobe lights flashed softly. Heavy, deep purple drapes hung at the windows. Tables lined the perimeter of the room with decorative candles lit up at their centers. Each table was flanked by two or three chairs, most of which were occupied by people who appeared to be engaged in conversation.

The music was toned-down, very restrained, in an almost indulgent sort of way. In the middle of the room couples were dancing slowly. The scent of whiskey and beer was strong in the air.

We took a seat at one of the tables with two chairs. A plain-faced woman walked up to us, wearing a white oxford shirt tucked in at the waist of a pair of khaki bell-bottoms. Her hair was long, in thin dreadlocks, and silver hoops dangled from her earlobes.

"Ah, Ndidi, we thought you had forgotten us!" the woman said.

Ndidi rose from her seat and greeted the woman with a hug. "I've been busy with school," she said.

"You can't mean it!" the woman replied teasingly. "You can't have been *that* busy! Looks to me that you've had plenty of time to be taking care of yourself. You're looking very fine," she said.

Ndidi brushed off the compliment and said, "This is my friend Ijeoma. Ijeoma, this is Adanna."

Adanna's face appeared pinched now, impish. "Soooo." She dragged out the word. "So this is who has been keeping you busy?" she asked, extending her hand to shake mine.

Ndidi ignored the comment. She said, "It's Ijeoma's first time here. I'm hoping you behave so that you don't chase her away."

Adanna laughed. "Okay, okay," she said. "I'll be on best behavior." She turned to me. "Welcome, Ijeoma. I hope you enjoy yourself. We have a good-sized dance floor. Feel free to make use of it. All I ask is you save at least one dance for me." She winked at me.

Another woman, in a short white skirt and a thick afro, had come to Adanna's side, linking arms with her and then leaning in and kissing Adanna on the cheek. Adanna turned to Ndidi and said, "Lucky there's no shortage of women tonight."

She winked at Ndidi, and as she did, she allowed herself to be coaxed away.

"How long have they been using the church this way?" I asked later, on the dance floor.

"A long time," Ndidi said. "Several years by now. This one is not even the first. The last one was destroyed by fire some years ago. It was just outside of town. Somehow, someone got wind that it was not a real church, and then a group of people got together and set fire to it. Luckily they set the fire in broad daylight and no one was there, so no one was killed. But this one is different. It's a real church during the day. People go to it to worship, which makes it an even stronger camouflage than that previous church. So far, so good. We are yet to be found out."

We continued to dance. After some time, I asked, "So, who is Adanna to you?"

Ndidi laughed. "No one at all," she said.

"She sounded to me like more than no one."

Ndidi began to protest, but then she seemed to think better of it. She said, "Well, we're friends. We teach together at the school. She's the one who first brought me here. She might be a little interested in me."

"You're not interested back?"

She shook her head. "She's a wonderful friend. But there's somebody else who is taking up my attention for now."

I knew that she was talking about me. And again I thought of Amina. A surge of anxiety came over me: why was it that I was having such strong emotions for this other woman who was not Amina? Again I felt myself the betrayer, equally as the betrayed.

My thoughts of Amina faded into thoughts of Mama, and of her Bible studies, and of the grammar school teacher's scolding, and of all those threats of stoning. Though I had not been convinced by any of Mama's interpretations of the Bible, I could not help the anxiety that was building in me, frantic and questioning thoughts: Just what are you doing in a place like this? What business does a respectable young woman have in an underground place like this?

The music grew loud then, overpowering my thoughts. Ndidi held me tighter, pressed her body into mine, and there was a reassurance in it. Never before had I danced this way with a woman, never before so freely. I banished all thoughts of Amina, and of Mama's Bible studies, and of the grammar school teacher's scolding, and of stonings. I told myself to enjoy, just enjoy. Enjoy, enjoy, enjoy!

We danced together for a long time, Ndidi and I, and I felt a sense of liberation that I had not until then known.

She walked me almost all the way to the bungalow, stopping a short distance from the gate. There, she said, "Now, I hope I can trust you to keep quiet about tonight. No one at all must know."

"Of course you can trust me," I replied.

She took my hand briefly. "Thanks for the good company," she said.

"Thanks for taking me," I replied.

"I'll be going home to Obigbo to see my parents and little brother this weekend. But maybe we can go out again next week when I get back."

"That would be nice," I said.

We stood there awkwardly staring into each other's eyes for a few seconds. In a different world, we might have leaned in and kissed each other on the lips. We might have held each other tightly the way that lovers do. But there was the matter of Mama being so close. She might suddenly appear and all hell would break loose. Anyone at all might suddenly appear, to the same effect.

"See you next week," Ndidi simply said.

"See you," I replied.

Watching her walk away that night, I felt more happiness than I had felt in a long time. If I could have sped up the hands of time, I would have done so, so that next week would be tomorrow.

46

W HERE HAVE YOU BEEN?" Mama hollered.

"I was just with Ndidi," I replied.

"Just with Ndidi? So why did it take you this long to come back? Do you know how late it is?"

It was not yet eleven, which was not very late in the grand scheme of things. But I did not bother to tell Mama that. Instead, I said, "I'm sorry, Mama. I just lost track of time."

"You lost track of time?" she scolded. "You lost track of time? One day, if you're not careful, time will lose track of you! And I hope you know what that means!"

Under her breath, she said, "Well, at least you were just with Ndidi. At least that one has a good head on her shoulders. I suppose it could have been worse."

Alone in my bedroom, I was full of thoughts of Ndidi. As I changed into my nightgown and climbed into bed, there she was, taking up all the spaces, right down to the cracks and crevices of my mind. I could not help myself, even with Mama in the next room over. I found myself having a physical reaction to her in my thoughts. I became so engorged, so swollen with desire, that the only relief I could think of was to pleasure myself, a thing that I had hardly ever done before—only once or twice in our secondary school in Oraifite. Never mind what Mama had said about Onan and the wasting of his seed, that the moral of the story was that any sort of self-pleasure was a sin in the eyes of God.

Never mind all of that. I did it anyway. I went about it very quietly, slowly at first and then faster and faster. Before long my throat was catching with fulfillment and relief, and there was not an ounce of guilt accompanying it.

I fell asleep with a sense of satisfaction, but I had slept only a couple of hours when I woke up with a start.

Memories of my Bible studies with Mama rushed back to me yet again, no matter how much I tried to put them away from my mind. Condemning words falling upon my consciousness like a rainstorm, drenching me and threatening to drown me out. I was the happiest I had been in a long time, but suddenly here was this panicked dream, as if to mockingly ask me how I could even presume to think happiness was a thing within my reach.

In the dream, I had lain curled up in a fetal position on the floor. Mama was hovering above me, waving her index finger like an angry schoolteacher, her eyes glowing with reproach and with tears. She was screaming, "A heedless fly follows the devil to the grave."

I woke up with the words reverberating in my mind.

> *A heedless fly follows the devil to the grave . . .*
> *A heedless fly follows the devil to the grave . . .*
> *A heedless fly follows the devil to the grave . . .*

I forced my eyes to close, forced myself to go back to sleep, but each time, the words returned in my dream and snatched me back awake:

> *A heedless fly follows the devil to the grave . . .*
> *A heedless fly follows the devil to the grave . . .*
> *A heedless fly follows the devil to the grave . . .*

47

IF YOU SET OFF on a witch-hunt, you will find a witch.

When you find her, she will be dressed like any other person. But to you, her skin will glow in stripes of white and black. You will see her broom, and you will hear her witch-cry, and you will feel the effects of her spells on you.

No matter how unlike a witch she is, there she will be, a witch, before your eyes.

The period of time after the church visit with Ndidi was the beginning of my witch-hunt against myself. At the moment when I had found a community that should have been a source of support and security, an unexpected sort of self-loathing flared up. In that moment, I began to believe myself a witch under the influence of the devil, and if Mama's exorcism had not worked, then it seemed that I owed it to myself to find something that would. Self-purification was the goal.

All night I had listened to Mama's voice — not her voice in real time, but her voice in the dream — warning me about following the devil to the grave. By the time day rolled around, my mind was infested with images of graves. I had become a little like a coffin: I felt a hollowness in me and a rattling at my seams.

Mama's voice was the source of all my turmoil, so I could hardly stand to be around her. At about noon, I asked permission to leave the shop. I could not tell her why. I simply requested an hour away. I carried the handbag I had packed for myself with my Bible and prayer scarf in it and headed to Mama's and my regular church.

When I got there it was empty. I sat for some time at the back of the church, my thoughts racing in no particular direction. I must have sat for half an hour before going up to the front. Just before reaching the pulpit, I knelt down, pulled out my Bible and prayer scarf from my bag. I tied the scarf around my head.

I opened the Bible, placed my palms firmly on its pages. I closed my eyes and prayed:

Dear God, what is the meaning of all of this?

Instantly I felt guilt stirring as a result of my daring to ask God this kind of question.

I tried a different tactic. I pleaded:

Dear God, I am a sinner, and I come before you to beg you to please show me the path to righteousness.

But what if I was not, in fact, sinning? What if I was subjecting myself to all this guilt for no reason at all?

Lord, I am confused. Please give me a sign. If there is any evil in my heart, please give me a sign so that I might recognize it and, in doing so, avoid it.

My eyes had been closed all along. I had hardly opened them when I caught a flicker of light in the direction of the pulpit, like a piece of jewelry reflecting the sunlight. Then it appeared that the flicker was growing bigger, approaching.

I grew eager and afraid at once, because this was, after all, the sign that I had asked for.

I heard the sound of footsteps behind me. I turned around.

I screamed at the sight, because if this was God's sign, then Mama was the evil in my heart.

48

MAMA RAN TO ME, muffled my screams. "What is the matter with you? This is the house of God, for God's sake! What is possessing you to scream this way?"

I collected myself. "I'm sorry," I said. "I was praying. I didn't expect anyone to come walking in."

"I've been running around looking for you. Of course I came! Do you realize you've been gone over two hours?"

"Two hours?" I asked, genuinely surprised.

She nodded. "What's the matter with you?"

"I'm just a little sick," I said. "I think I'll go back home and sleep. That should help."

She placed the back of her palm on my forehead. "Is it stomach trouble or a headache?"

"Mostly just a headache."

"All right. *Ngwa.* Let's go. I will walk back with you. I have some Panadol at home you can take. Hopefully it's not the onset of malaria. Obiageli down the road just came down with a bad case of malaria."

"I don't think it's malaria," I replied. "A small headache, that's all."

49

ESPITE THE PANICKED dreams, as soon as Monday rolled around, and as soon as we closed up the shop, I went to Ndidi's. It was like having an addiction to chili peppers, or to beans. You sensed that eating too much of them would overwhelm your system. That afterward there would be consequences. Your mouth would burn; you would surely get the runs. The dreams would come again. But you did it anyway.

I sat on her sofa listening to Fela Kuti on her record player, and again watching her mark her students' assignments.

I peered at her off and on, scrutinizing, because maybe God would give me a different sign where she was concerned, a clearer one, and if I looked closely, maybe I would see.

After a while, she must have felt the weight of my scrutiny. She lifted her eyes and very softly said, "Ijeoma, what?"

I allowed my eyes to drop. "Nothing," I said.

She went back to the papers in front of her. A few minutes went by.

She felt my gaze again and said, "Ijeoma, what's the matter?"

"I'm just checking to see if you're done yet," I replied.

She put her pen down, rose from the table, and came to me on the sofa. "And if I say I'm done, then what? Do you have special plans for us this evening?"

I shook my head. "No plans. Was just checking to see if you were done."

Now she was the one scrutinizing me, studying me with her eyes. She took my hand, began stroking it. "Well, if you have no plans for us, I might have a plan."

My throat was suddenly dry, and I felt heat rising in my cheeks. "What kind of plan?" I asked hoarsely.

She leaned in so that I could feel the warmth of her breath on my ear and on the side of my face. Her voice was strong even if it was only a whisper. She said, "This kind of plan."

She took my hand in hers and brought it to her waistline. In one swift motion, she unzipped her skirt at the side zipper. The skirt loosened, and she brought my hand inside. She wore no undergarments, not even a slip. Her skin where my hand landed was warm. But she moved it lower, pausing momentarily at the curls of hair that started low beneath her belly. She stopped only when my hand arrived at the wet flesh at the center. I felt a slight insecurity, having done this only with Amina before. What if the things that Amina had enjoyed were not the same things that would please Ndidi? What if I was somehow insufficient?

I would try anyway. I moved to her front, knelt before her. I pressed her wet flesh firmly with the tips of my fingers, then my fingers found themselves inside, enveloped by her warmth.

She gasped. The gasping transformed into moaning. I moved my fingers slowly in and out. I rubbed gently in small circles, slow at first and then faster, the way I had done with Amina and with myself.

Her hips moved along.

It did not take much time. She let out a cry, and I found myself overcome by emotion — warm feelings, feelings of affection, of happiness, of something like love; feelings of elation at being able to connect so intimately with her, at being able to elicit such an intense reaction from her. It was as if her pleasure was in that moment my own, ours, a shared fulfillment.

I held her, whispered her name, placed soft kisses on her face, her neck, her lips. If I could have stayed forever this way with her, there would have been no greater gift.

She let out another cry, and then her entire body stiffened in my embrace, with recurrent shudders, until finally she relaxed into my arms.

• • •

At home that night, the panicked dreams were worse than on all the preceding nights combined. Throughout my sleep I was confronted with Mama's scolding face, her reprimanding finger wagging at me, threatening to poke out an eye. The images of Mama were interspersed with a thunderous sound that, in the dream, was the voice of God, scolding also like Mama, reprimanding, condemning me for my sins. Each time I fell back to sleep, the same dream. Eventually I rose from bed, no longer willing myself to sleep. I pulled off my nightgown, changed into one of my day gowns. Dressed, I went back to bed and sat, not daring even to lie down. I sat there for hours, wide awake, waiting for day to break.

As the sun peeked through the sky and darkness turned to a light gray, I climbed out once more from bed, picked up my Bible and prayer scarf, and headed out of my room. It was still early enough that Mama would not yet have awoken.

I walked briskly out the front door and along the path leading across the yard. I stepped outside the gate and switched to a running pace until I arrived at church.

I went down the aisle to the front of the church, as I had done the time before. I knelt down before God. I would have prayed, but somehow I could not find the words to do so. I took a deep breath, slowly exhaling, attempting to steady myself that way. And then another deep breath. And another.

My breathing finally stabilized. I attempted once more to string together the words to form a prayer, but nothing came. I remained mute. Not a single word to express myself, not a single one to explain or to defend myself, not one single word to apologize and beg forgiveness for my sins. All I felt within me was a trembling from this questionable sort of guilt. A sense of defeat washed over me. Tears spilled out, forming tiny dark spots on the gray cement floor of the church. I took in a deep breath and then exhaled. The exhalation came out as a long, tumbling sigh. Somewhere in the middle of it, I remembered John 8. I knelt there at the front of the church and at last the words came out of my mouth, Jesus' words: *He that is without sin among you, let him first cast a stone at her.*

I felt a slow rising of relief. A steady dispersion of it, and then an overshadowing of that earlier sense of defeat. I exhaled once more. The air smelled of tears and sweat and that sharp scent of wet concrete.

50

I WAS GOING BACK and forth between the front and the rear of the store, dusting shelves and restocking, when I saw the man enter. His hair rose high above his head as if to form a black halo around him. He had a beard, a mustache, and sideburns trailing down his cheeks.

He headed toward the crates of drinks and picked up a bottle of Guinness. He wore a watered-down smile, the kind that matched the dull and wrinkled shirt he was wearing, the kind that matched the faded blue tie around his neck.

"*Ego one ka ifa bu?*" he asked Mama, holding the bottle out toward her when he had reached the counter. How much?

He had just collected his change and turned to leave when I recognized him. Also at that moment, I heard, "*Na wa-oh!*" The tone of Mama's voice was a mixture of glee and surprise.

"Chibundu!" she exclaimed.

At that moment he recognized her too.

He greeted Mama, and then he turned to me. "Ijeoma! Is it you?" He turned back to Mama. "Mrs. Okoli, long time!"

Memories flooded back, of Chibundu pulling my hair, of us climbing trees, of running around church together. Of him saying, "Look really closely at us so that you never forget that we were friends."

"Long time," Mama was saying. She had come around the counter and was greeting him with a hug, saying, "Welcome o. Welcome. *Nno.*"

His shirt was wrinkled and untucked at the waist. Ridges had formed on his forehead, age lines that made him seem far older than the image of him in my mind. But of course. He was no longer a boy.

Back in Ojoto, Mama never seemed to have a soft spot for Chibundu, but now it appeared that she did. She spent the remainder of that day, and the rest of the week, talking to me about him.

"He has done very well for himself. Imagine, little Chibundu, a graduate of the University of Ibadan and now doing Youth Service here in Aba! His mother and father must be very proud."

"Yes," I said. "They must be very proud."

51

T HERE WAS A beating yesterday," Ndidi said very softly one
evening. She appeared to be speaking to herself or into the
air, rather than to me.

"They were two men. I never knew them. They were friends of
Adanna from the university. For days they seemed to have disappeared, fallen off the face of the earth. And then yesterday she heard
something at the market, whispers about a pair of 'sissies' being
beaten by a crowd of people. She went to the bushes behind the dirt
road not far from where they lived, and she found the two of them
there, naked and beaten to death."

Her voice was soft and raspy now, as if her throat was parched.

"This sort of thing has always happened. Like several years ago
when they burned down that other church I told you about. But I
hadn't been going to that church, so the burning did not feel completely real. And no one died. This time it's different. This time it
basically happened right before my eyes, and I can't shake the feeling that it could easily have been me or you."

I went to her and wrapped my arms around her.

"We called the police. They couldn't even be bothered to do anything, not even to take the bodies away. 'Let them rot like the faggots
they are,' one of the officers said. The other one said, 'If they were
not dead already, we would beat them some more.' In the end, it was
Adanna and I who took their bodies," she said. "We carried them
and cleaned them and prepared them for burial. Imagine, holding
their bodies in my arms."

Her voice by now was a trembling whisper.

52

THERE HAD BEEN nothing extraordinary about the events of the first half of the following day: Mama and I worked at the shop as usual. In the evening I went to Ndidi's, where she and I ate some garri and okra soup for dinner. Afterward, Ndidi and I went to the church.

First we had danced in the middle of the floor, to the sound of Fela Kuti's voice, "Shakara Oloje" flowing loudly from the record player. Then we pushed ourselves deep into the corner of the church, at the rear, where the table of beer and jugs of kai kai and crates of soft drinks sat. We had become like all the other girls by now, kissing and fondling and making out in the dark.

I had not intended to stay so long. My plan had been to return home earlier than last time, before eleven p.m. Mama would scold me again for being late, but at least it would not be a new grievance. She might be worried, but not overly so, since it was something I'd done before.

But things did not go as I had planned.

The knocking at the front door of the church came when Ndidi and I stood making out at the rear of the dance floor. It might have been soft at first, but soon it was a loud banging sound.

We watched as several of the girls peeked out from the heavy drapes at the windows. A heavy hush fell over the place, and for a moment Fela Kuti's music was the only audible sound. Then there was the hurried scrambling of feet, and one of the girls, Chichi, herded the rest of the girls to the back of the church where Ndidi and I stood. "Shhhh," Chichi repeated, her index finger meeting her lips.

• • •

Outside, behind the church, it was that time of the morning when the moon is looming, the sky is still dark, and the cocks have not yet crowed. Midnight had come and gone.

Ndidi held my hand as we ran. The palm fronds were not quite covering the wooden slab at the entrance of the pit. We recognized the bunker that way.

In front of us and behind us, in the quiet of night, the girls, a dozen or so of us, lined up quietly to make our way into the bunker. Chichi pulled open the wooden slab and allowed us to climb into the hole.

We packed the bunker tightly like stacked-up tubers of yam. Chichi pulled the wooden slab back over the entrance of the pit. We stood quietly, our breaths hushed, the way we used to do those days during the war.

Above us, but a little distance away, we heard a scream, and then another. Then there were the sounds of men's and women's voices, talking, shouting, and then another scream.

Chichi raised herself, reached for the cover of the pit as if to open it up, but several of the girls pulled her arm back.

"They've caught someone," she whispered to us. She looked frantically around. "There must be at least a couple of us missing."

"Where is Adanna?" someone whispered.

Chichi reached again for the wooden cover.

The same group of girls pulled her arm back once more. "So you'll allow the rest of us to die to save one?" a girl asked.

"Shhhh," another girl said. "You don't want them to know where we are hiding." And of course the attackers would not have known unless we made it evident to them. These particular bunkers, I'd find out later, were very well concealed, palm covering and grass and all. Harder to detect than those of our war days. As if one or more of the girls had known to plan ahead. As if they had known that a raid like this would be inevitable.

Chichi no longer reached for the pit cover. We all returned to silence.

There was nothing else to do but to study the hole. All around, nothing but darkness, the smell of fresh earth, and in all that darkness the faint contour of bodies. Other sounds above us — of screams and cries and a man's thundering voice, as if reciting a prayer. In my mind, I saw the walls of the earth collapsing around us like the pillars of the Temple of Dagon, the walls of our pit crumbling all around us, and we, Samson-like in our decline, crumbling along with the walls. So was this how we would meet our end? An image of Mama came to my mind, Mama weeping before my dead body, Mama at my grave, mourning over me. Or perhaps she would not mourn. Perhaps she would be too angry to mourn. Perhaps she would not even bother with a burial for me.

By my side, Ndidi held my hand.

The sound of the screaming grew louder, and for a moment I thought I heard the thuds of feet approaching the bunker. But seconds and then minutes passed and no one came.

Everything seemed to settle above us. The screaming died out. The praying faded away. We stood rigidly breathing in the scent of our bodies, of our collective sweat. Breathing in the scent of our collective fear.

The knock seemed to come as gradually and steadily as the crawl of a snail. A tap, and then another quiet tap on the wooden slab of the bunker. We must have been inside for over an hour by then.

I watched — we all watched — as, above us, the cover was pulled open. There was the light of a kerosene lantern, followed by the squinting face of a woman. She called for us to come out.

We made our way out one by one. Back above ground, the smell of burning tires was strong in the air.

I recognized the woman who let us out as the one with the afro and short skirt who had led Adanna away during my first visit to the church. The woman had managed to hide in the small, cellar-like vault of the church and had not been found. Her face was tear-stricken. She was crying hard, coughing in fits, and she was pointing to something ahead.

We had hardly walked two yards when we saw, in the backyard of the church, a flame of orange and blue. A stack of burning logs.

Ndidi began to cry, and then all of us were crying too, because we had all seen what remained of the face, and we had all recognized her: Adanna in the midst of the logs, burning and burning and turning to ashes right before our eyes.

I arrived back home at about seven in the morning. Mama was out by the gate.

"Where have you been?" she hollered. "What in God's good name were you thinking to stay out all night? Do you know I have not slept a pinch? Are you that inconsiderate to make me wait up for you all through the night? Spending the night going back and forth from the gate to the bungalow and back, waiting for you. I was just getting ready to notify the police, and finally there you are. But what kind of thing was that to put me through? Do you not know better than to do that to me? Have I not trained you right?"

She caught her breath.

"That friend of yours, Ndidi, is she the reason for this? Tell me, is she? Is there something going on between the two of you?"

"Mama, I just fell asleep," I replied. "Can you please stop with all your suspicions? I lost track of time and fell asleep, that's all."

I brushed past her, went through the gate, not waiting to hear what she said next. I made my way to my bedroom, where I could be alone with my thoughts.

53

RAIN CLOUDS HOVERED in the sky, spreading themselves over the sun like an ashen film. Through the shop door and window, it was the pallid gray of evening time. But it was yet afternoon.

Two weeks, nearly three, had gone by, and still all the talk in Aba continued to be about the discovery of the church and the burning. No one could say who had made the discovery, or who had taken part in the burning, but everyone seemed to agree that all of it was necessary, that the discovery was aided by God, that an example needed to be set in order to cleanse Aba of such sinful ways.

Ndidi and I kept a low profile. I stopped visiting her as much. Sometimes three days passed before I went to her place. I never stayed later than eight p.m.

"Lucky for you that the grammar school teacher and I warned you of this," Mama said. She was standing behind the shop counter, writing my to-do list on a notepad, while I stood idly by her side. "That could have been you, Ijeoma. Imagine, not only would I be a widow, I would also have lost my only child."

I listened quietly, gazing out into the gray outdoors, praying that Mama would move on to some other topic. The last thing I needed was to be reminded that it could have been me. And by extension that it could have been Ndidi. Since the incident, every couple of hours or so, the image of Adanna flashed through my mind. The recurring reminder that one of us had lost her life in that terrible way. The reminder that Adanna had burned at the stake while the rest of us were allowed to continue to live.

I wanted Mama to stop her preaching, to stop the reminders.

As it was, I remembered the incident clearly enough on my own. I didn't need any more reminders. Just stop, I prayed silently. Please, God, make her stop.

In that moment, as if to answer my prayer, Chibundu walked into the store. By now he had gotten into the habit of dropping by during his lunchtime. His visits were becoming a source of increasing anxiety for me—the fact of this unwanted attention that I did not know what to do about, how to dispose of. But at least he never visited in the evening, for which I was grateful. My evenings were, until the burning incident at least, reserved for Ndidi, and I could hardly imagine a better way to spend them.

I saw my moment to flee. I left Mama's side, went into the stock room, and returned with a box of items to restock the shelves.

The beer cooler sat near the entrance of the store. Chibundu walked over to it, reached in, and brought out a bottle of Guinness. He straightened back up. The next step should have been for him to head to the counter to pay, or go to some other part of the store to pick up one or more items. But he did not move. He just stood there.

I had watched from behind the shelf as he reached in for the beer, but I had then returned to restocking, taking only momentary glimpses at him. My head was downturned in the direction of the box at my feet when I felt his gaze heavy on me. I looked up to find him still standing by the cooler, still gazing at me. In all the years that I was at the grammar school teacher's and at Obodoañuli Academy, Chibundu and I had not kept in touch. Perhaps this was one reason why conversations between him and me during these afternoon visits were awkward. So many years had gone by that he seemed only a little less than a perfect stranger to me. But it was also true that I realized Chibundu might still hold a romantic interest in me. And if he did, how would I handle the situation? I found myself balking at the thought of it. How should I go about conversing with him without accidentally giving the wrong impression? How should I navigate the whole thing without giving Mama any ideas about a match between him and me?

My eyes darted to Mama at the counter to see if she was watching.

I was relieved to find her head turned. She was flipping through the newspaper that lay open on the counter.

I looked back at Chibundu, who was now walking toward me. His footsteps were steady, striking in their evenness.

It was just as I feared. When he reached me, he leaned so that his body rested on the shelf from shoulder to mid-thigh. He smiled broadly and said, "*Omalicha.*" Beautiful. There was a mischievous look on his face as he said it again: "*Omalicha.*" All the while his eyes studied me, lingering on my hands, on my braids, on my face, before finding their way to my eyes.

"I've been thinking," he said when his eyes met mine.

"Thinking what, Chibundu?" I asked stiffly.

He laughed nervously, but still he spoke. "I've been thinking that every man needs a wife."

I breathed deeply, gathered myself, focused on not letting my alarm show.

He held the bottle of Guinness with both hands now, wiping off the condensation as he spoke. I did my best to avert my eyes from his. My gaze lingered on his clothes instead: a beige-collared shirt so tight fitting that the muscles of his upper arms threatened to burst open the seams. The collar of the shirt was rather wide and long. Either the shirt itself was not made to be buttoned all the way up, or it was too tight fitting to be buttoned up, or Chibundu had simply decided not to button the top two buttons — whatever the case, his dark, curly chest hair was exposed. From his neck hung a thin gold chain with a cross pendant. He wore a pair of gray-and-black-striped bell-bottom trousers.

His lips curved into a flirtatious smile. They were a little chapped, but his teeth beneath were flawlessly aligned: two rows of perfect little white squares. He said, "*Omalicha,* won't you agree that every man needs a wife?"

I laughed with discomfort, more a snicker than a regular laugh. "I suppose some women would also do well to have a husband."

"That's right," he said. "It goes both ways. Every man needs a wife, and every woman needs a husband."

I repeated, lingering on the "some," drawing it out for emphasis. "Yes, *some* women would do well to have a husband."

The clarification seemed to go over his head. He continued to wipe his bottle. I pretended to inspect the shelf for dust. There was the sound of wood scraping on the cement floor, and then a shuffling sound from the corner of the store. I looked up to find Mama approaching, nodding robustly, a wide smile on her face. I wondered why it had taken her so long to notice. I wondered if she had been in on the whole thing from the start.

"It's very good to see you children reconnect," she said, not quite winking, but almost.

"We thank God," Chibundu replied.

The blood vessels in my temples pulsed. My face heated up, and I felt a burning sensation in my cheeks. It seemed clear to me that I was the victim of a terrible conspiracy. A pawn in a scheme. "In fact, I came for a special request," Chibundu was saying now, looking at Mama. He turned back to look at me. "I've been thinking. Would you like to join me for dinner one night soon? I have been wanting to ask you for some time. I hope you don't already have another handsome young fellow in the picture. My disappointment would be too great."

Mama leapt in. "No, no, she does not have a boyfriend. You came just in time. Even one day's delay might have changed your fate," she said, smiling, patting him on the back. "Who knows, another man might have walked in and stolen her from you. But you are lucky, Chibundu my boy. Very lucky. Good timing."

He smiled.

I felt the anger in me mounting. I could say something to put them both in their place, to retract myself from any longer being a pawn. I could seize back control of myself just by opening my mouth and speaking my mind.

But for some reason, it was the same kind of issue that I had by now started to notice as a pattern in me: my mouth would not open up. I could not get myself to speak.

"What do you say? Tomorrow? Six p.m.?"

Mama did not miss a beat. "Yes! Certainly! *Da'lu.* Thank you o.

Ijeoma would like that very much. It's been so good to have you here in Aba, Chibundu. So very good."

"Wonderful," he said. He'd been looking at me as Mama spoke. He lifted his hand and squeezed me gently by the arm. "I will see you both tomorrow then. I must get back to work now."

He walked to the counter. I did not return to stocking the shelf. I looked back and forth between him and Mama. Mama was standing by my side, her arms akimbo, glowing like a pregnant woman.

I watched as Chibundu placed the money for his beer near the register, the glossy brownness of the Guinness bottle sticking out sharply from the light-colored skin of his hand. Then he made his way out of the door.

For the rest of the day, I longed for the closing of the store like a prisoner awaiting release. I felt terribly lethargic, as if all my energy had gone into simply surviving the incident with Chibundu and Mama.

In Ndidi's flat, my energy returned. "Can you imagine, just walking in there and basically proposing to me, and right in front of Mama!" My arms flailed all over the place as I spoke. So much anger.

We were standing in her kitchen. A frying pan sat on one of the stove's burners, slices of plantain sizzling in the oil in the pan. The air was humid from the heat of cooking, but the sweet scent of the plantains infused the heat with a gentle perfume.

She had flipped over the plantains with a fork so that the golden sides were facing up. She lifted the fork now and simply held it. She looked my way. The windows over the sink were open. A light breeze entered and caused a chill on my skin. She held my eyes with an ambiguous expression in her own.

She said, "With everything that has happened here lately — and now the arrival of this Chibundu — I can't help thinking maybe you should just try it."

She must have seen it in my eyes, how her words astounded me.

She still had that ambiguous look on her face, but she was determined to come off as resolute. "I'm serious," she said, no longer looking at me. "Go out with him. See how you feel. This kind of life is not for everyone. People like us are getting killed. And anyway, you might decide you like that other life better. The kind of life that he can give you — you know, man and wife."

"How can you even say that?" I asked.

"All I'm saying is that you never know." She looked at the plantains in the pan. She began gathering them one by one onto a plate. "You might like it. I really think that you should at least try it out and see. Have you ever?"

"Have I ever what?"

"You know, have you ever tried being with a boy?"

I shook my head. Of course I had never tried being with a boy. How could she imply that I even had a choice in the matter? How could she imply that it was that simple — that I should just go on and order myself to try things out with a boy? Had she? Was that how it worked for her? Anyway, if I had had any attraction at all to boys, would it not have expressed itself by now? What sense was there in my "trying it out"? My heart and soul and mind were centered around her. *She* was the one I wanted, and *she* was enough for me. She was the one I loved, the one who had a hold on my heart. It infuriated me that she was trying to push me away.

"Do it for me as a favor. If you don't like it, then at least I'll also know and will never have to worry about a boy stealing you away."

"You'll never have to worry about that anyway," I said.

"You never know," she said softly. "You might surprise yourself."

I remained quiet for some time, fuming. Finally I said, "Okay," more out of spite than out of acceptance. "You want me to go out with a boy? Okay. I will."

Of course, it would be just one date. It would really be a waste of time, but I'd do it anyway, if for no other reason than to be able to say that I had tried it out.

She nodded, gazing at me, her lips twitching slightly as if with nerves. There was something shaky, slightly nervous-sounding about her voice when she turned away and said, "Good. Just one date. It will be all the confirmation I need."

54

I SMELLED OF MAMA'S lavender perfume. She had insisted that I spray it on. She had found me a pair of her old earrings — the ones with yellow pebble-sized stones that dangled down like miniature globes.

I sat on the edge of the bed in my full slip, watching as she ransacked my drawers. "What are you still doing with this thing?" she asked, pulling out one of my old gowns. "Do you realize how old it is? *Biko,* you need to throw this nonsense out already! These are no longer the war days. We have moved on. Get rid of it."

She continued to riffle through the garments in the drawers. At last she settled on a long, beige dress with flower and leaf patterns printed along its hem. She held it out in front of her. The dress hung limply from her hands, all wrinkled. She shook it vigorously as if to shake out the wrinkles. She shook and shook, and then, giving up on that, she began tugging and stretching the wrinkles out.

"I should really iron this for you, but I don't think we have time." Still, as soon as she had uttered the words, she appeared to change her mind. I watched her walk out of the room. In the distance I heard the sounds of her fussing with the iron. About twenty minutes passed and she returned with the dress crisply ironed for me.

"It's really the perfect dress," she said. "It will show just enough of your neckline and your ankles. That should be enough to keep his interest. That's the way to do it. Show a little of the collarbone and a little of the ankles."

It was a three-quarter-sleeved dress. Mama said that the modesty of the sleeves was a good thing. Short enough that he could see my wrists and a portion of my forearm, which would also help in winning him over.

She sat on the edge of the bed and watched as I put on the dress. When I had slid it down my body, she stood and helped me to button it up, then took a few steps back and examined me. She walked back toward me and began fussing with the bodice and the hem.

"Yes," she said. "Perfect now. You look like the daughter I always envisioned you could be. Just perfect."

I remained silent.

She said, "You might marry him."

I rolled my eyes. "Mama, that's a big leap to make. Even if marriage were an option, don't you think you're hurrying things a bit?"

Her face now appeared sad, melancholic. Nostalgic. She said, "Not a day goes by that I don't wish your papa were here with me. Every minute counts. You want to take advantage of every minute while you can. Believe me, there are worse things than hurrying things."

It had been some years since Mama brought up the topic of Papa. The last time, it was with antagonism, resentment. Now it seemed she had let go of her grudge. Here she was, talking about him dotingly, with affection. I remained quiet, hoping that she would continue in that vein, hoping that maybe the time had come when we would be able to reminisce together, revisiting, fondly, old memories of Papa. But she did not say any more. Instead, she went back to the topic of Chibundu.

"He's a good man," she said.

I frowned. How could she really know? I said something that Papa used to say: "Isn't it the case that the most beautiful fruit might contain a worm?"

"Well," she said, "that might very well be. But isn't it also true that the cashew doesn't fall too far from the tree? His parents are good people. And it seems to me that if he's changed at all, it's been for the best. I think we both agree that he has grown into a fine young man. But let's not worry about that for now. For now, just go out and enjoy yourself. Smile often and make sure you show him how pleased you are to be out with him."

"And what if I'm not pleased?" I asked.

"Smile anyway. He's a good man, and you *will* be pleased. With a man, life is difficult. Without a man, life is even more difficult. Take it from me."

That evening, as Chibundu and I headed down the path that led to the front gate, I turned around to find Mama still standing at the front door. She was wearing a wide smile. Her arms were clasped in front of her, just above her chest, as if in prayer.

55

THESE DAYS, THE events leading up to the wedding still haunt me. They are blurry at times, but sometimes they are as clear as the sky on a sunny afternoon.

We were at the bus stop in Aba, as Chibundu was on his way back to Ojoto to visit with his family. He had asked me to walk along with him, and so I had. This was about a month after our date.

The bus had not yet arrived. I took a seat on a bench made out of several cement blocks and a single wooden plank. Chibundu refused to take a seat. He stood fiddling with his hands, wringing and unwringing them, wringing and unwringing like a child afraid of getting scolded.

"Chibundu, what's the matter?" I asked. "*Odikwa mma?*"

He cleared his throat and said, "I b-brought you here b-because . . . because I wanted to ask you something." He was stammering, though he was not a stammerer.

All his fidgeting was making me nervous. I had to look away.

Not far down the road, a hen was pecking at a crumb. A man in khaki-colored shorts was plucking a mango from a tree. Another man, a mechanic, was lying flat on a mat on the gravel-paved lot of the auto repair shop across the street, working on a Land Rover. Near him: metal pipes reflecting the sun, the trickling of black oil.

A minute went by. The mechanic slid out from under the car, walked around to the front. He opened the hood, appeared to be tinkering with something inside. The hen began to squawk.

"I — don't — know," I heard Chibundu say.

I turned back to look at him. "You don't know? What don't you know?"

"But I think—I think—I know I can." He put emphasis on the "know." It was something like the beginning of a pledge, a vow. But it was disheartening the way his voice was breaking, faltering, like an imperfect promise.

"You know you can what? *Gini ka inwere ike ime?*"

He cleared his throat, turned so that he was no longer looking at me. He had stopped fiddling with his hands. Now he was looking at the mango picker, who was walking away from the tree. Chibundu stared in that direction for some time. When he turned back to me, he was finally able to get it out. "I know I can make you happy," he said, instantly resolute.

We were looking at each other, eye to eye. "Make me happy?" I asked quietly, touched but also a little startled, because even then I must have known that the proposal would follow.

"Marry me," he said, crouching by my side. He took my hand in his, and he asked the question. "Will you? Will you be my wife?"

Sweat had formed on his forehead. He reached into his pocket, took out his handkerchief, and in that moment I noticed the contours of a small box in his pocket, below where the handkerchief had been. He dabbed away his sweat, then pulled out the box, opened it to reveal the ring. The golden band sparkled in the sun.

Soon he placed a gentle kiss on my cheek, and I allowed him to do so. It felt preordained, as if there were no way out even if I tried. How would I face Mama when it got back to her that Chibundu had proposed and I had declined? She would be devastated, would most likely be heartbroken at the fact that I had passed up the life she wanted for me—and perhaps the only opportunity that I was likely to have with a man.

And anyway, here was Chibundu, sweating before me, stammering, promising to make me happy. What if he actually could? What if I only had to give it a real try to see? Because when I thought of it, I *did* want to be normal. I *did* want to lead a normal life. I did want to have a life where I didn't have to constantly worry about being found out. What if Ndidi was right and that other life led to something like what had happened to Adanna, or to Adanna's two friends?

It was nearing the end of 1979. Sometimes we get confused about what happiness really means. Sometimes we get confused about what path to take to get to happiness. I looked at Chibundu, I nodded, and, wordlessly, I accepted his ring.

The next thing I knew, Chibundu was picking me up and twirling around with me in his arms, right there in the open air.

Only a month later, Mama was painting my eyelids silver and my lips a bright shade of red, and I was making my entrance as was expected of any Igbo bride: my jigida hanging from my midsection, extending down below my hips, waist beads of all different colors. I wore bangles on my wrists and ribbons on my braided locks of hair.

I entered the compound from the bungalow. I danced, waving my arms in the air, shaking my hips so that the jigida beads rattled and clinked above the wrappers beneath. The guests clapped and the drummers beat their drums.

Mama had left the gate wide open, an invitation to the villagers to come in and join the celebration. She stood near the gate as I danced, Chibundu's parents to her right and the grammar school teacher and his wife to her left. Ndidi stood at a distance from them, a woman apart, who, by all appearances, seemed to be enjoying the festivities. But I could tell from the way she stood, all alone there by the gate, that she was anxiously awaiting the moment when the festivities would conclude and she could leave. She had not bothered to greet Chibundu. The only person she took the time to greet was Mama.

The girls who formed my bridal party were just a group of Aba girls — daughters of some of Mama's friends whom Mama had recruited for the purpose of being bridesmaids. (I had insisted that I did not want any bridesmaids, and Mama had insisted that I should have them.) They danced in place. Soon, other members of the wedding party approached — Chibundu's groomsmen — breaking through the circle to throw their wads of naira bills at me. All the guests approached. The wads came apart. The bills danced about in the air like oversized feathers, then fell to the ground, spreading out like floor decorations around my feet. My bridesmaids crouched down and gathered them for me. I continued to dance, though all the while Ndidi was on my mind.

Toward the end of the celebration, Mama tugged at my shoulder, led me inside.

"You've done well. Very well," she said. All over her face was a rabid kind of excitement, which I knew must have been a struggle for her to contain. We went into the kitchen and she pulled out a stool for me, the one on which she usually sat to pound yams with the mortar and pestle. All over the kitchen was food—plates and trays and baskets of food covering all the counters. Garden eggs, their meandering green stripes seeming to creep like roots onto their yellow-gold skin. Kola nuts. Bowls of groundnut paste. Trays of meat pies and fried chin-chin. Jerry cans full of palm wine.

"What a wonderful day for all of us," she said. "The day we've all been waiting for."

I did not see fit to respond.

"Is something wrong?" Mama asked, but then she quickly brushed away the question, so determined was she that nothing would spoil this day for her.

I sat fussing with my hands, tangling and untangling my fingers. "Mama," I began, but I stopped. There was suddenly a startled look on her face, as if she already knew the words I was about to speak.

"This is the way things go," she said firmly. An exasperated laugh escaped from her. "The will of God."

She repeated it: "The wonderful will of God."

The white wedding came next, and there we were, in one of the small prayer rooms in the church. Mama slipped the gown over my head, zipped up the back so that its tight bodice hugged me. There was a bit of claustrophobia in its embrace. Sweat formed on my forehead. Several times I reached up and wiped it away. Eventually Mama folded a newspaper in half and began fanning me with it. "We can't have sweat spoiling this day for us," she said, her voice very impatient.

We stayed silent a while.

"What if it's not for me?" I said after some time. Perfect pleats ran down the waistline of the dress. I traced the pleats with my fingers, up and down, up and down. There was a tremor in my hands.

"What if *what's* not for you?" Mama retorted, like a dare. She looked down and observed my trembling hands.

"Marriage," I said. "What if marriage is not —"

I did not finish, because Mama's voice came booming: "Hush before you breathe life into your doubts! Marriage is for everyone! Remember, a woman without a man is hardly a woman at all. Besides, good men are rare these days. Now that you've found one, you must do what you can to keep him."

She studied me for some minutes, peering at me with hard eyes. Then she softened, shook her head slowly, and studied me some more. Finally she said, "*Nwa m, ke ihe ichoro ka m me?* My child, what do you want me to do? A woman and a woman cannot be. That's not the way it's done. You must let go of any remaining thoughts you have of that." She said it very softly, but firmly too. "If that's what this is all about, you must let go of it. It's not the way things are done." She took a deep breath, then exhaled, composed herself. "You'll see. This will all work out. *Bia ka ayi je.* Come, let's go."

Soon I was going through with the sermon, the prayers, the kiss, the handshakes, the smiles, the nods, and the tangential congratulations. Because that's what you do when you find yourself married to a man who both logic and your mother insist is the right man for you.

PART VI

56

�֍

Port Harcourt, Rivers State
1980

THE SUN WAS relentless, its heat so oppressive that even the flies appeared too tired to fly.

I forced one foot in front of the other. Even with my body heavy and distended at the middle, I continued to walk.

The woman in front of me was wearing a colorful wrapper and matching blouse and carrying a hen in her hand, its legs tied together by a string. The hen was clucking. A motorcycle sped by, blowing its horn and adding to the noise.

I crossed the tar-and-chip road, wrapping my hands underneath my belly like a brace. The road opened up on the right into a smaller, winding, dusty path. Along the path, two brown dogs were barking and a woman was shooing them away.

The church was a small rectangle of a church, unremarkable aside from its zinc roof, which shone like tinsel in the sun.

Inside, I took a seat at the front, in one of the pews, a simple bench like all the rest: one long plank set on two thin, cylindrical cement blocks. All over the place, the waxy scent of burning candles, though it did not appear that any candles were lit.

Every day for nearly two months I had been coming and taking a seat in that same spot. Every day the same routine, in the morning or in the early afternoon while Chibundu was away at work, until late afternoon just before he returned home. And I would continue to come, because all the women were talking about it still, even if nearly two months had since passed. The women did not seem to be able to stop talking about it: How the cursed mother's cries had been heard day in and day out in all the flats surrounding the clinic as she pushed and screamed and pushed and screamed. How, when the baby finally slid out, a sigh was heard, not just the woman's, but an exhale of multitudes, a collective flicker of relief. Everything should have been fine after that, and things were, in fact, fine. But then the midwife took one clean look at the baby boy's face and saw the horror that he was: a hole in his upper lip where flesh should have been, his left nostril spread wide and flat, not circling above the mouth as it should have been. Not surprising that it did not circle above: it could not be expected to. Not above what was an imperfect reproduction of a mouth, soggy and half-baked, like undercooked batter. A sight to see. A curse, they agreed. A bad omen. A harelip.

By the following morning the woman had fled. After two days of labor she had simply fled. Fled, of course, without her baby boy. And the boy? Maybe he would be sent away to some orphanage, or maybe one of the midwives would take pity on him and resign herself to taking care of him. But more than likely he would be left to perish, unwanted and unloved. Because this was the nature of such things, of anything that was outside the norm. They were labeled with such words as "curse," and wasn't it wise to keep curses at bay?

I settled into my seat on the bench. "Lord, have mercy," I whispered, as I had been whispering every day now for the previous two months. If there were ever another person to be cursed, to be punished in the same way as the harelip's mother, it was me. If it wasn't bad enough that I had lived in sin all those years, lying with woman as I should instead have done with man, here I was, carrying Chibundu's child, yet still allowing thoughts of Ndidi to linger in my mind. Thoughts of Amina, even. Thoughts of loving these two women.

Why was it that I could not love Chibundu the way that I loved Amina and Ndidi? Why was it that I could not love a man? These days, I've heard it said that the gender of your first love determines the gender of all your future loves. Perhaps this was true for me. But back then, it was not a thing I ever heard. All I knew in that moment was that there was a real possibility of God punishing me for the nature of my love. My mind went back to the Bible. Because if people like Mama and the grammar school teacher were right, then the Bible was all the proof I needed to know that God would surely punish me.

But if I were to go back to the Bible — to the New Testament specifically — what exactly were the consequences if we failed to do His will? Would God really carry out His will by way of punishment? Was not all our punishment taken care of by Jesus on the cross? What to make of God's grace in combination with His punishment?

Beyond welcoming thoughts of Ndidi, there was the matter of adultery. I acknowledged to myself that for all intents and purposes, I was an adulterer. Though I was not currently engaging in any physical acts with Ndidi, I knew well that, according to Matthew, *everyone who looks at a woman with lust for her has already committed adultery with her in his heart.* According to Matthew, I was in fact an adulterer.

And so, the visits to church. Prayer would be the tool if I were to dominate my thoughts and desires. Prayer as a method of dousing my desires. Prayer, like water on fire.

Prayer as a way to show God that He need not curse my child the way He had cursed the newborn at the clinic. If I could only pray enough, especially this last month of my pregnancy, perhaps all would be solved, done away with: the desires for Ndidi as well as the possibility of a harelip child.

Now the sunlight was making its way inside the church through the slats of the wooden shutters, sun rays spreading out in long, tapering lines across the cement floor.

I thought: So this is what it means to be married: to sit tensely in church, watching the sunlight spread itself all around me, with this constant fear of punishment. This must be married life: the daily attempt to pour out a basinful of hopeless desires. And yet the basin refuses to be emptied, as if the desires were wet cement that is already turning into concrete.

This must be married life: to sit in church with so much unrest, but at home carry on the pretense that all is just as it should be.

The clock inside the church was chiming half past the hour, playing a fragment of a tune, like a music box.

I saw a shadow on the cement floor at the periphery of my eye, a gray silhouette of a person, elongated and approaching from the center aisle of the church.

I was wearing my prayer scarf around my head. I tugged at it, out of a feeling of unease and apprehension over who it could possibly be.

To my surprise, Chibundu approached. It was rare that he attended services on Sundays, let alone visit the church on a weekday. Long gone was the churchgoing child he used to be. And yet here he was.

He took a seat next to me. We sat quietly on the bench for a while, then he said, "What is it? What's making you come here so often? Ngozi from next door tells me that she's seen you walking here quite a few times now."

"It's nothing," I said.

"How can it be nothing?"

"You should be at work," I said. I had been thinking of telling him for all the time since we were married, but I could never quite get myself to do it. Now I reasoned again that he'd been nothing but kind to me, so perhaps I could just tell him. In fact, maybe it was best I told him, in case the baby should come out cursed, a harelip or such. I should tell him and apologize. So that he would know that I was sorry for it.

"What are you doing away from work? Don't tell me they've sacked you," I said.

He shook his head. "No, they haven't sacked me. I had a consulting appointment in the area that finished early. I decided to stop home. You weren't there. Ngozi said maybe I could find you here."

Silence.

He said, "Whatever it is, it can't be that bad."

I had only been taking sideways glances at him. I turned now to look him square in the face. "It's bad enough," I said.

Another silence.

"Sometimes in Aba I used to catch Mama praying for me," I said finally. "I would walk in on her accidentally as she knelt in the parlor, praying over me."

He was moving one foot across the cement floor, swinging it gently back and forth like a pendulum. His shoe against the coarse floor made a scraping sound. I closed my eyes and listened to the sound. Then I whispered, "An abomination." I opened my eyes to catch the word's effect on him.

His eyes appeared to narrow. He looked suddenly deep in thought.

"An abomination?" he repeated, a question.

I nodded.

Surely he must already have had his suspicions. But there was no way I could have known this at the time. And he was not yet ready to let me know that he knew. He did not bring it up. Maybe he simply felt a need to avoid the truth. Or maybe his silence on the topic was, at that point, something he wanted to do as a favor to me, for my sake, by virtue of his love. Because he did love me, or at least he had loved me as a boy, that former boyish sort of love.

Or maybe his refusal to bring it up that day was a thing he did as a favor to himself, in order to allow himself the opportunity to continue to live out that old childhood love. Maybe he had, at some point before that day, decided that he could spend his whole life trying to fulfill a dream despite the unpromising circumstances.

Whatever the case, he appeared to think about the word "abomination," and then he said, "I myself, I'm no longer very much into church these days, as you know. See, I'm a businessman. And if you're a businessman, then one thing you know is that business is all about gathering as many customers as possible and retaining them. Religion is basically a business, a very large corporation. Take the

Anglican or Catholic Church, for instance. You have all these doctrines that are set up, and we are told that God is the reason for all
of them."

"Isn't He?" I asked.

Chibundu shook his head. "No. I don't think He is."

"Why not?"

"Because if you look deeply enough into those doctrines, you begin to see that the Church just wants to do whatever it can to get as
many followers as possible and to keep them under control. This
is the way business works. So the Catholic Church tells us that 'Be
fruitful and multiply' means 'Don't use contraceptives.' And people
actually soak it up and wind up having twelve children that they
can't possibly take care of. And they continue to have more children
for fear of using contraceptives and angering God. And really, it's
not even God who's making them do it. It's the Church that has in-
terpreted God's words to its own benefit. Because the Church wants
as many members as possible, as many followers as possible."

"But that's not us. We're not even Catholics. What's your point?"

"My point is that business is the reason for things like doctrines.
Business is the reason for words like 'abomination.' The Church is
the oldest and most successful business known to man, because it
knows not only how to recruit customers but also how to control
them with things like doctrines and words like 'abomination.' Bottom line is, take your abomination with a grain of salt. My sense of
it is that some things are called abominations that really aren't. And
anyway, like you said, your mama is praying over you. And here you
are, praying for yourself. If I were God, and if it turned out that you
were actually committing an abomination, then I'd forgive you."

"Don't you want to know what my abomination is?"

His face had been solemn as he spoke, very serious, but now his
lips curved into a slight smile, and he said, "Actually, no. I guess I
don't see the use in knowing. Whatever it is, it doesn't matter to me.
I'm your husband, and I know you well enough to know that you
are a good person, and that's enough for me." His arms came around
me, a quick embrace and then two soft pats, a little stiff. I closed my

eyes and imagined a less stiff embrace. Something soft and gentle, and indulgent even in its hesitation. There he was, hard and manly, offering me a reassuring embrace, and all I could think was that it was just a bit lacking. All I could think was that his embrace fell quite a bit short of what Ndidi's could have been.

"There are punishments for people who've done what I've done," I began again, pulling myself away from him. "Stoning and dro—"

He placed a finger over my lips, and just like that, he hushed me, canceled all the words that had been getting ready to make their way out of my mouth.

For a long time I sat there, twirling my wedding band around my finger. Chibundu continued to sit with me. A year of marriage and a baby on the way, and yet there was no indication that my love for him would ever develop into a romantic kind of love.

I thought about the journey we had made: A small boy and girl up in an orange tree. A clumsy kiss. The passage of time. An awkward proposal, a lackluster acceptance, a wedding ceremony, a wedding prayer, a wedding kiss.

Handshakes, smiles, nods. Congratulations.

I thought about what my life had become: Daily visits to church. Daily unrequited conversations with God. Speaking more and more to God, demanding that He speak back to me. *Dear God, can you please just open Your mouth and say something? Anything. I need Your guidance. I need you. I need. Dear God. Please, just open Your mouth and speak.*

In the end, after about half an hour of sitting there with me, Chibundu said, "I have to get back to work now, but I'll see you at home in the evening." He stood up, placed a kiss on my forehead, and turned around to leave. His footsteps thumped gently on the cement floor.

57

I ACKNOWLEDGE TO MYSELF that sometimes I am a snail. I move myself by gliding. I contract my muscles and produce a slime of tears. Sometimes you see the tears and sometimes you don't. It is my tears that allow me to glide. I glide slowly. But, slowly, I glide. It is a while before I am gone.

That first night of our marriage, I was a snail. We were all of us once snails.

In the beginning, we had stayed with Mama in Aba, and we had slept in my room, just for that first month of marriage, that one-month space before Chibundu got the Port Harcourt job. Mama had found a second twin bed and mattress, and pushed them together so that they appeared to be a double bed. She had spread new sheets that she had purchased as our wedding gift.

This is how our first night together went: Imagine a snail protected by its hard shell. Imagine a snail when it is alarmed. Imagine the snail retreating into its shell.

That first night, Chibundu called me to him. He was wearing remnants of his tuxedo — the tie, the white shirt, the trousers. He sat on the edge of the mattress.

I went to him, sat by his side. No alarm yet.

"You've made me a very happy man," he said, leaning over, wrapping his arm around me.

He leaned in further, began kissing me. I allowed him to do so.

"There is no more complete happiness than the one I'm feeling now," he said between kisses. "Look at me. I feel like I can fly."

A slight bit of alarm was rising in me now. "Go ahead and fly," I wanted to say. "Go ahead and fly, so long as you land far enough away from me."

Instead, I said, "We should try and get some sleep."

He laughed. Not disrespectfully. Almost appreciatively, for the sexual banter he perceived was going on. "*Nawa o!*" he said. "Women and their teasing! But of course, Ijeoma, you do know that sleep is the very last thing on my mind!" He made a sudden movement with his hands, and I watched as he began tugging at the front of his trousers. Then came that dreaded sound: just the sound of a man undoing his zipper, but it was as if a sharp object had somehow been jabbed into my ears.

A roomful of alarm. Alarm like fog, clouding up the atmosphere.

I pulled away so that there was at least a forearm's length of space between us. I folded my hands across my chest, looked up at the ceiling, not wanting to look at him. Uniform tiles formed large squares above, gray, like the paint on the walls.

Some time passed. A few more minutes. I lowered my folded arms from my chest, took his hand in mine.

Sometimes a story reminds you of a painting. Each time I tell this story, I see that old painting of a beach. Azure skies melting into a lighter shade of blue, melting into the pastel yellow of the disappearing sun, melting back into a sea-colored blue. A glass-looking slab of wood near the edge of the earth where brown and sea blue meet. There is a mountain range, craggy rocks, peeking in from the right side of the painting, and in the foreground there is the darkness of the cacao-colored earth.

The painting would be almost unremarkable if not for the rest of the objects in it: a plain-looking brown box, like a trunk. From the trunk, a growth, like a cancer, a stump of a tree, branches and all, but no leaves. And then a scattering of melting clocks, like wilted rags: one hanging from a branch of the stump, one hanging droopily from the trunk box, another hanging from an abstract-looking figure, a cross between a duck and a human face. Finally a burnt-orange clock covered in tiny black ants.

There I was, holding Chibundu's hand, and as I held it, the words came to me: "Too much ceremony has a way of taking the life, taking the joy, out of what is being celebrated."

The next thing I knew, Chibundu was staring at me with a look of shock on his face. I put down his hand and returned my hands to my sides. His eyes were steady on me, careful eyes, as if he was looking at some strange, new, unexpected version of me. And of course, to him, he was.

I left him where he sat and walked over to the window. I stayed by the window, still in my wedding gown. Every once in a while a breeze blew in through the open space. In the few instances that the breeze was strong, I pushed my face into it, as if it would somehow blow away all my agony.

Even when I heard Chibundu's soft snoring, I continued to stand by the window, wide awake.

Only when the sky turned from black to gray — only when I could hear the distant crowing of the roosters and hens — did sleep come to me.

I struggled to undo the zipper of my wedding gown, then I stepped out of it.

The knock came just as I had put on my nightgown.

I opened the door to Mama, standing with her wrapper tied across her chest, wearing a bright smile.

"Come, come," she said, waving me toward her and out of the room. "Come. You must tell me, how was it?"

"How was what, Mama?"

"*Nwanka!*" she said, feigning exasperation. This child! But there was a hint of a smile on her face. "'How was what, Mama?'" she said, mimicking me. "Of course you know what I'm asking! How was your first night as a wife?"

I shook my head at her, embarrassed that she should even ask. "Mama, I've barely slept."

"Of course not!" Her smile widened. "It's no surprise that you've hardly slept. All that happiness!"

Happiness was what she called it. But I knew that happiness was a word like madness, like sickness, like confusion, like loss, like death. Even like beautiful or pure or angelic or God. Happiness was a word that represented some deeper, unexplainable, heavy idea, the kind of idea that goes back and forth between two different worlds.

Still, there she was, pulling me by the hand in the name of happiness. She led me that way out of the room, down the corridor, and into the kitchen. The wedding ceremony food had been cleared off the counter. All that remained were empty plates and trays and baskets and bowls.

She pulled out a stool for me. With a slight nod of her head, she signaled me to sit. She cleared her throat. She had a placid, almost vacant look on her face. "So, you two have already begun, haven't you?"

"Begun what?" I asked.

"You know." A pause. "It's never too early to start working on a child."

"Mama!"

Her eyes focused now, her look no longer vacant. "Well, it's nothing to be embarrassed about," she said, staring straight into my eyes. "There's nothing more meaningful in a marriage than having a precious child of your own."

Our second night, Chibundu came again to me, wrapped his arm around me where we sat on the edge of the bed. There was more determination in his gestures, and in his eyes was the look of a man who was expecting to get what was denied him the night before.

I shifted away instinctively. His eyes turned soft, pleading, just as soon as I did. He began to stroke my shoulders. "It's not by force," he said in a whisper. "It's not something we should do by force. Just let me know when you feel ready."

That night, I saw the foolishness of my resistance in his words.

Just let me know when you feel ready. I knew in my mind that I might never feel ready. There was no sense prolonging my resistance. Anyway, better to have one person miserable rather than two.

That night, he moved closer to me, unzipped his pants. That night, I allowed him to make love to me.

58

OUR HOUSE IN Port Harcourt was a small, two-bedroom flat. It had peeling paint, leaking ceilings, buzzing fluorescent lights, cracking stone tiles. Holes in the walls, which allowed cockroaches to crawl in. Windows that could not be properly shut.

I sulked: Out of the way things had taken this unexpected turn. Out of the fact that I had gone and allowed myself to marry Chibundu. Out of the fact that his job had led us away from Aba, away from Ndidi.

He sulked: Out of the rigidness of his job. Out of the newness of his responsibilities.

And of course there was, again, the state of our new home. So many things old and falling apart as they were, it was a home that fueled our bad moods. If it could have done as much, the home itself would have sulked with us.

Our first month in the flat, Chibundu and I had taken time to tape up the peeling walls. We had taken time to seal the holes in the ceilings and the floors. For a while, the rain stopped dripping in and the cockroaches stayed away. But a month later, the problems returned, a crude reminder that patching would not be enough.

But Chibundu was hopeful too.

One evening, he came back from work not looking his usual miserable way. I had gone to the market that day, spent hours there, and had returned with only a batch of snails. Snails were what we would have had for dinner, if we had bothered to have dinner that night.

I rinsed the snails in a bowl and transferred them to a pot. The pot was still on the counter, not yet on the stove, when Chibundu called my name.

I could see him from the corner of my eye, his tall frame coming toward me. There was a slowness to his movements, as if the room were a pool of water and he was struggling to wade through it. But finally he arrived.

By the stove, he wrapped his arms around me and said, "One morning, you will look around the flat and see all the things that are wrong with it — the peeling paint on the walls, the cracks, the holes. You will see all those things, and yet everything will feel just fine."

"Impossible," I said, a little annoyed by the stupidity of the statement.

He removed his arms from around my body. He walked off toward the shelf in the farthest corner of the kitchen. He returned holding a tuber of yam. He reached for a knife and began peeling off the skin of the yam.

"Broiled or fried?" he asked as he peeled.

"Broiled," I said.

It was not unusual for him to cook. This was one of the things that made Chibundu different from so many other men I knew, even from Papa. Every once in a while he cooked, and even enjoyed doing so.

He cut up the yam into cubes, scooped them up, rinsed them off, spread them on a tray, and sprinkled some salt and pepper and coconut oil on them. All the while I watched. I watched as he bent over with the tray, sticking it into the oven to broil.

As he closed the oven, I turned from watching him back to the snails that I had been tending to on the counter. I carried the pot to the stove. I struck a match, lit the fire. Before I turned to leave, I bent over to peek into the oven, just to check that the yams were fine. From the small glass window on the front of the stove, I saw Chibundu's reflection, his legs crossed, arms folded. He was leaning against the sink watching me.

"What?" I asked, straightening up and turning to look directly at him.

"That morning," he said, "you will make your way out of the bedroom, through the parlor, and straight into the kitchen. You will find me here by the sink, beating some breakfast eggs for you. The fork will be clanking against the bowl. The windows will be open, and a breeze will be entering through it. Music will be flowing from the radio. Everything will be fine."

"And just how exactly will everything be fine?"

His face was earnest and hopeful as he stood there leaning his back on the sink. He said, "You will be somebody's mother, and I will be somebody's father."

I snickered, pointed to a crack in the wall. "Is that right?" I asked. "Are you sure you want to bring a child into this?"

"It's not so bad," he said.

By then there was the slight, sandy scent of snails in the air.

He straightened himself so that he was no longer leaning against the sink. He moved forward and took me once more into his arms. He pressed himself against me, and me against him. What else could he have done?

I buried my face into the nook between his neck and his shoulder. In that recess, I felt his body tighten. Soon his hands came between us, his fingers tracing the buttons on my blouse. He slipped the buttons out of their holes, one after the other. His hands made their way beneath my blouse, along the upper hem of my bra.

"Shhh. It's okay," he whispered, as I recoiled.

He planted a kiss on my forehead. The air was humid. The water in the pot of snails had come to a boil, the sound of gently popping bubbles.

He led me into the parlor. Our clothes trailed the path, my blouse and skirt mixing with his shirt.

On that tattered old couch, he caressed and kissed me some more, soft kisses, unhurried, even a little slow. All this time he'd been nothing but patient with me. Here he was, a man I wanted badly to be rid of. But I knew full well that he also held the key to my only imaginable escape: Perhaps by making me a mother, he would save me. Maybe motherhood would make me feel more invested in the marriage. Maybe motherhood would cause me to forget Ndidi. All of this I reasoned so that by the time he rooted me to the sofa, I had already relented. He planted a million and one more kisses on me, and when he moved to enter me, I made sure not to turn away.

59

W E HAD BEEN married for just over six months now, and living in Port Harcourt for five of those.

I stood up from the front steps, lifted myself from the weeds I had been picking.

What was it?

The headache was now beyond persistent. I could no longer continue. I marched into the kitchen, short of breath.

Something was changing in me. New qualities, a new restlessness.

Every day for all of that week, I had called Mama on the phone. Something was not quite right.

"What is it?" she asked.

"I don't know, Mama. That's the point. I don't know."

I found the teakettle and set some water atop the stove to boil.

I picked up the phone.

A breeze through the kitchen windows gently lifted the curtains.

I found a ginger root in the pantry. I scraped away the skin with a spoon, cut off a small piece, and allowed it to sit like a communion wafer on my tongue.

On the phone:

"Mama?"

"Yes, my child?"

"Mama, these days I have this feeling of being trapped in my body."

"Being in a new place is not easy."

"But Mama, it's been months already."

"It takes time to adjust."

"Mama, you're not hearing me."

"What, then?"

"These days, I smell too strongly the scent of wet earth. I catch a whiff of the rain before it starts to fall. Even the sun is a burning odor in my nose. Every scent is as sharp as a knife."

Outside in the backyard, swallows hovered around the guava tree. I observed them from where I stood by the window.

"So what do you think is wrong with you?"

"That's the point, Mama. I don't know."

She made her pronouncement one day over the phone: "Depression."

"I suppose it could be."

"Just think of all the things you have to be happy about in your life!"

"Like what?"

"Are you sad? Do you cry?"

"Mama, I'm too tired to cry."

"I can come stay with you two in Port Harcourt for a while."

"No, Mama. It's not necessary. I'm sure I'll begin to feel better soon."

"Of course you will."

"Yes, I think I should."

"The blind man wanted badly to see. He said, 'Today I will see.' But today he did not see. He said, 'Tomorrow I will see.' But tomorrow became today, and today became yesterday, and still he did not see."

"Mama, I'm sure I'll feel better soon."

"God helps those who know to ask for help."

"You are not God."

"No matter. I am coming. I will come and see what I can do. Whatever the problem, I'm sure I can fix it."

• • •

"Anyone home? Ijeoma? Chibundu? I told you I would come. I have shut the store, put up the Closed sign. Please don't tell me that I have done all that for nothing, coming all the way here and finding not even a soul to welcome me. Children these days! What is the world coming to?"

I swung open the front door. In the air, the too-sweet scent of the guavas, which hung in scattered arrangement from the branches of the tree, guavas ripe and yellow and nearly bursting with juice.

"Mama, welcome," I said. I opened the door wider to allow her in. The scent rushed in, stronger.

"How was your trip?" I asked.

No answer, but she entered. When she did, she remained near the entrance, would not take another step forward.

"Mama, why are you just standing there?"

She was scanning the flat with her eyes. After a moment she exclaimed, "I see the problem now! There is still so much to be done around here! Why have you two not taken the time to fix up the place? Well, we can certainly take care of all of this now. There's really no better cure for depression than hard work. We have our work cut out for us, but believe me, once things start to look nicer around here, you will surely start to feel better!"

Afternoon. Lunchtime. The thick scent of garri and Mama's okra soup.

"Look at you looking so miserable. When I was your age, I was wearing my marriage like a badge of honor. It's not every woman who is lucky enough to snatch herself a husband, you know. What's wrong with you that you still can't see that? God has been good to you, and you don't even have the common sense to see it."

"Mama, I'm not in the mood."

"Just as I thought you would reply." She rubbed the palms of her hands against each other as if my words were crumbs, as if to dust off the crumbs from her hands.

• • •

After breakfast of agege bread and tea. Chibundu long gone to work. My head full, a terrible dizziness, as if someone took a hammer and pounded and pounded until I blacked out, and now I was just coming to.

"I'm off to pick up some groceries from Mile One market."

"Mama, there's food already in the flat."

"Is that right? There's food already and yet your fridge is looking like someone took a bulldozer and gutted it out. Let me ask you, what will we be having for supper tonight?"

"We still have that pot of okra soup remaining. We can finish that off for supper."

"Ehn-hehn! So you want me to eat for supper what I already ate yesterday for lunch?"

"What's wrong with that?"

"What's wrong with that!"

"Yes, Mama. What's wrong with that?"

"I'll tell you what's wrong with that. For one thing, you're a newlywed. You should be making all sorts of food for your husband, not making him eat the same things over and over again."

"Chibundu doesn't mind."

Now she was opening and closing kitchen cupboards and drawers, inspecting for missing food items.

"Do you have beans at home? No. Do you have akamu? No. Do you have corn? No. Any oha leaves? Any ogbono seeds? No. What if I want to make egusi soup? Do you have water leaves? Any crayfish? Do you have palm oil?"

"We have other things."

"Listen, I won't spend time arguing with you. I'm thinking maybe we can make some moin-moin and eat it with akamu for supper tonight. Or do you think Chibundu would prefer some rice and stew?"

"Chibundu will be fine with anything."

"Very well, then." She picked up her handbag from the kitchen table. "I will see you in a few hours. This place needs to be made to feel like a home, not a boarding room. I will pick up some food, and then I will also see what I can begin to do about the rest."

I had fallen asleep on the sofa. I woke up to a tapping on my shoulder. The sun was streaming in through the windows.

She was hovering over me, pointing to the back wall of the parlor. I straightened up on the sofa and saw what she was pointing at: against the wall, a small Singer machine, propped up on a wooden encasement, a stack of threads, a pair of scissors, and some other sewing supplies on the table near it.

"Look what I brought for you!" Her eyes shone with self-satisfaction. She was waiting for my reaction, which I knew should be a mixture of shock and gratitude.

I replied weakly, "Mama, thank you, but you didn't need to."

She looked at me aghast. "I buy you a sewing machine — not just buy it, but also pay someone to carry it here for me — and you have the audacity to tell me I didn't need to? Where are your manners?"

She continued: "This is exactly the thing you need so that your guests will know that a woman lives here. I regret that the war came and made it so that I never had a chance to really teach you these things. But better late than never. It's never too late to learn how to keep a beautiful home."

"Mama, none of this is really necessary."

"The place needs some curtains, a proper tablecloth for the kitchen table. Some pillows for the sofa. What kind of place is this that you call a home, and yet there are no curtains on the windows, no tablecloth on the table? This is what the machine is for. And speaking of the sofa, why did you two go and buy secondhand? All those holes in it, and then add to it the peeling walls. Holes everywhere." She waved her hand as if to say none of it mattered now. "Lucky for you, all of these things can be fixed. Remember what I told you about the Aba house and how we fixed it up? We can do the same here. We will make you a beautiful home." She rambled on and on, all in that same vein.

· · ·

New curtains: a cornsilk-colored brocade fabric with an olive-green lace valance.

"This will be perfect," she said. "You see, these windows get a lot of sun. With brocade you won't have to worry so much about sun rot."

"Sun rot, Mama?"

"When the sun eats into and discolors the fabric. You won't have that to worry about. Not for a long time, anyway."

Other new additions: a coral-colored cover for the sofa, a matching tablecloth.

Food and more food, enough to leave the pantry overflowing, as if our flat were a rich, fat man's house.

In the hours when Chibundu was at work, we cleaned, fixed, rearranged.

I worked dutifully at my new machine, making decorative covers for our new sofa pillows, my eyes taking turns between the fabric that I was sewing and the large bold letters on the machine. SINGER. I pedaled, and I turned the wheel. The needle bobbed up and down, up and down, and I imagined that the sound from the machine was a song, and that the machine was singing sweetly to me. I lost myself in the features of the machine, in its curves, in the color of it, a shiny, unapologetic shade of brown, sticking out in regal fashion from its encasement of wood. I hummed along with the sound of its sewing, a different song each time.

We taped up the peeling walls, again. We sealed up the holes, again.

Those hours after Chibundu returned from work, he made sure to express to us just how much he was liking the changes. "Incredible!" he exclaimed. "Just incredible!"

We washed clothes, swept floors. We peeled yams and corn, soaked beans and palm kernels. When all of that was done, she made lists of items to be bought at the market. We went together to the market, bought the items, brought them back home to cook.

Another day done. Another day gone.

• • •

The afternoon of her second week in Port Harcourt, I was in the middle of preparing to go to the market when I noticed Mama looking closely at me. "You're looking very pale," she said.

I nodded. "I'm feeling very pale," I replied.

"You might hurry, then," she said. "There are quite a few more items to be bought and, afterward, food to be made."

I nodded.

She looked at me some more.

The plan had been that I go to the market on my own while she took care of other things. But now she said, "I could go with you."

I nodded. "That would be nice," I said.

She grabbed the market bag. We made our way out the door.

The bus station was just up the road from our flat. We climbed onto the bus, rode it until our stop, still a distance from the market but as close as the bus could get us.

As we walked the rest of the way to the market, I got a whiff of something roasting, something sweet, like ripe plantains. I ran to the bushes on the side of the road, parted the tall green shrubs, bent over, my hands at my knees. I allowed it all to gush out, to flow out of me, that disease that had been for all this time inside me.

Minutes passed before I noticed Mama standing at my side. She simply stood there, her feet visible through the overgrown grass. I straightened up, wiped my mouth with the backs of my hands. I could see tears in her eyes almost right away. She wrapped her arms around me, very unexpectedly, as soon as I was done wiping off my mouth. "You've done well," she said. "You've made your mother proud. Do you know what this means?"

I shook my head.

There is a story about a snake that, out of stubbornness, decided that it would not swim across the river. Near the edge of the river was a crocodile, getting ready to cross. The snake twisted itself into a tight ball and set itself atop the crocodile. The crocodile went ahead and crossed the river, too foolish, or just too plain oblivious, to realize that it was carrying a curled-up constrictor on its back. By the time the crocodile noticed, there was no use in fighting. The snake had unraveled itself and wrapped itself around the crocodile. It didn't take long before the snake devoured the crocodile. Then it let out one tumbling burp, and then another, brushed itself off, and said thank you to the crocodile in its stomach, not only for being its food, but also for helping it to cross the river.

Chidinma was by no means a snake, but only that she had come upon me the same way that the snake had come upon the crocodile. Somehow it had not occurred to me that all those weeks I was carrying a baby inside me. But of course, Mama was right.

60

I BEGAN THE FIRST of this particular set of letters the night Mama left, because that very night, Ndidi appeared to me, more vividly than ever, in a dream.

There were, in fact, two dreams. In the first, she was dressed in a calf-length romper, walking in slow, measured steps, all zombie-like, holding out her arms to me. It was outdoors, and above her an orange sun was peeking through the clouds and causing her to glow, almost electric-like, a human bulb. She was saying, like a chant, "One day I will need you to carry me on your shoulders the way Atlas carried the world."

The scene changed abruptly, and just as soon she was in a field of whitish-gray dandelion clocks. Above her, an overcast sky, clouds on the verge of raining down tears.

I woke up with a start, expecting to find myself also in the field. Instead, I looked to my left, laid my eyes on a set of rumpled sheets and a sleeping Chibundu by my side.

In the second dream, Ndidi and I were in that double-functioning construction of a church in Aba, seated face to face at one of its tables. She handed me a glass of kai kai. I took a sip and, not wanting any more, gave it back to her.

She pushed the glass back to me.

I said, "I've already had a taste. It's nice of you to offer, but I don't like its taste."

She said, "You don't drink kai kai for its taste. You're focusing on the wrong sense. You drink it to feel its effect on you. Feel, not taste."

• • •

Before leaving Aba for Port Harcourt, I left our new address with Ndidi. Within a week of Chibundu's and my arrival in Port Harcourt, I also made it a point to write Ndidi a letter, and then a couple of more letters, at three- or four-week intervals. But the days passed, and more days still, with no response from Ndidi. She did not have a phone in her flat, or else I would have simply called.

The absence of any kind of communication from her was not at all like an absence. It was instead a presence: of mind-pain, like a thick, rusted arrow shooting straight into my head, poisoning my mind with something like tetanus, causing my thoughts to go haywire, a spasm here, a spasm there.

If there were a muscle relaxant equivalent for the mind, I would have been first in line for it. But not having that option, I found other ways to cope. For instance, each time I spoke with Mama on the phone, I found relief in bringing up Ndidi's name. Just a few seconds of speaking about her was like a temporary medicine.

One phone conversation with Mama:

"Any new customers?"

"No, no new customers."

"None at all?"

"Well, there's that old vagabond who showed up one day out of the blue. Did I tell you about him?"

"No, I don't believe you did."

"Well, the long and short of it is that he showed up one day in the unexpected way that bird excrement drops from the sky. Can you imagine what it must be like to be at least fifty years old and yet manage to have made nothing of yourself? A fully grown man roaming about the place with nothing to his name!"

"Unexpected things happen to people, Mama. Tragedy happens."

"Well, regardless, it just infuriates me to no end that he keeps wandering around here, all drunk and reeking of whiskey and ale. Several times he's come by eating a large orange, sucking at the pulp, his cheeks puffed up, and all the while he grimaces as if he's sucking urine or catarrh, and then he spits out the seeds. Can you believe —he spits them all out right in front of my shop! Now, you know a shop owner's best friend is her broom, and so I race out with my broom and make to sweep him away. But the following day he's back again. *Tufiakwa!* Some people don't have any decency . . ."

Speaking of infuriation, something about the way she was speaking was starting to infuriate me. Out the kitchen window, a heavy rain was falling. There was a steady rapping above. I could not tell what amount of it was the sound of my head thumping and what amount was the sound of the rain beating on the roof.

Mama continued on about the man and about his lack of decency, as if decency were some kind of religion. Because I could no longer just sit and listen, I asked, "What if his behavior has nothing to do with decency?"

There was something red and bright and burning like firewood in her voice now, and she said, "How can it not, ehn? In fact, the first few times he came loitering in front of the shop, I went up to him, pointed a finger at him, and gave him a good talking-to. If you've ever heard a lecture on decency, that's what I gave to him, and still, Ijeoma, I tell you, the man is incapable of simple decency. Imagine, he still continues to place his raggedy, disheveled self right in front of my store! A person like that, in front of the store every day, will eventually cost me my customers!"

It was clear that she had a point. Still, a feeling of sadness descended upon me in hearing her words. I thought: The poor man. What if he had nowhere better to go? And I thought of Mama. How terrible the way she was actually trying to make herself the victim in someone else's tragedy.

I said, "But Mama, what if he turned it back around on you? What if he asked you, out of decency, to stop shooing him away with your broom? What if he explained to you that he was more than a fly and that he had nowhere else to go? What if he told you that *you* were the one being indecent by shooing him away?"

Her voice was very quiet now. "He really should try harder to find another place to go."

I could have said more, but instead I asked, "And what about Ndidi? Does she still stop in?"

"Every once in a while, but not as often as before," Mama replied.

I got off the phone with Mama and went about the remainder of my day the same way I always did. When night came, I sat in bed and wrote to Ndidi. Maybe I would send the letter, or maybe not. Either way, better to get out the things on my mind than to allow them to fester and grow mold and cause my insides to feel rotten. Better to get them out before they became the worst kind of wound: oozing with pus and with a pungent kind of odor, oozing and decaying and stinking up the place like a dead and decomposing body.

I could have waxed poetic, said something about my love for her being as large and wide as a whole country. I could have written sappy lines that floated thinly in the air without any grounding in reality. But it would have been risky to do so—to let out all of my emotion in a letter. What if someone else got ahold of the letter and exposed our relationship?

Anyway, it didn't seem to me that flamboyant flourishes should have any place in love letters. Love cannot live by poetry alone.

I simply wrote:

I am pregnant with Chibundu's child, and yet I keep thinking of you. Last night I dreamed you in a field of dandelion clocks, and in our church. Do you still think of me?

Chibundu, by my side, was snoring slightly. I folded the paper in fourths and then again into eighths and placed it in the wooden hand-painted chest where I kept my pens and pencils and my journal. I made sure to put the letter at the bottom, beneath the pens and pencils, even beneath the journal, where I was certain Chibundu could not see it.

I bent over the side of the bed, placed the chest in the bottom drawer of my bedside table, pushing it safely behind all the other odds and ends—a small sewing kit, a pair of scissors, containers of pomade, my Bible. I slid the drawer closed, set myself back down on my side of the bed, and allowed myself to drift peacefully into sleep.

61

CHIBUNDU WAS IN the bathroom carrying on with his morning rituals. I got up and walked out of the bedroom and outside the flat, the way I had begun to do those days.

I took my place out on the front stoop. Day was breaking and the sky was growing light.

My eyes found the hedges. These hedges were nothing as majestic as the ones in our old Ojoto house. But they were fine enough. I rose from my seat on the stoop and walked over to them. The leaves and flower petals were glossy with dew. I picked a small ixora flower and placed it in my hair. If my child were to be a girl, I would pick even more of them and place them like decorations all around her little head.

The night before, Chibundu and I had been at it like a baboon and a leopard, snapping at each other at the supper table, each of us threatening to pounce on the other.

"This food is tasteless," he said.

"Then next time you can make your food yourself."

"I go to work all day and you have the audacity to look at me and tell me that to my face?"

"I cook for you all day and you have the audacity to complain that the food is no good to my face?"

His lips folded out like two thick millipedes, one on top of the other. If he were Mama, this sort of complaint would be expected, and I would just take it in and let it come out my underside. But this type of complaint was not at all usual for him.

He continued to sit there, silently moping and fuming.

I watched him for some time, then finally I said, "What exactly is the matter with you tonight anyway? Did something happen?"

For some weeks now his eyes were appearing heavy, but now they were heavier than usual.

I said again, "What's the matter with you?"

"Nothing."

"How was work?"

"Fine."

After a while, he said, "Funny how life has a tendency to go unexpectedly downhill."

"Is something going unexpectedly downhill for you?"

"I've been thinking," he said.

"Aha!" I muttered. "That's what you've been doing wrong!" I added, "Don't you know that thinking is like carrying a large stone in your stomach? Not only the pain of it, but also the feeling of your insides being all muddled and clogged up. And I bet you've not just been thinking. I bet you've been overthinking. Imagine a tall heap of stones just sitting in you. Take it from me, I know."

He said, "I've been *thinking* that I'm not too happy about the way things are around here."

"You're not too happy about what, exactly?"

"And it's not just me. Even at work, everyone seems to be sad and depressed. It must be something in the air. Like everybody got caught in a monsoon and came to work all soaked and sulking from it. I know it's just the state of things. But I am determined to be happy. Where happiness is concerned, there's a lot to be said for simple determination."

I thought about it. Finally I said, "Yes, it's certainly true. There's certainly something to be said for simple determination."

I was sitting outside, clearing my head with the fresh morning air, daydreaming about a girl child with a crown of ixora flowers.

I felt a kick in my stomach, and then I felt exhilaration wash over me. I thought of God. Maybe this was the way that God was choosing to talk to me. Maybe He was choosing to speak through my child. So what was He saying? I tried to still my mind, so that maybe I could hear God's voice within me.

Try as I might, I could not clear my head.

I prayed:

Dear God, I am unhappy. Even as I carry my child, and even as the thought of this child makes me happy, I am yet unhappy. Dear God, I want to be happy. Please help me to be happy.

Maybe all I could do was carry on with my life the way it was. Become a mother to one or more children, follow through with all that motherhood entailed.

I rose and went back into the house to iron Chibundu's work clothes. I had lost track of time and stayed outside longer than planned. Chibundu would be out of the bathroom at any moment, wondering where his clothes were.

From the bedroom I could hear him in the bathroom, could hear those final sounds that meant he was about to come out: a gargling, a spitting. Soon he would turn the knob and the door would whine open. I quickly ironed the shirt and trousers and then spread them out flat across the bed.

I moved to the kitchen, began to fry his eggs and make his toast.

Minutes passed, and soon I watched as he came into the kitchen, fully dressed, briefcase and watch in hand.

He set his briefcase down on the floor, then sat, adjusting the watch on his wrist, hurried-like, as if he hardly had time, not even for that.

I joined him at the table, watched as he began to eat, scarfing down his food, barely chewing even a morsel of it.

"What's the hurry?" I asked.

"Nothing," he said.

"You're not late, if anything you're early, and yet you're rushing. Clearly, it's something. What is it?"

He smiled broadly. "Remember what I said about determination?

I have several appointments. Arrangements to make. Important things to be done."

"What kind of arrangements? What important things?" I wanted to know.

He rose from his seat, grabbing his briefcase from the floor. "Don't worry, you'll see" was all he would say.

On his way out, he stopped in front of me, placed a kiss on my forehead, and at that moment I thought: What did it matter whether he told me his important business or not? What did it matter if he withheld or disclosed? What did it matter that we were man and wife, supposedly one flesh? It seemed to me that there were no two married people more empty-feeling, no two married people more estranged from each other than the two of us. What was the sense, then, of that forehead kiss?

Man and wife, the Bible said. It was a nice thought, but only in the limited way that theoretical things often are.

That evening, I sat at the kitchen table, gazing out the window, waiting for him to return. On the table, our dishes and utensils and drinking glasses sat, all clean and set for use. On the stove, a pot of rice and chicken stew simmering on low heat. All that remained was for Chibundu to return and for the food to be served.

The sky had turned dark, a deep shade of orange mixed heavily with gray. Nearly an hour had passed since his usual return time, and about an hour and a half since I had finished cooking, yet he had not returned.

"Soon," I muttered. "Soon."

Another half an hour went by, and still no sign of him.

I went to the telephone at the entrance to the kitchen. The dial tone was strong and loud in my ear. I dialed his office number. His phone began to ring as I fixed my eyes on the empty dishes and the unused utensils. *Ring. Ring. Ring.* All that ringing and no one to answer the call.

I was now too hungry to wait. I hung up the phone. At the stove, I scooped rice out of the pot, sprinkled stew over it, returned to the kitchen table with my plate. Outside, the sky had turned darker, a murky shade of purple and black swirls.

I had just filled my mouth with rice and was in the middle of chewing when I heard footsteps and a fussing at the door. I swallowed the food in my mouth and went to the door.

I turned on the veranda light to see more clearly in the darkness outside. Chibundu's face was the first thing that greeted me. In one hand he was carrying a folded baby-blue stroller, in the other his work briefcase.

Behind him was a van, its driver in the middle of taking out a number of baby's things: a dark-wood crib, a small natural-colored Moses basket, a stack of cloth diapers, a Fisher-Price swing, a box on which were images of baby bottles.

I opened the door wide for him to enter, which he then did, transferring the briefcase so that he was now holding the stroller and the case all in one hand. With his free hand he stroked me on the cheek.

"After this baby will be another and another and maybe even another. All of these will be a good investment, passed down from one child to the next."

"Another and another and maybe even another?"

He nodded, smiling brightly, and now he was off, going back and forth from the doorway into the parlor, now he and the delivery-man, as they carried in the rest of the items.

When they were done with the unloading, and when Chibundu had paid the man and sent him off, the two of us sat alone in the parlor. Chibundu reached into the pocket of his trousers, took out an envelope, and handed it to me.

"This came in our post office box. It's for you."

On the envelope were two addresses, one of them ours, the other a return address. No name appeared above the return address, and I did not take the time to read what exactly the address was. I knew that something about the writing looked familiar, and that was enough for me to get my hopes up. How many times had I sat across from Ndidi at her table, watching her write notes on her students' essays? I should have known that the letter was not from her, but for that moment my mind somehow made itself up that it was indeed from her. My heart began to race, and I tore into the envelope like a wildcat clawing hungrily into a package of hard-earned meat, baring its teeth, getting ready to devour. Only when I had ripped apart the envelope and was at the point of folding open the card inside did my mind begin to place the handwriting. Inside the card, I read a confirmation, a brief message:

> We heard the wonderful news. Congratulations to you and Chibundu on the pregnancy! We are so happy for you and looking very much forward to soon meeting your precious bundle of joy!

At the bottom of the note, the grammar school teacher and his wife signed their names, bold curvy letters that screamed of excitement, letters that looked like the sound of "Joy to the World" or "Jingle Bells."

Until that day, I had never been so disappointed to see a pair of names on a greeting card. Beyond the disappointment, I felt anger at Ndidi, a full and overwhelming kind of anger like wasted energy, and I was out of breath with it, because what was I, chicken feed? What was I, the kind of thing you threw out after you were done using it? Toilet paper, an old toothbrush, shards of broken glass? Suddenly I was remembering how discarded the whole situation with Amina had left me feeling. It felt like the cruelest kind of déjà vu. Like the beginnings of a condemnation to a lifetime of the same kind of role.

That night, after Chibundu had fallen asleep, I took out my chest from the bottom drawer of the bedside table. I unfolded a sheet of paper and wrote to Ndidi:

> I banish all thoughts of you. I banish you. I banish you. I banish you.

I folded the paper back into fourths and eighths, and put it safely into the back of the bedside drawer.

62

I HAD CUT UP the peppers, the tomatoes, and the onions, and had finished grinding them for the stew, when the pain began. It had started the night before, that first pang disappearing quickly, and each time it returned, it was hardly a pain at all. But there it was again, excruciating, and I knocked over the mixture of peppers and onions and tomatoes, pinkish-red sauce scattering across the kitchen floor.

I calmed myself. Surely I had some time. No need to panic.

Chibundu was at work. I went to the phone, dialed his work number.

His voice came over the line. "Hello?"

"Chibundu," I said, "I think the baby's coming. *Obiawana.* She's coming. You have to come."

For a moment I heard several voices on the line. I could not make out what was being said, and whether it was to me.

"Chibundu! Are you there? Are you hearing me? I said the baby is coming!"

"Yes, yes!" he shouted excitedly. "I hear you. *Obiawana.* Baby's coming. I was just letting my coworkers know. How much time do we have? I'm on my way right now. I can be there before you know it."

"Maybe I should catch a taxi and you can meet me at the hospital," I said, thinking aloud.

"No, no," he said. "*Mba.* I'm coming right now. I'll be there right away. I'll catch a taxi and head there right now and we can take that same taxi together to the hospital." The line went dead.

I replaced the receiver and stood there, not sure what to do with myself as I waited for him. It occurred to me to go grab my hospital bag, to have it waiting at the front door for the moment Chibundu arrived. I took some steps in the direction of the bedroom, but then the pain came again.

I squatted, grabbing on to the table, bracing myself that way and waiting for the pain to subside. But the pain only grew worse.

I stayed there on the kitchen floor for what felt like hours, screaming, clenching and unclenching my fists, struggling to catch my breath.

I crawled toward the phone, reached for it, not sure who exactly I'd be calling and why, because surely Chibundu was already on his way. Even if I phoned his office again, he would not be there to take the call.

Soon, it seemed the world was closing up around me. Everything turned to black.

I looked up to see Chibundu entering the kitchen, his footsteps loud and drum-like on the tile floor. Just that one brief moment of lucidity and then things returned to black. Eventually I opened my eyes once more to find that I was lying on a hospital bed. More screaming, more clenching and unclenching of my fists. Pushing and more pushing, and feeling myself empty out, like the way a river empties into the sea.

63

THE FESTIVE ATMOSPHERE lasted the whole first week and into the second: the gathering of the neighbors, the gulping down of bottles of soft drinks—crates of them—and of gourds and jerry cans of palm wine. There was all the usual gift-giving, the well-wishing from family and friends. Mama and Chibundu's mother had come and had been waiting for me at the flat when I arrived from the hospital, all of them eager to welcome baby Chidinma home.

The first sign of trouble was when Chibundu refused to purchase a goat. Without the goat there would be no butchering, no digging of the hole, no letting of its blood into the earth. The roasting of the goat would have been the hallmark of the celebration, seasoning it with peppers and onions, and serving it for all to enjoy.

But Chibundu refused. Instead, he walked around moping, barely greeting the visitors.

Mama could not help but notice. She had taken the child and had been carrying her around the flat when she crossed paths with Chibundu. She returned to me immediately. "Whatever is the matter between you two," she said in a low voice, "you must find a way to work it out. Do you hear me?"

I was in Chidinma's bedroom—the nursery—sitting on a recliner. I took the baby from her. "I hear you," I said. "The only thing is that I actually don't know what the matter is."

"What do you mean you don't know?"

"I mean I don't know," I replied.

I began to rock the baby in my arms.

"He is your husband," she said. "Something is wrong, and you are telling me you don't know what it is?"

I examined my baby, no longer listening to Mama's questioning. Here was my child, my flesh and my blood. Tiny hands and feet. Nails as thin as paper. Eyes hardly more than slits. Her skin was smooth and soft, and her scent was sweet and pure, a little like the aroma of fresh coconut oil.

My breasts were swollen, and there was a rush of pain in them as her mouth latched on to me. But I also felt a mixture of gratitude and delight. I held her tight against my body. Despite the pain, she was cause for celebration. A beautiful baby girl, healthy, no harelip, no curse. Here she was, a little human being whom I would love the way I saw fit—love overflowing, love unrestricted. Chigoziem was the name that Chibundu had picked out in the event that she had been a boy. Chigoziem, because he would have been our little blessing, and through that name we would have been, in turn, asking God to bless him.

But she had wound up a girl, which was just as well to me. Chidinma was the name I chose for her. Chibundu had allowed me to choose the girl name, his only stipulation being that it somehow reflect his own. Chidinma was the name I decided on, for "God is good," because she was no curse of a child, no harelip. Through her, this perfect representation of me and of Chibundu, God had indeed been good.

64

I HAD NO SHORTAGE of help. Chibundu's mother stayed a week and did her best to help out around the house. Mama outdid her and stayed nearly two months, longer than I would ever have asked of her. She might have stayed even longer had I not encouraged her to go. Her shop was, after all, waiting. Two months was too long to keep it shut. Finally she conceded.

But I had been more than grateful for her stay, especially in those early days when I could not get Chidinma to latch on, and when there was all that pain.

Those days, she had brought a stool for me. "Here. Put your leg on this, it will bring the baby closer to your breast and make it easier for both of you."

It worked.

When the lumps came, Mama said, "It's nothing to worry about. Just a little lumping from congealed milk. A plugged duct. It will go away in a couple of days."

She saw to it that I fed Chidinma more consistently — at least every two hours — so that the duct would drain. She reminded me to switch positions so that there was not too much pressure on any one side.

She brought me a hot washcloth every few hours, especially at night, told me to lay it on my chest, as the heat from it would help to dissolve the clog. She saw to it that I drank lots of fluids, water especially. She made sure that I slept on my back or side so that I did not put extra weight on my breasts. Sometimes at night, those nights when I fell asleep in the nursery, in the double bed there that I sometimes shared with Mama, I woke up to her hovering over me, saying, "Ijeoma, you're lying too far into your front again. Turn around so that you're completely on your back."

65

I T WAS ALL Chidinma those days after Mama packed her bags and left. In the afternoon when, before giving birth to her, I'd usually be sitting in church, I instead tied Chidinma to my back with a wrapper and carried her on long walks, back and forth, with no real destination in mind.

Once, I waited until the evening to see if Chibundu wanted to come along. He was sitting in the parlor chewing on a garden egg. The question had hardly left my mouth when he looked sharply at me, his face twisted in a scowl. He responded that his work had rendered him useless for everyday life, that it wore him out so much that, he was sorry to say, he'd probably never have the energy to come along. Not in the evenings after he returned from work, and not in general, because didn't I see? Didn't I see that even on the weekends they were now sometimes calling him in? And those weekends when they did not, he preferred to rest, he said.

I had in fact noticed that he was starting to go in to work on some Saturdays.

I nodded, not saying a word, but it was clear that something had gotten into him. The way he was snapping more often than ever. As if all the world, and especially me and Chidinma, had become like thorns on his skin.

66

W E BECAME AS inseparable as moisture and air, Chidinma and I. Sometimes she hung in my arms, mindlessly suspended like fog. And sometimes she fell, but I was there to lift her back up. The months flew by. One month gone, and then the next, and still the next.

December arrived, and Mama was back again. All over Port Harcourt, the usual end-of-year festivities had begun. Masquerades —colorful ojuju dancers dancing to the beat of their metal ogene bells. Ojuju dancers dancing to the beat of clay udu drums, soft bass sounds forming the music that guided their steps. Ojujus in glittering gowns, shaking their ichaka gourds, causing the bead coverings to rattle. Frightening ojujus dressed in grass and raffia skirts dancing to the beat of some ekwe and igba drums. Ojujus with lion heads and covered in lion hides.

It was the season when the ojujus paraded on the roads, dancing and collecting money and sweets. The time of year when the children ran toward the ojujus, then ran away from them with fright, back and forth, back and forth, because between their bouts of fear was a heightened state of enjoyment. The ojuju dancers blocked the roadways so that even automobile drivers had to stop their cars and pay their passage in order to be allowed to go.

Neither Chibundu nor I had been particularly interested in celebrating Christmas, and Chidinma was too little yet to care. But by the end of her first day back, Mama was concocting ways to celebrate.

"We've not had a real Christmas since the year before the war came. I just imagined that maybe, with Chidinma here, we could get back to the way things used to be. How about a trip to Kingsway?"

"I don't know if it's a good idea," I said to Mama. We were in the parlor. Mama was looking at me with such excitement and anticipation. Chidinma was napping in my arms.

"You don't know if it's a good idea?" Mama asked.

She too had been a new mother, but it seemed that she had forgotten how hard it could be to go traipsing around with a small baby, how inconvenient it was to have to nurse outside of home.

Mama sighed, then painted the reminder: "Don't you remember the way Christmas festivities used to be, those days when your father would take us on those trips to Port Harcourt? I remember it like it was yesterday," she said, "the way we headed straight to Kingsway, and your little face full of excitement as you rode the toy train that ran through the entire shopping center, which dropped off all the children at Father Christmas's little alcove of a hut? Do you remember the gifts you got from Father Christmas?"

I remembered. One year, he had given me a set of plastic plates that could be used as Frisbees. I used them to play with my primary school classmates during recess and after school. Another year he had given me an oyibo doll, a baby with eyes so big and lashes so long that it had frightened me, and I had thrown it and ran. Father Christmas had then exchanged the doll for a children's tea set.

"I can just see it all over again, you and Father Christmas in that small, artificial hut of his, covered with small chunks of artificial snow. And your papa, the way he always crouched down to smile at you as you sat on Father Christmas's lap." Mama sighed a lengthy sigh.

Nothing could have made me feel worse than to hear her sigh this way. There was something incandescent about it, a sigh that glowed with a sad kind of nostalgia.

"Okay," I said. "We can go."

Mama smiled brightly and stood up to embrace me.

• • •

That December would become one of my most vivid Christmases of all time.

Mama led us all, Chibundu included, to Kingsway. She had insisted that he accompany us, because this would, after all, become a new family tradition, which he and I and Chidinma would spend years reminiscing about, just like she and I had just done.

At Kingsway, I rode on the little train, carrying a wide-eyed Chidinma on my lap. Mama and Chibundu waved at us as the train rode, very slowly, past them. Chidinma giggled and smiled back. The driver of the train, a young man with a chubby face, came around to help me out after the ride ended.

We did not stay at Kingsway very long, but for those couple of hours that we did, Chibundu beamed with what appeared to be happiness, reminding me of his former child self. We returned home with him carrying a full ghana-must-go. But instead of the bag's being filled with heavy produce — yam, cassava, maize, for instance — like those used in the markets, ours was filled with toys for Chidinma and gifts for us — dresses and shoes for me, shirts and trousers and ties for Chibundu — Christmas presents that Mama insisted on buying for us in order to ensure that we passed a good holiday.

For those hours at Kingsway, things were indeed looking up, but by nightfall, Chibundu was somehow back to his pouting self.

67

EVENING. I SAT in the parlor, cradling Chidinma in my arms, nursing her. She was then around seven or eight months old.

The windows in the parlor hung open, their curtains tied to the sides. The harmattan had arrived, and in the distance a dense swirl of dust hung like clouds descended upon the earth.

The room was cool, and the table fan atop the television sat, not oscillating, not rattling or buzzing the way it did on hotter afternoons.

The front door, like the windows, lay open. Outside, I could see Chibundu sharpening the blade of his machete with a stone. He always used the same stone — not really a stone, but a large piece of cement that had cracked and fallen off the side of the back steps. If you looked at it a certain way, it had a shape like the middle of a woman, from shoulders to hips — large breasts but a sunken belly. No matter how many times he ran his machete against it, the piece of cement seemed to hold its shape.

He moved on from sharpening the machete to trimming the hedges with it. He worked at the hedges with the fervor of a man killing a bush animal. I rose from the couch, moved closer to watch him work. The machete's blade glowed, even in the dim harmattan sun. The strokes of his arm sent green leaves and brown twigs flying all over the place. Every now and then a breeze blew, which caught the scent of chopped plants and carried it in through the open windows, seeming to deposit it right before my nostrils.

His thrashing made a loud sound. *Slash, slash, slash.* Quick, sharp, hacking strokes. Twigs and leaves falling dead in the yard. His machete rising and falling. He continued that way for some time.

The baby began to fuss. I stopped nursing her, stood up from the couch, and walked around the parlor, gently rocking her and patting her back to see if she was in need of burping.

A sound came, like the cracking of knuckles. Chibundu always cracked his knuckles after he was done with the hedges and the grass, but this sound was louder and more long lasting than his usual knuckle-cracking. After a while it went away.

The baby settled down. I made my way to the couch and took a seat, still keeping her in my arms.

I looked in the direction of the window. On the sill was a jerry can whose top half I had cut off to make a vase. Dried-up hibiscus flowers stuck out of it, some fallen red petals floating atop the water. Just outside the window, by the door, the movements of Chibundu's shadow.

The knuckle-cracking came again. But this time it was more like a knocking on the door: several slightly muffled thwacks at a time.

I rose to answer, but hardly had I taken a step when Chibundu opened the door and entered, the machete in his hand. It all happened so quickly and unexpectedly that I took a step back out of the surprise of his entry.

He walked toward where I stood near the sofa. The blade of the machete bumped one of the metal legs of the center table, making a scraping sound, a little like a shriek.

He was wearing a cotton singlet and a pair of old khaki trousers. Patches of sweat had formed across the singlet, dark areas of dampness all over. The fabric of his trousers appeared, in spots, a darker shade of beige. Behind him, the parlor door remained open.

He cocked his head a bit to the side. He lifted one eyebrow, a slight lift, looking at me the way he had begun to look at me those days, in a slightly astonished way. Finally he spoke. "Why didn't you open?"

"I didn't hear," I replied.

He cocked his head some more. "You didn't hear?"

"No," I replied. But of course I had heard the knuckle-cracking sounds. I had in fact heard, only I had not equated the sound to someone knocking. I said, "I'm sorry. I think I mistook your knocking for something else."

Mockingly, he said, "You think you mistook my knocking for something else." He repeated it, even more mockingly, very singsongy, "*You think you mistook my knocking for something else.*"

"I'm sorry," I said again.

"Now tell me, what am I to do with your sorry? Can I make soup with it? Can I pay bills with it? What exactly is your sorry good for?"

He turned in the direction of the kitchen. "I left my jug of drinking water in there. I needed you to bring it out to me. You didn't hear, so you couldn't bring it to me. You tell me you're sorry. It doesn't take a rocket scientist to see how useless your sorry is to me now."

He shifted his weight on his legs. He tapped the machete lightly on the tile floor, transferred it from one hand to the other, shifting his weight once more and just looking at me.

Chidinma was making babbling sounds. His gaze moved down to her.

"Speaking of the child, we should really try again," he said.

"We really should try *what* again?"

"Is she awake?" he asked.

"Something between asleep and awake," I said.

He nodded.

"We should try for a son."

I let out a sigh. It came out a little like a gasp.

"If the man who goes to the farm and comes back with no cassava is a true farmer, he will return to the farm, will put in the work necessary, so that one day he can return from the farm with cassava in his basket." He paused. "We will try again for a son, put in the work necessary to bear ourselves a son. I will have a son. I deserve that much from you."

I collected myself. I said, "Chibundu, I'm not really up to having another child, certainly not so soon. And besides, she's just as good as a son."

"Ha!" he cried out, very indignantly. "Is she really? Are you forgetting that girls cannot pass on the family name? If for no other reason at all, you will give me a son to pass on my family name."

"Chibundu, since when did you begin to care about all that nonsense?" I asked. "She's your child. Your flesh and blood. Your daughter."

"Yes," he said. "But she is no son. I want my son. I see the way you look at her, and the way she looks at you. She is all yours. I want my own. And maybe when he grows, and when you are too busy to answer my calls, he can be the one to bring me my jug of water. You'll have your girl, and I'll have my boy."

"Chibundu, I'm not —"

"What are you not? What exactly are you not?" He moved closer, so close that I could feel his breath on my face and the blade of his machete on my leg. "You owe me that much," he said in a steady whisper. "Do you hear me? You owe me that much."

Sometimes these days it seems to me that what happened next was no accident on Chibundu's part. But then there are other times when I tell myself that it was indeed an accident, that Chibundu could not possibly have known, which would explain the bewildered look on his face when he became aware of it. But the truth is that a man who sets out to destroy can still be bewildered, especially when he is forced to look his indiscretion in the eye.

In any case, he was by now hovering above me, so that his machete all of a sudden was pushing heavily on the skin of my leg. I tried to move away, but he would not allow it. He moved closer, pushing the big knife farther into my leg.

"Chibundu!" I shouted. "Any more and you'll tear open my skin!"

His eyes widened, and he gazed at me with a bewildered look on his face. Finally he took a few steps back, still staring, still bewildered. A long silent moment passed between us, after which he turned around, machete in hand, and walked out of the parlor door.

That night, after I had put Chidinma to sleep, I went into the bedroom and lay down to sleep. Chibundu was in the bathroom. I thought, How dare he have done what he did to me, to nearly tear open my skin with a machete? And who was to say he wouldn't one day do something like that — something harmful — to poor little helpless Chidinma? What was to stop him from doing it?

The bedroom ceiling light was still on.

First the sound of silence and then the sound of a turning knob. Chibundu appeared at the doorway wearing his pajama bottoms, drawstrings dangling down the front, like what should have been a temptation. He waited there by the door, just looking at me. I stared back.

"Are you just going to stand there?" I asked. "Aren't you going to come to bed?"

He continued to stand. I pulled the covers up to my chest and turned around so that I was no longer facing him. He flicked off the light switch by the door; the room went dark. I listened to the soft thump of his footsteps as he walked the short distance to the bed.

His body sank into the bed. More minutes passed.

I had begun to doze off when I felt the tap of his fingers on the back of my hand.

I knew what it must be. I pulled the blanket up to my chest, holding it tight, trying to ignore the tapping.

He tapped again. I finally turned to answer, repositioning myself so that I was now lying on my back, the blanket still high on my chest.

In the darkness, I watched as his murky, monster-like face came square above mine. His hands found their way to mine as he twisted the blanket out of my hold.

"The sooner we get to it, the sooner we'll be done," he said.

I stiffened.

His breath above me was chillingly warm as he settled himself on top of me. There was the rough movement of his hands and legs as the bottom of his pajamas came off. His hands returned to the space between our bodies, holding me in place as he lowered himself, and as he writhed himself into me.

68

THERE WERE TWO ways I always imagined telling him that I could no longer go on trying for a boy, that I could no longer even go on being married to him. At some point during the confession, I would also tell him that all the time I had been married to him, how could he not have seen, just how could he possibly not have seen, that I had been the whole while in love with somebody else?

Two ways. The first:

I'd be in the kitchen making supper, stirring Maggi seasoning or crushed tatashi into a pot of soup. I'd listen to the opening of the front door as Chibundu entered from work.

I'd move to set the dishes on the table. Near me, on the floor, Chidinma happily swinging in her Fisher-Price swing.

Chibundu would make a detour to the bathroom, followed by a detour to the bedroom. After that he would arrive at the table, looking tired and disheveled, the way he had begun to look, his shirt unbuttoned from top to bottom, his feet bare under his trousers.

Between us, our now-usual silence as he took his seat at the table, as I served him his okra soup and garri with contrived mindlessness, as if today were just another ordinary day.

I'd eat, and I'd watch as he ate, and I'd watch as he peered intermittently at me. We'd stay like that for a while, and then I'd vomit it all out on him, the way a drunk vomits up undigested food, the way he hurls out sprays of stomach acid, sloppy matter haphazardly jetting forth out of me.

What could he do? Perhaps he'd sit there and listen. Or maybe, even before I was finished, he'd rise angrily, thrusting the items on the table — his food, the hollow wooden centerpiece that sat in the middle of the table, the drinking glasses, all the silverware — to the ground. Maybe he'd walk up to me and slap me again and again, until he was feeling spent and purged and relieved. Until I was feeling spent and purged and relieved.

The second way I imagined it was this:

I'd wait until bedtime, until he was lying asleep next to me, soft breaths whistling through his nostrils like a distorted lullaby.

I imagined that I'd tap him, tap him until I startled him awake. Then I'd tell it to him. There'd be silence for some time while he registered the words. And then the shouting, the sound of his voice billowing out in the room, appearing to fill up even the tiniest cracks and crevices, and then seeping out slowly through the slightly open windows, scattering into pieces in the wind, fading and fading and diffusing until incomprehensible to the ear.

But perhaps there'd be no shouting. Just the singing of the crickets and the stillness of the night.

Perhaps he'd only turn back to sleep, and it'd be as if I'd not confessed a thing.

69

I WAS AT THE kitchen counter shucking corn, green and yellow leaves falling to the sink, yellow threads of corn silk everywhere. Near me, on the floor, Chidinma gabbling to herself in her swing. A large polythene bag lay open on the counter into which I should have been putting the corn leaves, but I was missing and making a mess all around. Next to the bag, a damp cloth with which I would eventually wipe away the mess.

The sun was already setting. The last I'd seen of Chibundu, he'd been sitting in the parlor, reading a newspaper and snacking on a bowl of boiled groundnuts. This was shortly after he'd returned from work, and even more shortly after we'd had our supper of rice and stew.

I wiped my hands with the cloth. I rose and walked to the parlor, where I'd last seen him, but he was not there. On the center table, next to his bowl of hollowed-out groundnut shells, lay a rag doll of Chidinma's, its legs dangling over the table's edge.

The curtains on the parlor windows were still open. The sky outside was dark.

I drew the curtains closed. I had been looking for him for no particular reason, but now I recognized that there was in fact a reason: I was ready, had now reached the point of readiness. Today was the day I would lay it all out on him.

I turned from the parlor and walked down the corridor to the bathroom. Perhaps he was there.

By the bathroom door, I leaned against the wall, waiting for him to come out. At the far end of the hallway, above the doorway of our bedroom, hung a white clock. It was eight o'clock in the evening.

Chidinma, in the kitchen, had been making loud, playful baby sounds which had been traveling throughout the flat. Now her sounds seemed to grow even louder, a definite fussing, no longer just play.

I returned to her in the kitchen, soothed her. "Hush, baby. Hush, little girl. What's the matter? Can't you try and settle down for me? Can't you see Mommy has something important to do?"

I carried her in her swing out to the parlor, where her rag doll still lay on the center table. I picked up the doll and handed it to Chidinma.

"Hush, baby," I said again in a whisper. "Be good for Mommy, you hear?"

I returned to the bathroom, took my position near the door. I had not stood there long before I noticed a sound coming out of the bedroom. I approached and saw Chibundu's shadow, like a bust on the wall, growing larger and darker the closer I got.

Chibundu sitting on my side of the bed, my wooden chest on his lap. Several letters unfolded and scattered on the bed around him. One of the letters hung from his hands. My pile of pens and pencils lay on the bed near where he sat.

I did not move past where I stood, just a few steps beyond the bedroom doorway. He looked up at me, rose from the bed. My wooden chest went crashing to the floor.

"I'm sorry," I said, taking a few steps back into the hallway and then coming to a stop.

He had been walking in my direction with the letter, but now he stopped too, staring at me with a rabid look. If his eyes were nails and he the hammer, he would have pinned me down in one fell swoop.

"I'm sorry," I said again, because I truly was sorry for what he had read.

He looked down at the letter in his hand. He read:

He is my husband, yes, but you are the one I love.

He looked back up at me.

I chuckled nervously. "I'm sorry," I said once more.

"You're sorry for what? What exactly are you sorry about? Tell me, I want to know."

My hands hung limply at my sides. I brought them to my hips as if to collect myself that way. There I stood, arms akimbo, struggling to find the words to speak.

He walked up to me, placed his hands on my cheeks. He was still holding the letter; the paper made a crumpling sound against my face. "It's just a silly letter, not so?" he said. His hands on my cheeks were tight, painful. His voice was steady and calm. "You'll tell me now that it's just a stupid letter. That nothing ever happened between you and this Ndidi." His voice broke.

I nodded, attempting to loosen my face from his grasp.

"Who is she anyway?" he asked.

In all the time that we had been in Aba, they had not formally met. Every once in a while there was a close encounter, he leaving the store just as she was entering, or vice versa—a cursory greeting here, a cursory greeting there—but never a formal meeting. And since she had been so standoffish, so withdrawn, and so sequestered at our wedding, they were as good as strangers.

"Who is she?" he asked again, my face still tight between his hands, his palms pressing into my face as if to bore a hole into my cheeks.

"She's just a woman," I said. "Just an old friend."

He chuckled wickedly. There was something fiendish about the look on his face. "Just an old friend?"

He let go of my face. He picked up another one of my letters and began to read a section from it:

. . . I can't wait for my baby to be here. I love the precious little thing already and can't wait to hold him or her in my arms. Poor Chibundu. I do care for him. But not a moment passes when I don't wish you were the one here with me, the one with whom I would raise my child.

He riffled through the letters, picked another, and read:

> *. . . Last night I dreamed of you. You were merging into me and I was merging into you. There were no clothes between us, nothing but our flesh and our warmth. And my lips reaching longingly for yours . . .*

The heat rose in my face. I felt naked, like my heart had been yanked out and kept out as public display.

I held my breath as he read the next one:

> *. . . My baby is here, Ndidi. She's here. My beautiful baby girl. It's hard to believe that I'm now a mother. It's so true what they say: there's been no better feeling than seeing her, than holding her in my arms. I love her so much that sometimes I am weak with love. I look into her little face and my stomach flutters. My only regret is that you were not here to welcome her into the world with me . . .*

And another:

> *. . . the only thing I want now is to make love —*

I cut in before he could read any more. "All that is foolishness," I said, chuckling nervously. "Just silly ramblings."

"Foolishness? Silly ramblings?"

"Yes, very ridiculous of me to have written them," I said. "That's why I never bothered to send them out. It's all foolishness, really."

"Well, then, you might as well stop hiding them in that box. You might as well just throw them out."

"Yes, you're right," I said. "I will throw them out, yes. That's exactly what I will do."

I squirmed free of his grasp, took the paper from him. I would have folded it back up, stuck it back in the chest with the rest of them, but his eyes were steady on me, and somehow I felt I owed that much to him. I looked one last time at the letter, then turned so that my eyes met his. I ripped the letter into shreds, one tiny little piece at a time.

We continued to stand there. Finally he turned away from me, walked over to the bedroom wardrobe. His work briefcase sat in front of the wardrobe. He picked up the briefcase, placed it on the bed, popped open its snaps. He lifted out some piles of paper, a stack of folders. Underneath was a wad of about a dozen envelopes, held together with a tan rubber band.

He extended the stack of envelopes to me.

"You might as well have these now," he said. "They're yours."

I struggled to understand what was happening. Chibundu tried to explain himself: "I thought maybe if I kept them away from you . . . I hadn't realized that you . . . that you reciprocated her feelings. I was so sure that you didn't . . . and if I kept these from you . . . there would have been no sense in giving them to you . . ." His voice faded away, as if utterly confused, or as if he were unconvinced of his own rationale.

I snatched the envelopes from him.

I looked down at the top envelope, about to open it, when I saw that its side had already been opened, neatly, carefully, as if to carry out the pretense that it had not been opened at all. All the rest of the envelopes were the same way.

In the moment that followed, I recognized the handwriting and cried out in surprise, and in anger. My hands shook as I held the letters.

"Chibundu, where did these come from? How long have you been keeping these? Why didn't you give them to me?"

Surely they must have started to arrive *after* the first two or three months that we moved to Port Harcourt, because those first few months I had been vigilant about checking the mailbox. No way would Chibundu have intercepted those letters before I got to them, so vigilant was I. But then months had gone by, and not a thing from Ndidi, and eventually I had resigned myself to checking the box only once in a while — once or twice every couple of weeks. Somehow the timing must have worked in Chibundu's favor, so that he managed to get to the box before me on the days when Ndidi's letters came in. But for every single one of her letters?

I said, "Chibundu, how is it that you got ahold of all these letters before I did?"

His jaw tightened as if he was not going to explain, but he explained anyway. "The first one I stumbled on by accident. I opened it just by accident. But after I read it . . . I began going to the post office every afternoon during my lunch break, early enough to get to them before I knew you would. Each time I saw an envelope with her writing, and with her return address, I took it. The rest of the mail I left in the box for later, either for you to get or for me to pick up on my way home from work."

I was aghast. "That's a breach of confidence and trust!"

"I didn't mean to . . . I was afraid . . . I couldn't risk . . ." His voice broke. He gathered himself, then he said, "Ijeoma! You're the one who has broken my confidence and trust! You stand there and you lie to me and tell me you never sent a letter to her? Never? Not once?"

Immediately I recognized that he had caught me in my own lie. He grabbed the letters from my hand, riffled through the envelopes. He must have memorized them, which ones were which, because it took him only a couple of minutes to land on the two letters that he was looking for. He read:

My darling Ijeoma, just as I thought I might never hear from you again, I received your letter in the mail. Not a day goes by that I don't think of you . . .

"And what about this other one?" he asked.

My dear Ijeoma, I received your second letter in the mail today. What was I ever thinking to encourage you to marry? Yesterday, I ran into your mother and she couldn't stop gushing over the fact that you are pregnant. I've never felt such anger at the thought of anything as the thought of Chibundu having his way with you . . .

He stopped there, and he said, "So, you see, I'm the one who should be asking the questions here. You lied to me and said you never sent a letter to her. But you know, Ijeoma, if I'm to be honest too, then I should admit that I actually knew you had written to her, only somehow I really hoped that you had just written back to tell her to stop, because what business did you have writing to reciprocate her feelings? You're a married woman, Ijeoma! Do you hear me? You're a married woman, for God's sake!"

I wanted to scream at him at this point, and remind him that I had tried to tell him, that day long ago in church. Had he forgotten? I felt the urge to explain that I had not in fact tried to keep it from him, not really. Yes, I had hidden it, but also I had not hidden it.

He went on. "Imagine my surprise to find all those stashed-up letters in your drawer today. Imagine! Now I can see clearly that I was wrong in what I was hoping. So, what is it, Ijeoma? You really love her? How long has this thing between you and her been going on? How long were you both . . . before I married you? And how long after? How long?"

"Chibundu, I only wrote three letters," I said. This time I was speaking the truth. It was risky enough to send those three. After all that time of not receiving anything back from her, I could not have sent more. "Just three," I said. "I stopped myself from sending the rest."

By now Chibundu was frantic. He cried out, "You have finished me! You have finished me completely! How could you? How could you?"

Suddenly he regrouped himself, regained his composure. His voice took back its steadiness. He said, "You can do whatever you will with those letters. You can even continue to write to her. But don't you forget for one moment — not for one tiny moment — that you are *my* wife. You are *my* wife, for God's sake. I can do things to make your life miserable. Do you hear me? *You are my wife.* Whatever you do, don't provoke me, or I will see to it that you pay the price."

70

I LAY IN BED unable to get my limbs to move, my mind heavy with the realization of what I had become: the equivalent of a washrag, worn and limp, not from overuse, but rather from misuse and manhandling.

Chibundu was maneuvering himself about the room with an energy that seemed to say that everything was just the way it should be. Now he was pulling on his shirt and trousers, whistling as he did. Now he stood before the dresser mirror, humming the tune of a song I did not recognize, arranging the collar of his shirt, then tying his tie around his neck.

Chidinma was most likely wide awake in her room, playing with her toys and waiting for me to come and collect her. Instead, I continued to lie in bed.

The scent of his cologne was so strong in the room that it seemed as if someone were chopping wood and crushing the leaves and blowing the aroma out in the air with a fan.

He turned away from the dresser and began walking toward me. He took a seat on my side of the bed. There was a sallowness to his face, something a little like old age. I observed the way the crow's-feet seemed suddenly to have deepened around his eyes. I observed the way his hair seemed grayer than ever before.

He sat so that he was facing the windows, his eyes lowered to the floor. The silence between us was loud.

"I admit I was a little rough on you last night," he said. "We are husband and wife, and it shouldn't have to be that way."

"Chibundu—"

"I've been thinking, and my sense of it is that there's a way in which you can just tell yourself to love me instead of her. I shouldn't have to force myself on you night after night. I am your husband, and it shouldn't have to be that way."

"Chibundu, that's not how it works."

"How do you know if you don't try? You can just try. It shouldn't be that hard to love me. Or am I that unlovable?"

"Chibundu, it's not that—"

"Tell me, what exactly can she give you that you don't think I can?"

Silence.

"I don't hate you for it," he said. "I really don't. You know already that I don't believe all that nonsense about abominations. Maybe there's something special about that kind of love, about a man loving another man, or a woman loving another woman in that way. Maybe there's something appealing about it. But what makes me so angry is that I loved you first. Before there was her, there was me. And more than that, you made me a promise. Marriage is a promise, not just to marry, but also to love."

I took his hand, began stroking it gently.

He looked down at our hands together, followed my movements with his eyes. He said, very softly, "I am your husband and you are my wife, and I just know that we will make it work. I can feel it in my bones, in my lungs, in my heart. You'll see. We will make it work. None of that thing with Ndidi matters. We can still make it work."

No string of words could have been more devastating than those. The desperation from which they came.

There was a sudden sharpness to his voice. "The answer is simple. You haven't tried enough. If you put your mind to it, I know you can love me the way a woman is supposed to love her husband. You will try harder. And if all else fails, I really do want my son. You really must keep in mind that you are my wife. If all else fails, you will at least give me my boy."

● ● ●

The remainder of that morning, after he had left for work, and for all of that afternoon, I found myself caring for Chidinma with an aloofness that even she must have felt—watching her, but barely watching.

Evening arrived. I tied her with a wrapper to my back and went out to pick up some missing ingredients for the stew I should already have finished but was yet to make. Outside, along the road, birds were zigzagging across the sky, sparrows and orange-blue trogons stopping to perch on the trees and on the roadside. A small boy was throwing a ball to his friend. Several girls were skipping rope. A woman was calling out to a man on a motorcycle. Everyone looked like puff-puffs, fat and round and chock-full of all the energy that I felt myself drained of.

"Aunty, good evening," Anuli, the shop owner's daughter, greeted me when I entered the shop.

"Good evening, Anuli," I replied.

She was a girl of around sixteen or seventeen, a pretty face, and very bright: sharp-witted, sharp-mouthed, always a clever observation just waiting on the tip of her tongue. And her proverbs: as if she were a village elder reincarnated in the body of a girl, she was always ready to spew out something wise.

She appeared to study me with her eyes. "Ah, Aunty, you no dey look well o. You dey sick?"

I averted my eyes, not feeling in the mood for conversation. Mustering as much cheerfulness as I could, I asked, "Biko, you fit give me some fresh tomatoes and Maggi?"

The baby on my back was making small noises and squirming around.

Anuli went to the rear of the store and brought out a bowl of tomatoes. I looked through the bowl, picking some out for myself. She left me for a moment, and when she returned, she placed a box of Maggi seasoning cubes on the counter.

I reached into my purse and pulled out some bills.

As she collected the money, she said, "Aunty, whatever the matter, just remember that it is the same moon that wanes today that will be full tomorrow. And even the sun, however long it disappears, it always shines again."

I smiled slightly at her. She smiled back. Her smile was more than a little like consolation.

Back at home, I cooked the stew with Chidinma still tied to my back. Afterward, I retreated from the kitchen to the parlor and set Chidinma down. I moved the center table to the far end of the room, where she could not be injured by the table's sharp corners. I gathered a handful of her toys and put them on the parlor floor, on the area of rug on which the center table usually sat.

I stood for some time just watching her play with the toys. Then I took a seat on the sofa to give my back a rest. She gabbled delightedly as she hit the button of a toy book that immediately set music playing, and as she fussed with a set of plastic building blocks, I faded away into a series of incoherent thoughts. I must have fallen asleep to the sound of her gabbling and of her music book.

I woke up slowly to silence. Not a sound in the room. My eyes darted to the rug, to that space where the center table had sat, looking for Chidinma, but she was gone.

It was as dark inside the house as outside. I stayed a moment on the sofa while I called out to her.

"Chidinma!"

No answer.

I rose from the sofa and went straight to the light switch. How late was it now? Had Chibundu already arrived home and eaten and afterward put Chidinma to bed?

"Chibundu!"

No answer.

I turned in the direction of the kitchen. I saw her then, quietly sitting by the sewing machine in the corner.

The pincushion sat with the bobbins on the cloth plate, far

enough away from the needle bars. The cushion was in the shape of a garden egg. Yellow-gold skin with meandering stripes of green. Its stem, twig-like, stuck out of its top. Chidinma had somehow climbed her way up to the machine to be able to grasp it in her hands.

She was holding the garden egg now, very near to her mouth, pins and needles glistening silver in the bright gold and green fabric of the cushion. Threads dangling from it like beautiful ribbons, a little like serpents, tempting her with their devilish charm.

She was not at first aware that I was watching her. Then, for whatever reason, she looked up, and her gaze caught mine.

I watched as she stuck the garden egg, pins and all, into her mouth, the pincushion deforming her mouth, one whole corner buried away.

She looked wide-eyed at me, green and red and black threads dangling from her mouth. And for some unknown reason, I could not get my feet to move.

I stood where I was. "Chidinma," I whispered, and again, in a whisper, "Chidinma."

Suddenly Chibundu entered the parlor, and he walked up to us in our little corner. He looked at me, and he looked at her, and at the threads dangling out from her lips.

It's hard to say how much time passed, but I know that he shook his head (at me, or at her, or at all of us?), before going to her. He prodded and dug the cushion out of her mouth, with enough force that it either startled her or hurt her. She began to cry.

He picked her up and cuddled her as he replaced the garden egg on top of the machine.

I stood just staring idly, neither at her nor at Chibundu, but at the machine. It had been some time since I last used it. I now found myself engrossed in it. The spool of thread was sitting on the holder. Bobbins in cases, like medicine in capsules, surrounded the cloth plate. I thought of the handwheel. Just one. Not two. Not like a bicycle. If I were to have used it then and there, I imagined the way it would move: the needle, sharp in its movement. Needle up, needle down. Up and down, like a nod. Like an affirmation. Maybe yes, everything would be fine. Or maybe yes, one wheel was enough. No marriage of two. Just a single person would do.

Maybe yes, sometimes one was enough.

71

IJEOMA!" CHIBUNDU CALLED from the front yard.

I sat in the parlor, watching Chidinma play with her rag doll and sewing up a seam that had come undone on one of our sofa pillow covers. It was a Saturday afternoon, just after lunchtime, the time of day when the sun, traveling in and out of the puffed-up rainy-season clouds, should have caused light and dark reflections to dance about the walls. The time of day when the rainy-season rains should have been pelting our corrugated aluminum roof like music. It was the time of day when afternoon siesta should have been on everyone's mind, the thought of it as sweet as cake.

But all around the air was still, and not a drop of rain. For a while now — more than a handful of months — it seemed we had all grown too rigid for afternoon naps.

This particular afternoon, it was even as if the sky had grown too rigid to allow for rain. And yet no sun, either, in sight.

Chibundu had left long before siesta time. He had been gone all morning, in fact, and had not bothered to say where he was going, but now his voice came booming from outdoors.

"Ijeoma!"

I tied the last stitch to a stop, rose from the sofa, gathered Chidinma and her doll into my arms, walked out of the house to answer his call.

Outside, the air was thick.

A short distance away, farther into the gravel but before the gravel met the hibiscus bush, Chibundu stood in front of a deep blue 504. The sky was overcast, but the way the black tires and the car's body glistened, it was as if the sun had suddenly come out, just for a moment, to cause it to shine that way.

Chibundu opened up his arms wide, like a magician who had just demonstrated a trick. Or as if he were a character from one of those books that Amina used to read, *Ali Baba and the Forty Thieves* or something to that effect. Abracadabra, his arms seemed to say.

"What is this?" I asked.

"What do you mean, what is this? Do you not see that it's a car? I have gotten us a car. What do you think? Can you imagine, we now have our very own car! See the way I'm making sure to provide for you? See the way I'm doing my best to give you a comfortable life? No more walking if you don't want to! No more taking the bus or taxi! Now we have our very own car!"

I smiled.

"Now, there's one more thing," he said, and he went to the back of the car, opened the trunk with a key, and pulled out a red toy car, sharp-looking, a cross between a Jeep and a Land Rover. It was the kind of toy car that was big enough for a child to sit inside and drive: a car with a set of real-looking tires, a set of real-looking doors, and a real-looking windshield — all of those real-looking things, but made of plastic rather than from the materials of the real thing. There was a wide opening at the top, which was too wide to be accurately called a sunroof, and too enclosed for the car to be accurately described as a convertible.

Chibundu laid the car down in the yard and stood behind it, smiling an impishly wide smile.

"Here is what we *really* need!" he said. "A good-luck charm! Something to help bring the boy along."

I set Chidinma down so that she was standing by my side, her hand in mine. She was now almost a year old and was newly learning to walk — one wobbly step carefully placed before the other, like an old man without his cane.

It was not hard to imagine her in the toy car, in the driver's seat, driving alongside me as I walked to Anuli's father's shop, or around the neighborhood to another of the small shops.

The girl slipped her hand out of mine and went to the toy car, leaned against it, placed her hands on its red body. Chibundu was, at this point, back at the big car—the real car—not looking at me and Chidinma, but rather wiping something—road dust, perhaps—off the driver's side door.

I allowed Chidinma to remain with the toy car, and I set off toward the veranda, intending to sit on the front stoop and watch her play. When Chibundu was done, he could instruct her on how to ride the toy car. It would be a nice bonding moment between the two of them.

I had taken only a few steps when I heard Chibundu's voice, loud and scolding: "*Oya,* Ijeoma, come carry your daughter away from here! If she thinks this car is hers to play with, she better think again. Ijeoma, do you hear me? You better come carry her before she gets any nonsense ideas in her head."

I turned around to find Chibundu pulling Chidinma away from the car, shaking his head at her, reprimanding.

"For your brother, not for you," he was saying. "Even from the land of the unborn, he will see how much we want him to come, he will see how much I am preparing for him, and he will come."

I hurried to Chidinma and lifted her into my arms.

Chibundu looked up at me. "Our son will come. Our son will surely come." And he smiled widely again.

He wrapped his arms around me as we lay in bed that night, and just as I thought he had fallen into sleep, he pulled me to him. I closed my eyes tight and pretended to be asleep. I parted my lips and allowed a small sound like a snore to come out of my mouth. Every once in a while I made the sound appear to catch, so that it gave the impression of a deep kind of snoring, of someone who was well into sleep.

Eventually I felt the pressure of his hands on me subside, and a little later, I listened to the tranquil sound of his own snoring.

72

W<small>E WERE IN</small> bed again. The lights in the room were out. Moments earlier he had lain down beside me. Now he spoke. "You think I don't know that you're awake?"

I ignored him, continued to pretend to be asleep.

He pulled on my hair.

"Chibundu, please," I shouted.

"'Chibundu, please' what?"

"I'm trying to sleep. Please just let me sleep."

"You'll sleep when you're done."

I shifted farther away from him, very close to the edge of the bed. A moment later, I felt his weight lift from the bed. I listened to his footsteps. I heard the flick of the switch. Light flooded the room.

I remained where I lay, very still on the bed, listening to a rustling sound that could only have been coming from him. Soon he was stamping his feet and coming around the bed, and I opened my eyes to find him standing before me, his wallet and some naira bills in his hand.

"*Ngwa,* tell me, how much do you want? How much does it cost to get you to do it tonight?"

"Chibundu!" I exclaimed.

"Tell me, if it's not enough that I'm your husband, maybe I can pay you to do it. Tell me, how much should I pay?"

"Chibundu, stop. I'm not a whore."

He laughed loudly. "You're not a whore! Are you sure about that? You're not a whore? So why is it that I have to fight to sleep with you? You must be a whore. You must be giving it to someone else, which is why you have nothing left for me."

I ignored him.

He moved forward. I felt his presence heavy over me. He threw the money in my face. The bills scattered around me, on the bed and on the floor.

He dug back into his wallet. This time he filled his hands with kobo coins. He tossed them in my face. The coins fell, making sounds like tiny bells as they hit the floor.

He stood there looking intently at me, waiting for me to react. I only continued to sit where I was, only continued to look intently back at him. I must have felt so tethered to him, so tethered to my life with him, to the superficial normalcy of it. That tethering way in which what is familiar manages to grab ahold of us and pin us down. Marriage to him was what I now knew as normal and familiar, so that even with this terrible treatment of me—calling me a whore, throwing money in my face, and the rest—the thought never once occurred to me that these were grounds on which I could now pack up my bags and leave.

Finally he turned away. The lights went back off. A little later, I felt his weight back on the bed.

73

I BEGAN TO SPEAK to Chidinma absent-mindedly those days.

"Your father wants for you a brother," I'd say, rubbing my belly. "Chigoziem will be his name."

I spoke in a monotone those days, because by then I had begun to grow numb. As much as I didn't want it to happen, it was happening. Often my only thought was of how much longer I could carry on that way. How much longer could I continue to exist in this marriage with Chibundu? I was convinced that I would only grow deader were I to stay in it. I would only grow more numb. And who would take care of Chidinma if things went that way? Who would take care of her if I became like the living dead?

Chidinma sat in the tub and watched my hands ride up and down my belly. She just watched, quietly peering at me, her small hands tightly gripping the side of the tub.

Those days there had begun to be a frightened look on her face—the look of a child who was afraid that she'd soon be let go, that she'd soon be discarded by the people who should have loved her most. Or maybe I only imagined it so. To me, it was the look of a child who somehow knew that she had been placed in the care of a mother as lukewarm as the water in which she sat.

I lathered the washcloth, soaked it in the tub of water. I squeezed it just above Chidinma's head so that the water trickled down like raindrops.

"Chigoziem," I said. Her eyes plunged down to my belly. She pressed her little lips together, and appeared to frown at me.

"Who is in there?" I asked.

"Chi-do-dem," she murmured.

I leaned over, kissed her head, kissed the small brown curls of hair on it.

74

OUTSIDE, THROUGH THE open front door and windows, a dog was barking somewhere down the road. Between the barking, the sounds of children laughing, talking, shouting. Day was turning to dusk.

We were experiencing a power outage — NEPA was becoming less and less reliable these days. I had (as was becoming my habit) moved the center table to the side in order to allow Chidinma to play on the carpet. On the table was a candle set atop a tin can, its flame flickering, dimly lighting the room. We had already eaten supper, and Chibundu was out with some of his work friends. He was going out with them more and more, arriving home just in time to crawl into bed.

Chidinma rose from the carpet. She had been sitting for all of half an hour, tugging not at her rag doll but at another one of her dolls: a little unclothed plastic one. She tugged, pulling its plastic arms and legs out of their sockets so all that remained were the torso, the head, and a thick wad of stringy artificial hair.

She stood, holding the doll by its hair, and settled herself squarely on her own two feet. She began wobbling toward me, trembling like the candle's flame, the doll's hair swaying from side to side in her hand.

When she reached me, she let go of the doll, allowing it to fall to the floor. Her hands reached up, her mouth formed the word "Mama," and I knew that she wanted me to hold her. This was the way she begged me to pick her up. I slid down from the sofa onto the parlor floor, lifted her, and set her down on my lap.

The song came to me:

> *Nkita Chikwendu*
> *Tagburu Chikwendu*
> *Ebe ha na'azo anu.*
> *Ha hapu Chikwendu*
> *Kwoba nkita oria.*
> *O di kwa mu wonder.*

The story came next. I thought of all the details of it, the way Papa used to tell it to me:

Once upon a time there was a little boy named Chikwendu, a homeless orphan who managed to find himself a beautiful little dog as a companion. The dog was always by his side. They played together all through the day, and at night Chikwendu could be seen sharing his sleeping mat with his dog.

One day a tall, dark, and handsome stranger from a faraway village was traveling through Chikwendu's village, carrying a basket of roasted meat on his head. All day, Chikwendu had not eaten, and now he sat on the side of the road, begging passersby for something to eat.

From across the road, the stranger caught sight of Chikwendu in his threadbare pants and no shirt, all skin and bones. Immediately he thought, How hungry this boy must be. He took pity on Chikwendu and crossed the road to where Chikwendu and his dog sat. There, he lowered his basket from his head and pulled out a piece of roasted meat from within, which Chikwendu accepted with delight. It was a small piece of meat, but the boy was grateful all the same. He rose to his feet and thanked the stranger with all the energy he could muster.

As the stranger walked off, Chikwendu sat back on the ground and began eating the meat. His dog by his side was at that moment growling softly, a light, barely perceptible rumbling of a sound.

It was not that Chikwendu did not want to share. He had always made it a point to share all his food with his dog. But this time, the piece of meat was so small that Chikwendu could not even begin to imagine how to set about cutting off a bit of it for the dog. Chikwendu simply allowed himself to eat the meat. The next food he got, he promised himself that he would give to the dog.

But the dog could not possibly have read his mind. And so, just as Chikwendu was putting the last morsel into his mouth, the dog attacked. So began the struggle. A gash here, another gash there. Barking and loud growling, teeth sinking into flesh. Tumbling and rolling of bodies along the side of the dirt road. Sometimes it was Chikwendu who wound up on top, and sometimes it was the dog who got the upper hand. Chikwendu screamed and screamed, and the dog barked and barked, and the villagers heard the noise. By the end of it all, a crowd had gathered, and they stood around watching as Chikwendu and his dog lay still on the ground, unmoving, from injury and from exhaustion, their bodies covered in blood. The tiniest piece of uneaten roasted meat lay on the ground, still giving off its strong scent.

Perhaps it was the whiff of the meat that had had an effect on the villagers, the same way that it had had an effect on the dog. Perhaps the smell had somehow driven the villagers crazy too, because they now stepped in, but instead of tending to the boy, they got on their knees and took turns tending to the dog. Instead of tending to Chikwendu's wounds, or at least to both the boy's wounds and his dog's, they all gathered around the dog, and it was on the dog's wounds that they rubbed their ointments and wrapped their plasters. They carried on tending to the dog, leaving Chikwendu there on the road to die.

Chidinma could not yet have understood, but as soon as I was done with the story, she looked up at me with an expression of fear on her face. She sat that way, her face upturned and gazing fearfully at me.

I finished by singing the song again, the way Papa used to finish the story off for me:

Chikwendu's dog bit him
While they were fighting
Over a piece of meat.
The people left Chikwendu
But treated the sick dog.
It really is a wonder.

75

I SAT ON A damp stool by the tub, rinsing off the soap bubbles from her hair and body.

Again, a story:

Obaludo's mother worked as a trader of goods and knew well that during market days the spirits came out of the spirit world to do their own trading. On these market days, she made sure to leave her three daughters with food, and with careful instructions on how to prepare the food, so as not to have to go out of the house and risk coming face to face with the spirits, for the spirits were known to do harm to children in any number of ways.

This particular day, Obaludo's mother brought out some snails and a small tuber of yam and gave them to Obaludo and her sisters. "The snails release liquid," she said, "so you must roast the yam first, or else the snails will quench the fire."

She was careful to repeat the warning, especially for the sake of Obaludo, the beautiful daughter, whose beauty she knew was the envy of so many villagers and spirits alike.

Then Obaludo's mother left.

Hours passed and finally suppertime arrived. The girls set about cooking their meal, only they had by now forgotten their mother's warning. They started off with the snails instead of the yam. The snails had hardly finished cooking when the fire was quenched. And now they remembered the warning that their mother had given to them. But it was too late.

Their mother would not be returning for several hours yet. They were hungry, and the thought of waiting so long was like torture to them. Together they decided that they had no choice but to go in search of fire.

They fought over who would go for fire.

The two younger sisters consorted and decided that the best thing would be for the eldest sister to go. *Nwaegbe,* the younger two sisters begged, *please won't you go and get us fire.*

But she refused.

They begged Nwaegbe again: *Elder sister, please won't you go and get us fire.*

Again she refused.

Now the first and youngest sisters consorted among themselves. Finally they reached a decision: that the second sister, Nwaugo, should be the one to go. They presented their case to Nwaugo. They pleaded, *Nwaugo, please go and get us fire.*

But like Nwaegbe, the second sister refused.

Knowing that there was no one else to ask—that she was the only remaining option or else they would starve—Obaludo decided to go for the fire herself.

At first the roads were clear. Obaludo had begun to think that she would make it there and back just fine when, as her mother had warned, she met with a spirit.

The spirit began. "Tunya!" it said.

Obaludo replied to the spirit, "Tunya to you too!"

The spirit said, "Tunke!"

Obaludo said, "Tunke to you too!"

The exchange continued like that for some time. Obaludo could not have known it, but in the moments during which they exchanged those words, the spirit was taking away her beauty and replacing it with its own ugliness.

I sang the song softly as I bathed Chidinma:

> *Obaludo, Obaludo, Nwa oma,*
> *Obaludo*
> *Obaludo, Obaludo, Nwa oma,*

Obaludo
Nne anyi nyele anyi gi na ejuna,
Obaludo
Si ayi bulu uzo ho nwa gianyi
Na ejuna ga emenyula anyi oku
Obaludo
Anyi bulu uzo ho nwa ejuna
Obaludo
Ejuna emenyusiala anyi oku
Obaludo . . .

Beautiful Obaludo, beautiful child,
Beautiful Obaludo, beautiful child,
Our mother gave us yam and snails,
Told us: Roast first the yam,
For the snails will douse the fire,
But we disobeyed, went first for the snails,
And the snails put out our fire,
Obaludo . . .

Midway through the song, I heard something like the shifting of a door in the distance, and I thought: a breeze blowing, causing the front door to rattle. I didn't think much else of it.

I heard no footsteps, but when I turned around, I found Chibundu leaning against the bathroom doorframe, watching us with something terribly sad in his eyes. These days I can't help thinking maybe it was the way Jesus looked upon the world as he hung from the cross. *E'li, E'li, la'ma sa bach tha'ni?* My God, my God, why have you forsaken me?

Or maybe, as according to John, simply: *I thirst.*

76

I WON'T SPEND TIME explaining why, after seeing Chibundu like that in the doorframe, I relented and gave in wholeheartedly to trying with him for a boy. Where did God come from? Before God there was whom? What is the purpose of life? Why am I here? Where am I going?

Some things can't easily be explained.

All you need to know is that, seeing him that way at the door, I succumbed. No more pretending to be asleep. No more fighting him off at night. I made up my mind to try and get pregnant again. As if just getting pregnant was a kind of guarantee that it would be the boy child that he so desperately wanted, the boy child on account of which I now felt myself Chibundu's hostage. But I prayed it would be so, prayed enough for both of us, enough for at least ten others. If he would only get his son, then maybe I would finally be excused from any more of those nighttime obligations. Maybe I could finally be released from this captivity of a marriage. If only the baby would come quickly, and not only come: if it would just be a boy. Please, Lord, I begged.

In that cushion of time when the harmattan imposed itself once more upon the dry season, I became with child.

If I will not spend time explaining why I gave in to Chibundu, I also will not spend any time describing the details of the pregnancy. I will instead cut, like a zip line, from point A straight to point Z and say that I had not carried the baby for three months before I lost it.

This was the way the losing went: I felt a pain one evening in the parlor as I was in the middle of lifting Chidinma. I stopped in my tracks, still holding her in my hands, afraid that any additional movement would only worsen the pain.

I tried to wait it out. But minutes passed and the pain persisted.

I set Chidinma down. It was still early in the evening, and I thought, Chibundu is not home yet. Also I thought, God, please let Chibundu come home and claim his baby before there's nothing left to be claimed. I was only three months into the pregnancy, but I imagined a little boy in Chibundu's likeness. He would have his father's ogbono-shaped eyes, his button nose, his lips — the way they pursed out thickly like two millipedes when he was upset. He would be like his father in so many ways. But he would not have any of that pent-up anger of Chibundu's, and in being born, he would wipe away all of his father's old anger.

There we were, standing in the middle of the parlor, Chidinma's little hand now in mine. And the pain turning into something sharper and many times more painful than all the moments before. Then, out of the blue, a cutting pain set in, and I felt myself reflexively squeeze the little hand in mine. Chidinma began to cry. What could I do? I simply listened to the sound of her crying, listened to it as from a deep, hollow tunnel, more like listening to an echo than to the sound itself.

I thought: Let him come and claim his baby before there is nothing of a baby to be claimed.

I moved one foot in front of the other, but then I felt myself drain out, the opposite of a suction, as if a plug in me had suddenly been unplugged. I looked down, and beneath me I saw a pool of blood spreading out in clumps on the floor. Then there was a heavy odor of raw flesh all over, saturating the room, threatening even the air in my lungs. To this day, I can see it in my mind: little Chidinma standing by my side, crying and wallowing in the clumpy puddle of her mother's blood.

Everything turned to gray. And then all of it faded to black.

• • •

I awoke to Chibundu's face hovering above me, stroking my forehead, telling me that everything would be fine. He was carrying Chidinma in his arms.

My hospital bed was near a window. Outside, the sun was setting, purple clouds blooming in a bed of gray, something like a bruise on pale skin.

How long had I been there? Hours? Days?

Chibundu continued to stroke me. Then, seeing that I had awakened, he said, "Soon the doctors will have you back to normal. One hundred percent. They say we can try again." He shifted Chidinma in his arms, leaned closer to me, and said, as he had now taken to saying, "If the man who comes back with no cassava is a true farmer, he will return to the farm and put in the work necessary, so that one day he too will return from the farm with cassava in his basket."

I grew lightheaded with the sound of those words. They appeared to whirl around in my head, causing me to grow anxious, making it a struggle to breathe.

Following the miscarriage, Chibundu could almost always be found outside in the front yard, dusting, polishing, holding long drawn-out conversations on the veranda with that good-luck charm of a car. It was as if he was coaxing it to do better, reasoning with it: what good is a good-luck charm if it fails to do its job? His posture betrayed his disappointment in the car.

The way I saw it, if his good-luck charm had not worked, perhaps he would have no choice but to let me be. And anyway, wasn't it the nature of people that after obsessing over something for so long, eventually they moved on? No matter how fervently we set our minds on a venture, if time after time that venture proved too hard to attain, sooner or later it only made sense to move on to something else.

Maybe.

For the umpteenth day in a row, I walked out to the front yard to call him in for supper, only to find him with the car.

Chidinma was with me. She had learned by now that the toy car was not for her. She had also learned, perhaps, that many things could be taken away as soon as they were given. Even a mother's affection. She stood rigidly by my side, not moving toward the car.

The previous weekend, Chibundu had invited one of the neighborhood boys to drive the car, a little boy, about four or five years old, by the name of Somto. Chidinma and I had come out to find the boy huddled tightly in the driver's seat, his knees sticking up in front of the steering wheel, his legs too long for the car.

Still, he drove, and Chibundu followed behind, heartily clapping. Finally he lifted the boy out of the car, set him down on the ground, and patted him on the head. The boy wrapped his small arms around Chibundu's legs in return, gratitude for this unexpected opportunity to drive the little car.

Now, a week after the incident with Somto, Chibundu lifted the car from the veranda and set it down in the yard.

Looking up at me, he said, "It was a mistake on my part not to share this with the girl. What was I thinking? How could I have been so foolish? It would probably have brought us the good luck we wanted if only I had shared it with her. After all, she would have been his sister, and that's what siblings are supposed to do. They are supposed to share."

He was looking at me as he spoke. I wanted to tell him that there was no indication that the baby had been a boy. At three months, it had been too soon to tell.

His eyes turned to Chidinma.

"Come here," he said to her.

Chidinma remained where she was.

"Come," he said, and this time he reached for her, lifted her in his arms, and set her into the front seat of the car.

As he instructed her on what to do, moved her hands and legs this way and that, I examined her face, looking for signs of gratification from having been finally given this opportunity to do what long ago she had wanted.

Her face showed no happiness. She sat stiffly, apprehensively, one hand hesitantly placed on the steering wheel, the other tugging nervously at one of the plastic hairpins that decorated the tips of her braided hair.

The car finally began to move, but only because Chibundu took to pushing it along by hand. There she went, little Chidinma, gripping the steering wheel and being pushed around in the toy car that was never meant to be hers.

And there was no sign of gratification in her.

Later that night, she curled herself in a tight ball in bed, as if she wished to disappear. Her eyes remained open, steady on me, deep in contemplation.

Time passed, and then, in a muted and dismal way, she let out a sigh. I watched as she turned her body away from me. In that instant my eyelids became a little like the windshield wipers on a car. I tried to blink away the moment of her turning from me. I blinked, and I blinked, and I blinked. But still, I could not blink the image away.

77

L EGEND HAS IT that spirit children, tired of floating aimlessly between the world of the living and that of the dead,
take to gathering above udala trees. In exchange for the dwelling,
they cause to be exceptionally fertile any female who comes and
stays, for even the briefest period of time, under any one of the
trees. They cause her to bear sons and daughters, as many as her
heart desires.

Back in Ojoto, some years before the war came, I heard of this
legend from one of my schoolmates, a pudgy little bright-eyed girl
whose head was shaped like a flattened loaf of bread. She had a scar
on the very top of her forehead, running horizontally from left to
right. All the children at school whispered that it was because she
had fallen out of her parents' second-story window when she was
a baby. But no one ever asked her about it to her face. And no one
ever knew. Her name was Osita.

One lazy afternoon while we sat on the steps of the classroom
during afternoon recess, she begged me to go with her, after school
let out, to the udala grove that was not far from the school. She and
I, we must have been eight or nine years old at the time.

We made ourselves seating places under the trees: piles of leaves
placed one next to the other, and we lingered there on our seats,
under the trees.

"We have to remain here until the count of a hundred," Osita
said.

"Why a hundred?"

"Because a hundred is a very long time to stay under the tree. A
hundred because that way we can be sure that we will receive every

single drop of our blessing from the hands of the spirit children. Not like when we drink a bottle of soft drink and there's still that tiny little bit left in the bottle. With this, we have to try and get even the tiniest drop of our blessing."

She began to count, painfully slowly, as if the numbers were flour, as if she had measured them and was now gradually sifting them out of the sieve. One . . . two . . . three . . .

Because nine was not too young to prepare, she said. Because sooner or later we would each become somebody's wife, and as wives, it would be our obligation to be fertile, to bear children for our husbands, sons especially, to carry on the family name.

I went along with her in all that she proposed we do, even if to me the gap between legend and reality was not one that my mind was prepared to leap across. To me, the legend was a little like making a wish: it was anyone's guess if the wish ever came true.

My last night under Chibundu's roof, I dreamed of udala trees.

In my dream, I saw Chidinma dressed in a yellow dress with a sequined bodice and a hem of lace. On her hair was a ribbon, which the wind lifted gently from her head. Around her was a circle of gray and beige stones, big stones, about the size of cement blocks. Set atop of each stone was a tall, white wax candle, seven or eight of them in total, their flames burning blue and orange and yellow, and flickering this way and that in the night.

Her expression was mournful and sad, and there was a paleness to her face.

She stood under one of the udala trees, a tree much taller and more fruitful than any I had ever seen before. It was speckled throughout with udala fruit of a brighter than usual orange. Its leaves glowed by the light of the candles, a dark shade of green.

Other trees lined each side of the trail leading up to where she stood, trees hovering above: palm, iroko, cashew, and plantain trees. Behind Chidinma, the trail appeared to taper into the lake beyond, which then tapered into a vanishing point somewhere in the distance, in the bluish-black horizon. The moon, obscured as it was by clouds, asserted itself just enough to leave the tips of the trees silvery and bright.

Near the tip of the trail, not quite close enough to where the earth gave way to water, there were even more burning candles.

I approached Chidinma with horror, and as I did, I saw that she was standing with her feet not quite touching the earth, like a ghost floating above the ground. How could it be? I lifted my eyes to check. I saw, dangling from the udala tree, a wiry rope leading to the wiry noose that was tied around Chidinma's neck. Somehow I had at first failed to see it, but I saw it now, extending down from the branches of the udala tree, and Chidinma, my child, dangling from it.

I made to run for her, but my legs were heavy, as if they were being pulled down by wet mud. I forced them to move, keeping my eyes on her. I saw the moment when she lifted her eyes to me. She was wearing that familiar expressionless look on her face, and then her lips curved into a slight smile, something sinister, nothing like anything I had ever seen on her.

A book appeared in her hands. It was my papa's old Bible — that small one from long ago, with the black leather binding and yellowing pages. As she hung from the tree, she began reading from the Bible. I listened to the words that she read, but I could not make them out.

I was too late. By the time I reached her, her eyes had fallen closed. Her skin was still warm, but a coldness was setting in.

A new dream followed, and in it, I saw Chidinma all grown up: a beautiful woman with a rich brown complexion and full, shapely lips, and her eyes very sharp. She sat outside in a yard full of udala trees, holding a child in her arms.

All around were the sounds of helicopter and bomber engines, the thudding sounds of running feet, of things crashing into the earth. War sounds.

From where I stood, I screamed at Chidinma to get up from where she sat, to hurry so that we could run and hide in the bunker. It was nighttime, dark all around except for dull moonlight. "Chidinma, come!" I screamed. Chidinma looked up at me and caught my eyes with her own. Her eyes glowed in the darkness, appearing angry and wild.

Just then the child in her arms began to choke. Chidinma looked down at the child. But she did nothing more than look. I could have done something to help the choking child, but there seemed to be an invisible fence between me and the scene in front of me. I could no more reach in to grab Chidinma and drag her to the bunker than I could help soothe the choking child.

In her arms, the child gasped and gasped, bringing its hands to its neck, its pleading eyes turning up toward Chidinma. Its face appeared to swell. More gasping, more pleading with its eyes. Still, Chidinma only watched. She did not do a thing to help the choking child.

Sometimes a decision comes upon us that way—in a series of dreams, in a series of small epiphanies. Imagine that there is a murmur of a sound, something from somewhere in the distance. It is not quite noticeable, but the minutes go by and the sound gets stronger: *quonk, quonk, quonk,* and finally you look up and see a skein, a flock of geese, a perfect V up above in the sky.

I woke up with a start, frantic, drenched in sweat, gasping for air. It did not seem that I was at home, or that I was on my bed. I stared blankly around, trying to make sense of where I was. It was then that I made the realization: Chidinma and I were both choking under the weight of something larger than us, something heavy and weighty, the weight of tradition and superstition and of all our legends.

The bedroom took shape around me: the floral sheets and the wooden side table and the dresser on which I saw my reflection in the mirror. The dark curtains on the windows. Chibundu by my side.

I sat up in bed, set my feet firmly on the floor. The solution to my problems became clear. Why had it taken this long for me to act? There's a way in which life takes us along for a ride and we begin to think that our destinies are not in fact up to us.

Chidinma's crying now rang out in my mind. But the bedroom door was closed, so if she had truly cried, I could not possibly have heard. Still, her cry rang out.

Chibundu lay sleeping on his side of the bed, his snoring reverberating like a horn. I rose, quickly gathered some things into a bag, being very careful not to wake Chibundu. I tiptoed out of the room, carrying the bag with me. I went straight for Chidinma's room.

In her room, I bundled her against my chest, tying her in place with a wrapper stretched across my shoulder. She had been asleep when I came to her, but now she opened her eyes, and she squirmed a little, giving off her usual baby scent, of talc and fragrance, sweet and soft, a little like incense.

I carried her that way out of the room, into the parlor, and out the parlor door.

Outside, darkness wrapped itself around me like grace. The leaves were thrashing in the breeze, and along the road, by the side of a small shed, a woman was pouring soapy water out of a bucket. A man was sweeping the front stoop of his own shed.

At the taxi stand, I stood while the oga in a blue-and-black agbada and sokoto directed me to a cab. I walked, all the while rocking Chidinma in my arms.

Sitting in the taxi as it drove off, I thought once more about the way that life so often takes us the long way around. But perhaps it didn't matter, long or short, as long as we eventually found our way to where we needed to be.

The taxi dropped me a short distance from Mama's gate. Up the hill a light was shining like a bonfire.

I walked, not at all sure what I'd say when I reached Mama's gate, or when I was inside the gate, or when I knocked on the door and

Mama opened it for me. Maybe something about wanting to be alone, like her. Wanting to be rid of all attachments to people, save for the ones I chose for myself.

I passed a small patch of land, sprinkled here and there with green moss. I passed a tall iroko tree, and a chicken with red patches on its head, walking circles around the iroko tree.

Just before I reached Mama's gate, I stopped. On the side of the road where I stood was a tree stump. I took a seat on it. There, I prayed silently, asking God to forgive me for abandoning my marriage. I prayed for what might have amounted to seconds, or minutes, or perhaps even hours.

I stood up and, feeling ambitious and a little brave, brushed off my wrapper, ridding it of all the dust it had gathered on the walk. I brushed it fervently, as if to start my life anew.

Epilogue

Aba, Abia State
January 13, 2014

I N A LIFE STORY full of dreams, there are even more dreams. From time to time Amina still comes to me at night. Three particular dreams. Each one takes its turn, and each turn, like a habit, recurs.

In the first, I have found my way back to Oraifite, to Amina's and my old secondary school there. The visit takes place in the evening. I get off the bus and make my way to the river. The sun is setting, causing the water to glisten. I find that spot where we once sat, and I grab a handful of sand and watch the grains trickle out from between my fingers, just as Amina had done that time long ago.

This is the first.

In the second dream, I have trekked all the way down to the grammar school teacher's house. The place has long been abandoned, but I approach anyway, make my way across its front yard, across the weeds that are creeping up, covering the path leading from the gate to the entrance of the house. Weeds on concrete, drowning the cement.

I enter and pass quickly through the house, go by way of the kitchen into the backyard. In the near distance, I see the old hovel, and a short distance from the hovel, the tap, the silver one that once glistened in the sun. Rust has built up all along the length of it. Grasshoppers skitter freely around.

I approach the tap, advance a few steps toward it, and suddenly there is Amina, just as she used to be, fetching a bucket of water.

I run to her, wrap my arms around her though she is still holding the bucket, and I ask, desperately, "Do you remember? *Do you remember?* This is where we walked. This is where we worked. This is where we grew. This is where we laughed. This is where we made love. *This is where I learned love.*"

Hardly have I finished speaking the words, and she vanishes, the way that people sometimes do, even from our minds.

Gowon had said in his speech: *The tragic chapter of violence is just ended. We are at the dawn of national reconciliation. Once again, we have an opportunity to build a new nation.*

Forget that Gowon was a Northerner. Forget that his name is synonymous with the war and its atrocities.

But remember the war and its atrocities, and remember the speech, and remember that aspect of national reconciliation, and of the building of a new nation.

Forgive Gowon. Forgive Ojukwu. And forgive the war.

The third dream is as follows, and it is this one that, by far, recurs the most:

I am up north to visit Amina. Up there the sand is gray and fine, not reddish and heavy like the sand down south. The plains are grassy and stretch for miles on end, and on them cattle graze, their tails swinging in the sun, under the watch of Hausa and Fulani herdsmen.

In addition to the herdsmen are Hausa and Fulani vendors, dressed in traditional caftans and headscarves and shawls, carrying trays of bananas, of bread, and of nuts on their heads. There are Igbo and Yoruba vendors too: women in lace blouses or bubas, matching wrappers on the bottom; men in agbadas. And still others: men and women garbed in European and American clothes: dress shirts and T-shirts, trousers and skirts and shorts.

Amina meets me at the bus stop. Though her face and her long braids are masked by the veil, and though her body appears shape-less in the long flowing gown she wears, I recognize her all the same. She is young, shamefaced, guilt-ridden, and there is fear trailing af-ter her, tacked onto the soles of her feet.

I attempt to appease her, to tell her that those things we did were not so bad, if bad at all. I attempt to say that soon there'll be no more fears of stoning, that soon all those stories of villagers sending lov-ers to drown in the rivers will be ancient, almost forgotten, like old light, barely visible in the sky. The words have just made their way out of my lips when a lorry passes by, a long, bulbous one, its engine racketing and rattling so loud that it drowns out my voice. And not just the buzzing and the bustling of the lorry, not just the clamor and the clangor, but also the fumes and the smog, black clouds ris-ing. And we are breathing in the fumes, coughing and choking on all the fumes. And then another lorry. And another. And another. More fumes. More coughing. More choking. My words get lost in all of that ruckus, my sweet, consoling words becoming like sugar in the rain, like ghosts, like the sheerest of cobwebs: melted, vanishing, imperceptibly thin. Useless words, lost words, words as good as if they were never spoken at all.

Several years ago — 2008 — reports had it that a bunch of God-preaching hooligans stoned and beat several members of a gay and lesbian–affirming church in Lagos, bashed their faces, caused their flesh to become as swollen as purple-blue balloons.

Mama put down the newspaper from which she was reading about it and exclaimed, "*Tufiakwa!*" God forbid! "Even among Christians, it can't be the same God that we worship!"

Chidinma has been based in Lagos for the past three years.

Last year, a prefect found two female students making love to each other at the university in Lagos where Chidinma teaches. It happened in one of the student hostels, so Chidinma was not there to see it, or else she might have stepped in, might even have risked her own life as she did. She is, after all, of that particular new generation of Nigerians with a stronger bent toward love than fear. The fact that she herself is not of my orientation does not make her look upon gays and lesbians with the kind of fear that leads to hate. Besides, she knows my story too well to be insensitive to the cause.

In any case, the two female students' schoolmates, some of whom were Chidinma's own students, decided to take matters into their own hands. They stripped the lovers of their clothes and beat them all over until they were black and blue. They shouted "666" in their faces, and "God punish you!" Those who did not participate in the beating stood around watching and recording the incident with their mobile phones. No one made any move to help the women. They only stood and watched.

When she heard of it, Mama said, "God forbid! What has this world turned into?"

After a while, she joked, "You know, it really is a shame that our president, the really good-looking man that he is—between that handsome smile and his fashionable fedora hats—it's too bad he doesn't do anything to correct the situation. Such a waste of good looks. A handsome face has a way of persuading the masses. The least he can do is try and use his good looks for a noble cause."

Later, I asked Chidinma whether she had mentioned the incident to her father. She had. Chibundu's response? "Well, that's life. These things happen."

Chibundu still lives in Port Harcourt, but every once in a while he comes to Aba. Over thirty years of distance has led to a polite sort of estrangement between the two of us. Perhaps he still holds a grudge about the way our marriage turned out; perhaps he does not.

For some years after I left, he continued to implore me to go back to him. He arranged several meetings in the span of those years —with Mama and his parents in addition to the two of us—to try and see what could be done to salvage the marriage, but all of the meetings were to no avail. Through all of it I was indebted to him, because he was at least considerate enough to keep from revealing to his parents any information about me and Ndidi. After all these years, it still does not seem that he has revealed a thing to them or anyone else. If there is one way to describe him these days, it is that he generally appears resigned.

Growing up, Chidinma used to ask why her papa and I did not live together.

"Some papas and mamas love each other but not in the marrying or living together kind of way," I often used to say. She would nod, and after some time she'd ask, "But why?"

I'd simply repeat, "Because some papas and mamas love each other but not in the marrying or living together kind of way."

Though they've certainly had their rough patches, she has always loved her father; I know she feels a latent sympathy for him on my behalf. For several years now, she has expressed to me her concern that he is lonely. She wishes that he would remarry, because that might make him seem less lonely to her.

There was some talk, maybe seven or eight years ago, about Chibundu's plans to marry a young Yoruba woman by the name of Ayodele. The woman was only a few years older than Chidinma, and she, according to Chidinma, was the kind who loved to throw large, elaborate parties. Perhaps Ayodele and Chibundu did not see eye to eye on those parties, or maybe there was some other problem, but in the end there was no wedding.

Sometimes I feel that Chibundu is too busy pitying himself to fully invest in a new relationship. But of course I could be wrong.

There is the story of a man who was so distracted while driving his car that he drove it straight into his neighbor's yard, killing the neighbor's little daughter who was playing there in the yard. The neighbor came out screaming, shouting at the man, "Look what you have done! You have gone and killed my child! How could you do this to me? I will not let you get away with it! You've gone and killed my innocent little child!"

The driver got out of his car, and upon hearing his neighbor's words, he immediately took offense. He said, "How dare you talk to me this way! Why are you shouting at me? You have no right to shout at me! Do you not see that I've had a lot on my mind? I'm sorry, but I am a businessman and I've been traveling so much, taking care of so many things. I'm sorry, but do you even know how stressful life has been for me? Do you even know?" He went on and on in this vein, screaming at his neighbor whose child he had just killed, making excuses for why he drove into the yard, making excuses for the tragic accident, how terribly hectic his life was. How unfair it was for the neighbor to shout at him that way. *I'm sorry but this, I'm sorry but that,* and on and on and on. To him, he was the victim; he was the one to whom wrong had been done.

I suppose it's the way we are, humans that we are. Always finding it easier to make ourselves the victim in someone else's tragedy.

Though it is true, too, that sometimes it is hard to know to whom the tragedy really belongs.

Chidinma must have been thirteen or fourteen at the time that I revealed to her that Ndidi and I were more than friends. It turned out to be an underwhelming kind of revelation, almost a nonrevelation, because unbeknownst to me, the girl already knew. And somehow it did not matter to her.

As for Ndidi, looking back on it, it seems almost inevitable that I would return to her, and that we would try and salvage what was left of our relationship.

These days, I think a lot about something Mama used to say: that a bicycle has two wheels. And, of course, it does. Ndidi is one, and I am the other. We have now shared decades together, and though there can be no marriage between us (a relationship like ours is still too dangerous a thing, let alone a marriage), we feel ourselves every bit a couple.

Outside of Mama and Chibundu and Chidinma, Ndidi and I have done our best to keep the whole thing a clandestine affair, a little like it used to be. We keep separate quarters, but we do spend many of our nights together. Sometimes I go to her flat, and other times she comes to mine, which is not far from Mama's bungalow, the same one in which, with help from Mama, I wound up raising Chidinma.

Some of those nights when we are together and in bed, Ndidi wraps her arms around me. She molds her body around mine and whispers in my ear about a town where love is allowed to be love, between men and women, and men and men, and women and women, just as between Yoruba and Igbo and Hausa and Fulani. Ndidi describes the town, all its trees and all the colors of its sand. She tells me in great detail about the roads, the directions in which they run, from where and to where they lead.

"What is the name of the town?" I ask.

Sleep threatens to overtake her, and sometimes she forgets that she does not want to say a name. One night, she mumbles that it is Aba. The next night it is Umuahia. With each passing night she names more towns: Ojoto and Nnewi, Onitsha and Nsukka, Port Harcourt and Lagos, Uyo and Oba, Kaduna and Sokoto. She names and names, so that eventually I have to laugh and say, "How is it that this town can be so many places at once?"

Her voice is soft like a hum, and the words come out quiet like a prayer. She is older now. Both of us are. The years have flown by, and there is an aged roughness to her voice. She says, "All of them are here in Nigeria. You see, this place will be all of Nigeria."

Hebrews 8: God made a new covenant with the house of Israel, and with the house of Judah, not according to the covenant that He made with their fathers. If that first covenant had been faultless, then no place would have been made for the second. With that new covenant, He made the first old. And that first one was allowed to vanish away.

It is this verse that fills my mind these days. This, it seems to me, is the lesson of the Bible: this affirmation of the importance of reflection, and of revision, enough revision to do away with tired, old, even faulty laws.

Sometimes I sit with my Bible in my hands, and I think to myself that God is nothing but an artist, and the world is His canvas.

And I reason that if the Old and New Testaments are any indication, then change is in fact a major part of His aesthetic, a major part of His vision for the world. The Bible itself is an endorsement of change. Even biblical covenants change: In the New Testament, no longer the need for animal sacrifices. Change. No longer the covenant of law, but rather the covenant of grace. Change. A focus on all mankind rather than a focus on the Jews. Change. So many other changes, if a person were the list-making type.

Many days I reason to myself that change is the point of it all. And that everything we do should be a reflection of that vision of change.

Maybe the rules of the Bible will always be in flux. Maybe God is still speaking and will continue to do so for always. Maybe He is still creating new covenants, only we were too deaf, too headstrong, too set in old ways to hear. Yes, there are the ways of God that have already been made known to us, but maybe there are also those ways in the process of being made known. Maybe we have only to open our ears and hearts and minds to hear.

It is a comforting thought when I reason it like that.

At the door, I had knocked, Chidinma in my arms. Mama opened, a questioning look on her face.

"Mama, I can't. I can't anymore," I blurted out.

She stood there just looking at me. Finally she lowered her eyelids, out of what seemed to be disappointment. Her questioning look was no longer questioning.

"Mama, I can't," I said again.

A soft breeze blew from behind me, entering through the door and stirring the tip of the white headscarf that Mama was wearing on her head. Causing it to quiver as if it were a miniature flag.

Chidinma was now awake, her head upright, but she was quiet, her face turning back and forth as she looked between Mama and me.

"Mama, please let me in. I can't anymore with Chibundu."

Mama lifted her eyes. She took Chidinma from my arms, carried her with one arm. I did not expect it when her other arm came around my shoulders. We walked together into the parlor and toward the sofa. The baby was making a valiant attempt at speaking —a series of babbling words—and Mama said, "It makes no sense to send you back this late at night." We had been standing side by side, but she turned to look directly at me now.

"All right," she said. "All right." This was an understanding. Discernment like tepid light, very understated, but an understanding nonetheless.

And now she began muttering to herself. "God, who created you, must have known what He did. Enough is enough."

Who knows how long she'd been deliberating it this way.

She cleared her throat, and she finished: "*Ka udo di, ka ndu di.*"

Let peace be. Let life be.

Author's Note

On January 7, 2014, Nigeria's president, Goodluck Jonathan, signed into law a bill criminalizing same-sex relationships and the support of such relationships, making these offenses punishable by up to fourteen years in prison. In the northern states, the punishment is death by stoning. This novel attempts to give Nigeria's marginalized LGBTQ citizens a more powerful voice, and a place in our nation's history.

According to a 2012 Win-Gallup International Global Index of Religiosity and Atheism, Nigeria ranks as the second-most-religious country surveyed, following very closely behind Ghana.

Acknowledgments

Many thanks to:

My classmates at the Iowa Writers' Workshop, and my professors: Paul Harding, Marilynne Robinson, James Alan McPherson, Lan Samantha Chang, Allan Gurganus, and Ethan Canin.

Connie Brothers, Deb West, and Janice Zenisek at the Iowa Writers' Workshop.

Michael Martone and Robin Hemley at the Overseas Writers' Workshop.

Lisa Zeidner and the English/creative writing faculty and staff at Rutgers University, Camden.

Daniel Grow, Linda Barton, Charlotte Holmes, and Aimee La-Brie at the Pennsylvania State University.

Greg Ames, Peter Balakian, Jennifer Brice, Jane Pinchin, and Tess Jones at Colgate University.

The creative writing faculty at Purdue University, especially Porter Shreve and Bich Minh Nguyen.

The Bread Loaf Writers' Conference.

The editors at: *AGNI, Apogee, Coffin Factory, Conjunctions, Granta,* the *Iowa Review,* the *Kenyon Review, The New Yorker, Prospect,* the *Southern Review, Subtropics* (special thanks to David Leavitt), *Tin House,* and *TriQuarterly.*

Christopher Merrill, Nataša Durovicová, Kelly Bedeian, and Ashley Davidson at the University of Iowa's International Writing Program.

The O. Henry Prize Stories.

Lambda Literary and the Astraea Foundation for Justice.

The Caine Prize, for its tremendous support of African writing, especially Lizzy Attree and Jenny Casswell.

Rolex Mentor and Protégé Arts Initiative, especially Jill Morrison, Michael Ondaatje, Miro Penkov, Neal Hovelmeier, and Togara Muzanenhamo.

Congregational United Church of Christ, Iowa City, especially Reverend William Lovin.

Chika Unigwe, Sarah Ladipo Manyika, Uwem Akpan, Chimamanda Adichie, Maaza Mengiste, Tayari Jones, NoViolet Bulawayo, and Rita Adedamola Mogaji.

Rae Winkelstein, Montreux Rotholtz, Emily Ruskovich, Naomi Jackson, Christa Fraser, Amanda Briggs, Bryan Castille, and Lori Baker Martin.

Marc Benda.

Mrs. Brenda Nickles.

Granta, especially John Freeman, Patrick Ryan, Ellah Allfrey, Yuka Igarashi, Ted Hodgkinson, Rachael Allen, Sara D'Arcy, and Anne Meadows.

Houghton Mifflin Harcourt, especially Jenna Johnson, Nina Barnett, Summer Smith, Simmi Aujla, Chelsea Newbould, and Larry Cooper.

The Wylie Agency, especially my superb agent, Jin Auh, as well as Tracy Bohan and Jessica Friedman.

Ludwig Wittgenstein ("The limits of my language mean the limits of my world").

"Things congealed by cold shall be melted by heat." Creech's Lucretius, in *The Works of the British Poets: With Prefaces, Biographical and Critical,* Vol. 13 (London, 1795), p. 663.

The BBC and its documentaries on the Nigeria-Biafra War.

Yakubu Gowon, "The Dawn of National Reconciliation," broadcast from Lagos on January 15, 1970.

The works of Flora Nwapa, Chinua Achebe, Wole Soyinka, Edwidge Danticat, Alice Munro, Kazuo Ishiguro, Ian McEwan, and Marilynne Robinson — my predecessors, my guiding lights.

And Jackie Kay's "Road to Amaudo," where I first read the saying "*Ka udo di, ka ndu di.*"

My most heartfelt thanks and love to:

Chidinma Okparanta, Chinenye Okparanta, and Chibueze Okparanta, my siblings, my best friends.

Constance Okparanta, for her strength, for her love, for her war songs and war stories, for her folktales, without all of which this book might not exist.

Aunty Ifeyinwa, you are always in my heart.

All our elders, for the proverbs that carry on to this day.

Last but not least, God and the Universe, for conspiring together to make this book the assured expectation of things hoped for, and the evident demonstration of realities, though not beheld.